I0831456

WOMEN'S WORLD THE FALL OF Y

TEDD NGUYEN

Contents

WOMEN'S WORLD
THE FALL OF Y

Prologue: The Last Whisper

The world didn't end with fire or war. It ended with a whisper. A slow unraveling. A quiet erasure of half its heartbeat.

No one noticed at first. The virus came like a thief, slipping through cities, touching lives with unseen hands. It wasn't violent, not like the plagues of the past. No burning fevers, no bodies piling in the streets. Just a cough here, a headache there—nothing that would make anyone pause.

But then the men began to disappear.

It started with sickness, young and healthy bodies breaking down without explanation. Then the births stopped—sons, once so eagerly awaited, were lost before they could take their first breath. Hospitals filled with mothers grieving children they would never hold. Scientists scrambled, governments lied, and the world's pulse weakened. By the time the truth came, it was already too late.

The Y chromosome was dying. And with it, half of humanity.

Now, the cities stand quieter, their streets walked only by women who carry the weight of survival on their shoulders. Some cling to the past, to the memory of fathers, brothers, and sons. Others look ahead, toward a future that must be rewritten.

Because the old world is gone. And what comes next will be something entirely new.

1

The Silent Shift

The year was 2040, and the world trembled beneath a stillness that masked its frantic pulse. It wasn't a silence of emptiness—cities still thrummed with the raw energy of life. Horns screamed through gridlocked streets, children's laughter ricocheted off the cracked concrete of playgrounds, and drones wove their ceaseless hum into the urban sky. Yet beneath this clamor, a tension coiled tight, an unspoken tremor that seemed to vibrate through every living soul. The world teetered on the brink, peering into a chasm it couldn't name—a storm brewing in the marrow of humanity, its first whispers stirring five years prior, now swelling into a roar poised to break.

It began in the winter of 2035, innocuous as a shadow slipping through a crowd. A virus crept into the world, cloaked as a common cold—a scratchy throat, a fleeting cough, a fever that flickered out in a day or two. It drifted through homes and offices, a polite intruder leaving only sniffles and crumpled tissues in its wake. Hospitals dozed undisturbed; morgues gathered dust. Most people didn't even bother to visit a doctor. Why would they? *It was just a cold.*

But it wasn't just a cold.

Dubbed *Chromovirus-X* by a handful of intrigued scientists, the virus was a chameleon, a master of subtlety. Unlike the pandemics of history—those brash reapers that scythed through millions—it didn't blaze with fever or drown lungs in fluid. It was patient, embedding itself into the human genome like a seed in rich soil, lying dormant, undetectable even by the sharpest diagnostic tools. For years, it lingered as a ghost, a benign quirk dismissed by experts as a footnote to the flu season. By the time its true nature surfaced, it had already claimed every corner of the globe, a silent conqueror woven into humanity's very fabric.

The first signs of fracture emerged in the spring of 2040, faint as cracks in glass. Young men—vibrant, unbreakable men in their prime—began to falter. A 28-year-old mechanic in Tokyo woke to a marrow-deep ache, soon diagnosed as leukemia. A 32-year-old teacher in São Paulo collapsed mid-lesson, his lymphoma a sudden thief. A 25-year-old runner in London stumbled mid-stride, prostate cancer gnawing at his youth. These were diseases of twilight, not dawn—rarities in men so young. Doctors murmured about misfortune, toxins, statistical outliers. But as spring bled into summer, the outliers became an onslaught. Across cities and continents, men in their 20s and 30s fell like leaves in a gale—cancers blooming with vicious speed, defying every medical precedent. By July, the male population was unraveling, and denial was no longer an option.

The medical world stirred, unease rippling into panic. Labs buzzed with sleepless urgency as researchers clawed through data, seeking a pattern, a cause. What they unearthed was a nightmare sculpted in DNA. *Chromovirus-X* wasn't merely a virus—it was a predator, and its prey was the Y chromosome. Over five silent years, it had infiltrated male genetics, dismantling them with surgical precision. It didn't kill outright; it corrupted, triggering cancers as a cruel byproduct of its deeper sabotage. The virus was erasing maleness itself, strand by unraveled strand.

Women bore its mark too, though its grip on them was a subtler venom. By late 2040, a harrowing truth crystallized: the virus had slipped into their reproductive code, twisting it into a barren maze. Pregnancies that promised sons ended in blood and silence—miscarriages striking with clockwork precision, often before the first ultrasound could catch a heartbeat. The rare male infants born alive were frail miracles, their lungs too weak to hold the air, their lives slipping away in hours or days. Mothers wept over empty cribs, their grief a growing chorus. The virus had snapped the thread of male lineage, leaving humanity's future dangling by a fraying edge.

The world tilted toward extinction, one fading pulse at a time.

Dr. Elena Hayes had seen it coming—not the full shape of it, but the shadow. A geneticist at the Sydney Institute of Advanced Genomics, she was a wiry figure in her late 30s, her gray eyes sharp as scalpels, her mind a blade honed by restless curiosity. While her peers brushed off *Chromovirus-X* as a triviality in 2035, Elena felt a gnawing unease. She'd tracked it alone at first, her nights swallowed by data, her instincts screaming where science stayed silent. She mapped its dormancy, sequenced its stealth, and when the first cancers flared in 2040, she didn't wait for permission. She requisitioned a team, commandeered a lab, and plunged into the abyss, chasing a truth she feared more than she admitted.

"It's not a virus," she told her team in August, her voice taut as she stood before a screen glowing with genetic code. The conference room was a tomb of flickering lights and stale coffee, the air heavy with dread. "It's a weapon. It's targeting the Y chromosome—disassembling it—and it's rewriting female fertility to reject male embryos. This isn't random. It's deliberate." She paused, her gaze locking onto each exhausted face. "And we're running out of time to stop it."

Her words ignited the scientific community, a flare in the dark, but the wider world remained shrouded in denial. Governments, paralyzed by the specter of mass hysteria, smothered the crisis with vague assurances—"*ongoing studies*," "*isolated anomalies*." Behind locked doors, leaders whispered of containment, of control, but how do you cage an enemy that lives in every cell? How do you fight a war already lost?

The illusion held until autumn, when the cracks became chasms. Men vanished from the streets—not by decree, but by attrition. Workplaces echoed with absence; playgrounds grew quieter, the laughter thinner. Families mourned in private, their losses a tide washing through homes—sons claimed by cancer, brothers by despair, fathers by a force without a face. Women huddled in fragile circles, their voices low as they asked the unanswerable: Were they the last to cradle a shared world? Would their daughters inherit only echoes?

Yet defiance burned amid the ashes. Elena's lab became a crucible, its machines alive with purpose, its team a sleepless army. She didn't just study the virus—she attacked it, testing inhibitors, splicing countermeasures, risking unorthodox trials that skirted ethics for the sake of speed. The odds towered over them—billions infected, a genome in freefall, a virus that morphed with every move—but Elena refused to yield. She wasn't just fighting for science; she was fighting for the mechanic in Tokyo, the teacher in São Paulo, the runner in London—for the unborn sons slipping away. Humanity's thread was hers to hold.

Time, though, was a relentless foe. *Chromovirus-X* tightened its chokehold, its mutations a dance of chaos outpacing every defense. The Y chromosome's collapse was no longer a theory—it was a tolling bell, rung in the bodies of the dying and the graves of the never-born. The clock was merciless, and the threshold near.

Dusk fell over Sydney, the sky bruising purple and gold. Elena sat alone in her lab, the screen's cold glow carving shadows into her face. Before her sprawled a galaxy of code—billions of base pairs, a battlefield of life and ruin. Her latest trial had failed, the virus shrugging off her best weapon like water off stone. Exhaustion clawed at her, but she leaned closer, tracing a faint anomaly in the sequence—a whisper of hope, fragile as a thread. It wasn't a cure, not yet, but it was a foothold. To seize it would take more than brilliance or grit—it would take a leap into the unknown, a gamble with stakes she couldn't fathom.

Elena exhaled, her breath steadying. Miracles were scarce, but she'd forge one if she had to. The world couldn't wait.

2

The Fading Equation

The clock on the wall ticked past midnight, its soft rhythm swallowed by the cavernous silence of the Sydney Institute of Advanced Genomics. Elena Hayes sat hunched over her desk, bathed in the cold, sterile glow of her computer screen. Shadows stretched long and jagged across the lab, pooling in the corners where the dim overhead lights couldn't reach. Beyond the hum of the refrigeration units—guardians of the dwindling stockpile of viable genetic material—the building was a tomb, its once-bustling corridors now hollowed out by absence and despair. Elena's fingers hovered above the keyboard, trembling not from the chill in the air but from the weight of the numbers staring back at her.

Her left hand slipped into her lab coat pocket, brushing against the cool, familiar shape of an ivory pocketknife. Its surface bore the faint grooves of an engraved whale, a quiet gift from Daniel that anchored her when the world spun too fast. She didn't pull it out—didn't need to. Its presence was enough, a tether to him amid the storm.

The latest data set was a brutal tableau of loss. Another spike in male mortality rates—8.7% in the past week alone, a jagged upward slash on the graph that mocked every ounce of effort she'd poured into this fight. Another dead end in their search for a cure, the viral mutations slipping through their models like water through clenched fists.

She leaned back in her chair, the creak of its springs loud in the stillness, and pressed her palms to her temples. Fatigue gnawed at her, a relentless ache that seeped into her bones and coiled around her spine. She couldn't remember the last time she'd slept more than a few fitful hours, snatched in stolen moments between experiments. Coffee, once a lifeline, now sat cold and bitter in a mug beside her, its magic long since faded. But sleep was a luxury she couldn't indulge—not when every tick of the clock dragged the world closer to a precipice, not when her own husband, Daniel, flickered like a candle in a storm.

Daniel. His name alone was enough to tighten her chest, a vise of love and dread squeezing the air from her lungs. Eight years he'd been her anchor, the steady heartbeat to her restless mind. His laughter—a warm, rumbling sound that could cut through even her darkest days—had once been her refuge. Now, it was a ghost, faint and fleeting, drowned out by the virus that had taken root in him as it had in countless others. She saw it in the way he moved, the subtle wince he tried to bury when he thought she wasn't watching, the deepening hollows beneath his hazel eyes. He was slipping away, piece by piece, and all her years of training, all her late nights and breakthroughs, couldn't stop it. Not yet.

Her hand drifted instinctively to her stomach, resting on the faint swell beneath her lab coat. Two months pregnant. The knowledge had once filled her with a wild, trembling joy—visions of a family of three, a child with Daniel's crooked smile and her stubborn streak, a future they'd build together brick by brick. Now, it was a cruel jest, a fragile hope dangling over a chasm of loss. The virus had claimed so many unborn sons, snuffing them out before they could draw breath, and the thought of her child joining that silent legion was a blade she couldn't bear to touch. She wouldn't let it happen. She couldn't.

A soft knock at the door shattered her reverie, pulling her back to the sterile present. She turned, blinking against the glare of the screen, to see Dr. Marcus Keller framed in the doorway. Once, he'd been a wiry spark of a man, his bright blue eyes alight with curiosity and defiance. Now, he was a shadow of himself—gaunt, hollowed out, his shoulders slumped beneath the weight of too many defeats. The white streak in his dark hair, once a quirky badge of distinction, seemed to have spread, threading silver through the chaos of his unkempt curls. He clutched a tablet in one hand, its screen dimmed, as if he couldn't bear to look at it any longer.

"Elena," he said, his voice a quiet rasp, barely audible over the hum of the lab. "We've lost another one. Dr. Haddad passed an hour ago."

Her breath snagged in her throat, sharp and cold. Dr. Tariq Haddad—brilliant, irascible, irreplaceable—had been a cornerstone of their team. A geneticist with an almost uncanny ability to tease patterns from chaos, he'd been the one to spot the first anomalies in *Chromovirus-X*'s behavior, the one to push her when she wavered. He'd been more than a colleague—a mentor who'd guided her through her early years at the Institute, a friend who'd shared late-night coffees and dry humor over endless data runs. She could still hear his voice, gruff and teasing, telling her to "stop chasing shadows and start cutting through the noise." Now, he was gone, another name etched into the growing tally of the lost.

"How many does that make this month?" she asked, her words barely a whisper, as if speaking them louder would make the truth too real.

Marcus hesitated, his gaze dropping to the floor. "Seven," he said finally, the word heavy with resignation. "Tariq was the last of the senior staff besides us. The junior researchers are dropping too—either to the virus or to burnout. Most of the other labs have shuttered. The government's pulling funding, Elena. They're calling it a lost cause."

Anger flared in her chest, hot and sudden, curling her hands into fists at her sides. "It's not a lost cause," she snapped, her voice cutting through the stillness like a whip. "We just need more time."

"Time?" Marcus echoed, lifting his eyes to meet hers. There was no fight in them, only a dull, weary bitterness. "Time is the one thing we don't have. The virus is accelerating—spreading faster than we can map it, mutating faster than we can predict. And with the team shrinking, it's only going to get harder. We're bleeding out, Elena, and there's no one left to stitch us up."

She shot to her feet, her chair scraping harshly against the tiled floor, the sound a jagged protest in the quiet. "We can't give up," she said, her voice trembling with a ferocity she clung to like a lifeline. "Not now. Not when we're so close."

"Are we?" Marcus's question hung between them, sharp and accusing. "Because from where I'm standing, it feels like we're just spinning our wheels—throwing darts in the dark and praying one hits the mark. We've been at this for months, Elena. Every lead evaporates, every model fails. How long do we keep pretending we're making progress?"

The words stung, slicing through her resolve with surgical precision. She opened her mouth to argue, to fling back a defense forged from desperation and hope, but the truth lodged in her throat like a stone. He wasn't wrong. Months of relentless work—nights bleeding into days, meals forgotten, lives unraveling—had yielded nothing but ghosts of breakthroughs, fleeting promises that crumbled under scrutiny. They were chasing a phantom, and with every step, it slipped further from their grasp. But what was the alternative? To surrender? To sit idly by as the world collapsed around them, as Daniel faded, as her child's future dissolved into ash?

"We'll find a way," she said at last, her voice steadying with a resolve she forced into being. "We have to."

Marcus didn't reply. He just nodded, a tired, mechanical gesture, and turned to leave. His footsteps echoed down the empty hallway, a slow, fading drumbeat that seemed to carry the weight of his doubt with it. Elena watched him go, a knot of dread tightening in her gut. How long before he, too, was lost to the virus—or to the despair that was claiming them one by one? How long before she stood alone in this shrinking fortress of science, the last soldier in a war already lost?

She sank back into her chair, the fight draining from her limbs as quickly as it had surged. Her gaze drifted to the small photo frame perched on the edge of her desk, its edges worn from too many restless touches. It was a snapshot of her and Daniel, captured on their last anniversary. They'd gone to the coast, escaping the city's clamor for a weekend of salt air and quiet. In the photo, they were pressed cheek to cheek, her dark hair tangled with his sandy curls, their smiles wide and unguarded. The sunset behind them had painted the sky in streaks of orange and pink, a promise of a tomorrow that now felt like a fading mirage. She traced the edge of the frame with a trembling finger, the memory a lifeline and a wound all at once.

Her hand moved to her phone, hesitating over the screen before she dialed Daniel's number. He picked up on the second ring, his voice a soft warmth that pierced the lab's sterile chill.

"Hey, you," he said, the words tender but threaded with exhaustion. "Still at the lab?"

"Yeah," she replied, forcing a lightness into her tone she didn't feel. "Just finishing up. How are you holding up?"

"I'm fine," he said, too quickly, the lie bare in the strain beneath his words. "Don't worry about me. You've got enough on your plate."

Her throat tightened, a lump she couldn't swallow. "I'm always going to worry about you, Daniel. You know that."

He chuckled, a faint echo of the sound she'd fallen in love with, and it twisted her heart into knots. "I know. Stubborn as ever. But you need to take care of yourself too. And the little one."

The little one. Her hand drifted back to her stomach, a wave of guilt crashing over her like a tide. She'd been so consumed by the fight—by graphs and genomes and the relentless march of the virus—that she'd barely paused to feel the life stirring within her. Two months along, a fragile spark in a world going dark. What kind of mother could she be if she couldn't shield her child from this nightmare? What kind of wife, if she couldn't save the man she loved?

"I will," she said, the promise ringing hollow even to her own ears. "I'll be home soon, okay?"

"Okay," he murmured. "Love you, Elena."

"Love you too."

The call ended, and the silence rushed back in, heavier now, pressing against her ribs. For a moment, she let it overwhelm her—the fear that clawed at her insides, the grief for Haddad and the others, the crushing weight of a responsibility she hadn't asked for but couldn't set down. Tears welled in her eyes, blurring the lab into a haze of light and shadow, and she let them fall, hot trails down her cheeks. But only for a moment. Then she drew a shuddering breath, wiped her face with the sleeve of her lab coat, and turned back to the screen.

Her fingers brushed the pocketknife again, its whale etching a silent vow beneath her touch. The data glared back at her, unyielding, a riddle woven into the strands of human existence. Somewhere within it lay the answer—a way to stop the virus, to save Daniel, to give her child a world worth inheriting. She didn't know if she could find it, didn't know if she had the strength left to keep searching. But she knew one thing with a clarity that burned through the haze of doubt: she wasn't going to stop. Not tonight. Not ever.

The weight of tomorrow pressed down on her, vast and unyielding, but Elena Hayes straightened her spine and began to analyze the latest virus's strains.

3

The Whale's Promise

Five weeks before the clock struck midnight in the hollowed-out Sydney Institute, the lab pulsed with a fragile semblance of life. Machines whirred their steady hymns, keyboards clacked in staccato bursts, and faint laughter drifted from the break room like a memory clinging to the air. But for Elena Hayes, the world had shrunk to a single, glowing screen, its sterile light casting jagged shadows across her face. Her hands trembled as she stared at the test results, her breath snared in her throat, caught between disbelief and a wild, trembling joy. Pregnant. The word burned into her mind, a flare against the storm that had shadowed their lives too long. Her hand drifted to her stomach, pressing against the faint promise beneath her skin—a spark of awe, a shiver of terror. This was real.

Daniel found her moments later, framed in the break room's doorway, his doctor's coat hanging loose on his thinning frame. His hazel eyes narrowed with a flicker of concern, catching the pallor on her face. "Elena?" His voice was soft, steady, a tether she'd clung to through years of chaos. "Are you okay?"

She looked up, her lips curving into a smile—radiant yet brittle, like glass kissed by dawn. "Daniel," she said, her voice quaking on the edge of tears. "We're going to have a baby."

He froze, the words sinking into him like stones into still water. Then, in two strides, he crossed the room, his arms folding around her, pulling her close. "You're serious?" he whispered, his voice splitting with raw wonder.

She nodded against his chest, tears spilling hot and fast down her cheeks. "The test—it's positive. It's real, Daniel."

He drew back just enough to cradle her face, his thumbs brushing away the damp trails, his own eyes shimmering with a vulnerability she rarely saw. "A baby," he murmured, the word a fragile thing he tested against the air. "Our baby."

For a moment, the world beyond them dissolved—the hum of the lab, the weight of the virus, the relentless march of loss. There was only this: his warmth, her trembling hope, a future flickering to life between them. They held each other in the quiet, a fragile island in a sea of ruin.

That evening, as dusk bruised the Sydney sky with streaks of violet and gold, Daniel led her through the city's labyrinthine streets. The clamor of horns and drones faded as they slipped into a narrow alley, where a small shop crouched like a secret carved from time. A bell chimed faintly as they stepped inside, the air thick with the musk of polished wood and steel. Shelves sagged under the weight of trinkets and tools, each one whispering stories of hands long gone.

"What are we doing here?" Elena asked, her brow creasing as she scanned the cluttered space.

Daniel's lips quirked into a half-smile, shadowed with intent. "You'll see."

He guided her to a glass case at the back, where pocketknives gleamed under a soft, amber glow. His fingers lingered over one—a sleek, silver blade, its handle carved with the graceful arc of a whale, tail flared as if plunging into unseen depths. The craftsmanship sang of care, the whale a quiet force carved in ivory.

"This," he said, lifting it with reverence, "is for you."

Elena's breath caught as she took it, her fingers tracing the whale's curves—delicate yet unyielding. "Daniel, it's beautiful," she whispered. "But why?"

He hesitated, his gaze softening, hazel eyes catching the light like sea glass. "You've always loved whales," he said, his voice low, steady. "You told me once they were survivors—diving through the dark, finding their way no matter the odds. And now..." He paused, his hand brushing hers. "Now you're carrying our future. I wanted you to have this—a reminder that we'll find our way too."

Her chest tightened, her grip on the knife firming as his words sank deep. "Daniel..."

He squeezed her hand, his touch a lifeline. "This baby changes everything, Elena. You're going to be an incredible mother—I know it."

Tears welled again, not of fear but of a love so fierce it ached. She leaned into him, her head resting against his shoulder, the knife clutched to her chest like a vow. "Thank you," she breathed. "For this. For us."

They left the shop hand in hand, the knife a quiet weight in her pocket, its whale a promise carved in silver. That night, tangled in the sheets of their bed, her fingers drifted to it again—tracing the etching as her mind spun with fragile dreams. A child with Daniel's crooked smile, her stubborn fire. A family forged against the tide. She pictured telling them of whales—of resilience, of paths carved through shadow.

But even as hope flared, a chill lingered at the edges. The virus prowled beyond their walls, its silent predation claiming lives by the day. She turned to Daniel in the dark, her voice a fierce thread of urgency. "We have to keep fighting," she said. "For this baby. For their world."

He nodded, his hand finding hers beneath the covers, warm despite the faint tremor she pretended not to feel. "We will," he promised. "Together."

Five weeks later, that night was a fading ember—the knife now her sole tether to its light. Daniel's laughter had dulled, his strength ebbing as the virus tightened its grip. The baby she carried was a fragile pulse in a fracturing world, its future teetering on her resolve. As she sat alone in the lab, the whale's promise pressed against her palm—a vow to navigate the abyss, to fight for the spark within her, for the man slipping away, for a tomorrow that refused to die.

The road ahead was a shadowed sea, but Elena straightened her spine, the knife's weight a quiet fire, and turned back to the battle she couldn't abandon.

4

The Fraying Edge

The days bled into one another, a relentless haze of exhaustion and despair that clung to Elena Hayes like a second skin. Time warped and twisted—stretching thin in the lab's quiet hours, snapping cruelly taut with every fresh toll of loss. Her world balanced on a razor's edge, a brittle dance between the work that devoured her, the grief that gnawed at her marrow, and the fragile life stirring within her, tugging her toward a hope she could barely grasp. The Sydney Institute of Advanced Genomics, once a thrumming heart of discovery, had shriveled into a husk. Empty desks lined the corridors, dust settling thick where brilliant minds had once wrestled with the unknown. The virus had reaped its harvest—colleagues, friends, the frayed threads of a community she'd clung to. Yet amid the wreckage, a scant handful of women endured, their resolve a guttering flame against the swallowing dark.

Elena sat at her cluttered desk, the glow of her monitor casting stark shadows across her face. The latest data sprawled before her in a tangle of graphs and genetic sequences, each line a testament to their unraveling world. The virus was mutating faster now, its tendrils sinking deeper into the human genome with predatory precision. What had once taken years to erode—the slow unraveling of the Y chromosome—now consumed its hosts in months. Weeks. For some, like

Daniel, it was a matter of days, a countdown measured in shallow breaths and fading light. She stared at the numbers, her vision blurring at the edges, until they blurred into a single, damning truth: they were losing. Not just the battle, but the war.

Her hand drifted to her stomach, a reflex that steadied her against the abyss. Two and a half months along, the swell was still faint, a secret whispered only in the quiet of her body. The baby—her baby, Daniel's baby—was a fragile vow, a thread of light woven into a world tearing at the seams. The virus hadn't turned on women—not yet—but the fear coiled tight in her gut, a shadow that hissed in the silence. What if it shifted again? What if it reached for her, for them? The thought was a blade she couldn't dodge, no matter how fiercely she gripped her reason.

Her fingers brushed the pocket of her lab coat, tracing the cool edge of the whale-engraved knife nestled within—a gift from Daniel, a silent promise from brighter days. She didn't draw it out; its weight was enough, a tether to him when all else slipped away.

"Elena?" The voice sliced through her spiraling thoughts, soft but insistent. She looked up to see Dr. Priya Sharma in the doorway, her lab coat hanging loose on a frame whittled by sleepless nights. Priya's dark eyes, once ablaze with quiet fire, were dulled by weariness, yet their determination held firm. She clutched a tablet, its faint glow a harbinger Elena couldn't yet read. "The latest sequencing results are in. You need to see this."

Elena nodded, pushing herself to her feet with a grunt of effort. Her body protested, every muscle weighted with exhaustion, every joint aching with the strain of too many hours spent upright. Grief had etched itself deep—a dull ache in her chest that flared with Daniel's name. His decline had sharpened in recent days, a plunge that had wrested him from her grasp. The hospital's verdict was ironclad: no visitors, not with the pregnancy, not with the risk. It stood as a fortress she couldn't storm, and the distance bled her dry—each unanswered call, each night alone in their echoing apartment, a fresh wound.

She trailed Priya to the main workstation, a sprawl of screens and machinery humming with mechanical life. Dr. Synclair Nguyen, Dr. Amina Okoye, and Dr. Clara Hayes—her sister—stood silhouetted against the flickering displays, the last remnants of a once-thriving team. Synclair's sharp mind cut through chaos like a blade, her pragmatism a lifeline. Amina's calm sifted order from noise, her insights a spark in the gloom. Clara, a quieter presence with gray eyes mirroring Elena's own, brought a steady hand to their dwindling ranks, her role unspoken but vital. Priya, ever the heartbeat, tethered them with her unyielding faith. Together, they were a sisterhood forged in the crucible of collapse.

"What do we have?" Elena asked, her voice scraped raw by sleeplessness and silence.

Clara tapped the screen, pulling up a sprawling genetic map that pulsed with color-coded markers. "The virus has mutated again," she said, her tone clipped, professional, but laced with an undercurrent of dread. "It's targeting not just the Y chromosome but other parts of the genome as well. Cancer rates are skyrocketing, and the timeline has accelerated. What used to take years now takes weeks. Days, in some cases."

Elena's stomach twisted, a nauseous lurch that had nothing to do with the pregnancy. "And women?" she pressed, her voice tighter now. "Any signs it's affecting us?"

"Not yet," Amina replied, her gaze steady as it met Elena's. Her voice was a low, measured calm, but her fingers fidgeted with the edge of her sleeve—a telltale sign of the unease she buried. "The data's clear so far, but it's too unpredictable. It's adapting, learning."

Priya leaned forward, her brow creased with worry. "We're running out of time, Elena. The male population's collapsing faster than we can track, and if it shifts to women..." She trailed off, the unspoken hanging heavy in the air. "If we don't stop this soon, there won't be anyone left to save."

The words landed like stones, sinking into the pit of Elena's chest. Her mind raced, a storm of images flashing behind her eyes—Daniel in his hospital bed, his once-strong frame reduced to a fragile shell; the baby, a heartbeat she hadn't yet heard but felt with every fiber of her being; the world beyond these walls, fraying at the edges as families dissolved and cities grew quiet. They were fighting a tide that rose higher with every wave, and their makeshift dam was crumbling.

"We need to try something radical," Elena said at last, her voice cutting through the silence with a clarity that surprised even her. "Something we haven't considered before."

The others exchanged glances, a ripple of tension passing between them—hope warring with skepticism, desperation with fear. "What did you have in mind?" Synclair asked, her arms crossing as she fixed Elena with a piercing stare.

Elena hesitated, the idea taking shape in her mind like a half-formed dream. She took a deep breath, steadying herself against the enormity of what she was about to suggest. "We've been focusing on repairing the damage the virus does to the Y chromosome. But what if we bypass it altogether? What if we find a way to... rewrite the genetic code? To create a workaround that doesn't rely on the Y chromosome at all?"

The room stilled, the weight of her words settling over them like a shroud. It was a concept that danced on the edge of science fiction, a leap into uncharted territory that defied everything they'd been taught. To rewrite humanity's blueprint—to sidestep the very structure the virus had turned into a weapon—was audacious, reckless, perhaps impossible. But they were out of moves, pinned against a wall with no retreat.

Priya broke the silence first, her voice tentative but firm. "It's insane. But it might work. If we can pull it off, it could be the lifeline we need."

"It'll take everything we've got," Amina added, her gaze flickering to the screen as if already calculating the odds. "Resources, time, people—we're already stretched thin."

"Then we stretch thinner," Elena said, her resolve hardening into steel. "We give it everything."

The pact was silent, sealed in the glint of their gazes. They turned to the screens, fingers darting, voices weaving as they charted the uncharted. For the first time in weeks, a spark flared—fragile, fierce—a ember defiant in the gloom.

Hours later, exhaustion dragged Elena's bones as she stood outside the hospital, her breath clouding in the night's chill. The city stretched before her, its lights fainter, its rhythm slowing. She pressed a hand to the glass barring her from Daniel's room, her palm cold against the divide. He lay beyond, a wraith of the man she'd loved—his chest rising in shallow gasps, his vitality stolen by the virus's relentless march. The sight fractured her anew, a splinter in a heart already breaking.

She longed to push through the doors, to kneel by his side and thread her fingers through his, to whisper the words she'd held back for too long. But the risk loomed large, a specter she couldn't ignore. The virus was a phantom in the air, on every surface, in every breath—and the baby was her shield, her tether to a future she refused to let slip away. She stood frozen, torn between love and duty, until a nurse approached, her voice gentle but firm.

"Elena, you shouldn't be here. It's not safe."

Elena nodded, her throat too tight to speak, but her feet remained rooted. Not yet. She couldn't leave him yet.

The call came in the gray hours before dawn, a shrill intrusion into the fragile peace of the lab. Daniel's condition had plummeted—he was fading, the doctors said, his time measured now in hours, perhaps minutes. Elena didn't pause to think. She grabbed her coat, the fabric still damp from the night's drizzle, and bolted from the Institute, her heart a wild drumbeat in her chest. The streets blurred past her as she ran, the hospital's stark silhouette rising against the lightening sky like a sentinel of loss.

Nurses barred her path at the entrance, their gloved hands outstretched, their voices a chorus of caution. "You can't go in!" But she shoved past them, her desperation a force stronger than reason, stronger than fear. She didn't care about the virus, about protocols, about anything but reaching him. One last time.

The room was a tomb when she stumbled in, antiseptic biting the air, the heart monitor's beep a fading thread. Daniel lay swathed in white, his skin waxen, his sandy curls dulled against his brow. He was so small beneath the tangle of tubes, a ghost of the man who'd once held her through the dark. But his hazel eyes found hers, flickering with a spark of life, and a faint smile curved his lips.

"Elena," he rasped, his voice a threadbare whisper. "You came."

"Of course I came," she said, tears spilling hot down her cheeks as she crossed the room in three strides. She sank to her knees beside him, taking his hand in hers, its warmth a fading echo of the strength she'd always known. "I'm here, Daniel. I'm here."

He lifted a trembling hand, his fingers brushing her cheek with a tenderness that broke her all over again. "You shouldn't have come," he murmured, his gaze clouded with love and sorrow. "The baby..."

"The baby will be fine," she said fiercely, clutching his hand tighter, as if she could anchor him to her through sheer will. "I couldn't let you go without seeing you. Without saying goodbye."

His breath hitched, a ragged sound that tore at her, and for a moment they simply looked at each other, the weight of eight years—of laughter, fights, quiet mornings, and unspoken dreams—passing between them in silence. Then, with a strength she hadn't thought he still possessed, he tugged her closer, pulling her into an embrace that smelled of hospital antiseptic and the fading trace of his cologne. She buried her face in his shoulder, her arms wrapping around him as if she could hold time still, as if she could keep him with her just a little longer.

"I love you," he whispered into her hair, his voice breaking. "Take care of our baby. Promise me."

"I promise," she sobbed, muffled against him. "I love you, Daniel. Always."

They clung to each other, suspended in a moment that stretched and stretched, a fragile eternity carved from the chaos. But the heart monitor's rhythm faltered, its steady beep slowing to a mournful cadence, then falling silent altogether. His arms slackened, his breath stilled, and the warmth of him began to ebb away. Elena held him until the silence was absolute, until the absence of him settled into her bones.

She stayed by his side as the gray dawn crept through the window, her hand resting on her stomach where the baby stirred—a faint kick, a whisper of life amid the ruin. She didn't know if it was a boy or a girl, didn't know if it would face a world without men or become another casualty of the virus's wrath. But it didn't matter. This child was her tether, her defiance, her reason to rise from this grief and fight.

When she finally stepped out of the hospital, the morning air was sharp and cold, the city waking to a day that felt emptier than the last. The weight of the world pressed down on her shoulders—Daniel's loss, the virus's relentless march, the fragile hope she carried within her. It was a burden that threatened to crush her, a fraying edge she teetered upon with every step.

But Elena wasn't ready to fall. Not yet. The virus was out there, mutating, killing, carving its path through humanity. She didn't know if a miracle existed to stop it, didn't know if science alone could save them. But if there was no miracle to be found, she would forge one—hammer it from the ashes of her loss, temper it with the fire of her will, and wield it until the end.

She turned to the rising sun, tears drying on her cheeks, and started back toward the lab.

5

The Threads of Tomorrow

The lab lay cloaked in a stillness that felt almost sacred, broken only by the low hum of refrigeration units and the sporadic beep of a monitor tracking data streams that never slept. Clara Hayes sat at her desk, her fingers hovering over the keyboard, poised yet unmoving, as if the act of typing might commit her to a truth she wasn't ready to face. The screen before her glowed with the latest data set, a relentless cascade of numbers and genetic markers that painted a picture as grim as it was familiar. *Chromovirus-X* prowled the world beyond these walls, its mutations a ceaseless dance of destruction, its hunger for lives unquenched. Five years of fighting, of clawing at the edges of a cure, and they were no closer to stopping it than when the nightmare began.

Five years. The span stretched behind her like a lifetime carved from loss, each day a brick in a wall of exhaustion that threatened to bury her. Clara leaned back in her chair, the creak of its springs sharp in the quiet, and pressed her palms to her temples. Fatigue was her constant shadow now, a deep ache that seeped into her bones and coiled around her spine, untouched by the bitter coffee cooling at her elbow. Sleep was a ghost, a luxury she couldn't claim—not when humanity teetered on oblivion, not when her niece, Maya, five years old and fierce with Elena's spark, looked to her with wide, trusting eyes, counting on her to stitch the world back together.

Maya. Her name kindled a fleeting warmth in Clara's chest, a fragile ember amid the gray. But guilt surged in its wake, cold and heavy. She'd vowed to Elena—her sister, her compass—that she'd shield Maya from this unraveling chaos. The promise had spilled from her lips five years ago in a hospital room, Elena's hand frail but fierce in hers as complications from Maya's birth stole her away, mere months after Daniel's death shattered their fragile hope. How could Clara keep that vow now? How could she offer sanctuary to a child so small in a world where every dawn cracked humanity's frame a little wider?

Beyond the lab's reinforced walls, the world was a husk of its former self. The male population, once half the pulse of civilization, had thinned to a scant few million, scattered like leaves on a dying tree. Some endured through a rare, baffling immunity, their survival a riddle science couldn't crack. Others had fled to bunkers or remote outposts, dodging the virus's grasp for years—until it hunted them down. The decline was a slow bleed, draining the globe of its lifeblood. Cities that once thrummed with clamor now stood silent, their streets choked with absence, their steel-and-glass skeletons staring blankly at an indifferent sky.

The collapse had rippled outward, a stone dropped into a pond already drained dry. The global economy had shattered, its intricate web of trade and innovation reduced to bartering for scraps. Technology, once a beacon of progress, had stagnated, its brightest minds felled by the virus or diverted to the primal task of survival. Women had risen to fill the void, stepping into roles long dominated by men—engineers, leaders, protectors—but the shift was a jagged, uneven thing. The weight of responsibility pressed down with a force that bent spines and cracked spirits, and the absence of men left a chasm no amount of resilience could bridge. It wasn't just the loss of bodies; it was the erasure of a dynamic—of fathers, brothers, sons—that had shaped the human story for millennia.

Sperm banks had emerged as sanctuaries of hope, their frozen vaults guarded with a fervor that bordered on reverence. They held the last whispers of a future where men might yet walk the earth, their contents a fragile lifeline for a species on its knees. But even that lifeline frayed with every passing day. The virus had twisted further, its mutations seeping into women's reproductive systems, rendering male fetuses unsustainable. Every pregnancy was a roll of the dice, a quiet prayer whispered over swelling bellies—and more often than not, the answer was silence, a miscarriage that hollowed mothers and dimmed the odds.

Clara had stood at the genesis, a soldier in Elena's ragged army, poring over data beside her sister through endless nights. She'd watched Elena fight, watched her falter, watched her die—complications stealing her breath as Maya's cries pierced the air, a cruel coda to Daniel's loss months before. Elena had been her anchor, her mirror, the one who'd nudged her through doubt and held her through despair. Losing her was a wound unhealed, a piece of Clara buried beneath their failed war. Yet Elena lingered—in the lab's hushed corners, in her voice's echo, in the fire Clara clutched like a lifeline.

Maya was the living echo of that loss, a mirror of Elena in miniature. At five, she bore her mother's sharp cheekbones and piercing gray eyes, the same unyielding spark that had defined Elena's spirit. But there was Daniel in her too—his quiet strength, his steady resilience, a softness that tempered the fire. Clara had fought to carve out some semblance of normalcy for her niece, filling their small apartment with picture books and lullabies, shielding her from the worst of the crisis. She'd woven bedtime tales of a world before the fall, when parks rang with children's laughter and fathers lifted their daughters to the sky, hoping to preserve a flicker of wonder in Maya's young heart. But Maya was too perceptive, too attuned to the silences that followed Clara's forced smiles. The truth bled in, a shadow they couldn't escape.

One evening, as the sun dipped below the horizon, casting the lab in a wash of bruised purple, Clara sifted through a box of old research files—relics of a time when hope had still felt tangible. Her fingers brushed against something unexpected: a leather-bound journal, its edges worn soft by time, tucked beneath a stack of faded printouts. She pulled it free, her breath catching as she recognized the hurried, angular scrawl of Elena's handwriting. Her sister's words spilled across the pages in a torrent of ink, a chronicle of desperation and defiance.

"*Day 147: The virus is mutating faster than we can track. Daniel's condition is worsening, and I don't know how much time he has left. I can't lose him. I can't lose our baby. There has to be a way to stop this.*"

Clara's chest tightened, a vise of grief clamping around her ribs. She'd lived those days beside Elena, watched the toll etch itself into her sister's face—the sleepless nights, the trembling hands, the quiet moments when Elena pressed a palm to her stomach, whispering to the child who would become Maya. But seeing it in black and white, raw and unfiltered, brought the pain crashing back like a wave. She flipped through the pages, another entry leapt out: "*Day 215: If we can't save him, I'll save her future. Rewrite the code. Outrun the virus.*" The words cut fresh, a shard of Elena's soul bared in ink—hypotheses scratched and redrawn, viral sketches crowding the margins, pleas to keep fighting. Each entry was a shard of her sister's soul, a testament to a fight she'd refused to abandon, even as her strength waned and Maya's first cries echoed through the hospital.

"I promised her," Clara murmured, her voice a fragile thread in the empty lab. "I promised I'd find a way." The words tasted of ash, a vow she'd made at Elena's bedside as machines beeped their final farewell, Maya cradled in her arms, a newborn orphaned by a world unraveling. She'd failed then—failed Elena, failed Daniel, failed the fragile life entrusted to her care. But the journal was a lifeline, a tether to her sister's mind, and she dove into it with a hunger she hadn't felt in years.

Page by page, she pieced together the early days of the virus—Elena's meticulous records of its spread, her theories about its origins, her obsession with the outliers. There had been men who'd defied it, men like Thomas, whose immunity had baffled them all. Elena had tracked them, interviewed them, drawn their blood in search of a key. And then there were the sperm banks—Elena's notes detailing their preservation efforts, her hope that they might hold the genetic code to humanity's salvation. But the questions loomed larger than the answers. Why had some survived when others perished? Could that immunity be harnessed, replicated? And what would become of them when the last men faded away?

The journal ignited something in Clara—a spark of purpose that cut through the fog of her despair. She needed answers, and they weren't here, buried in dusty files. They were out there, in the remnants of a world she'd avoided for too long, cloistered with Maya in the safety of routine. Her search led her to Thomas, one of the last known survivors, a man whose name had surfaced again and again in Elena's notes. He lived on the city's ragged edge, in a crumbling farmhouse surrounded by overgrown fields, a relic of a life the virus had spared only by chance.

Clara found him there on a windswept afternoon, the sky heavy with clouds that mirrored the weight in her chest. She'd left Maya with a neighbor—a rare, trusted friend who'd taken to watching the girl when Clara's work demanded it—promising to return with a story and a hug. Thomas was older than she'd expected, his face a map of weathered lines, his hair a shock of gray streaked with the remnants of black. But his eyes were sharp, piercing blue, and they studied her with a quiet intensity as she approached the sagging porch, the wind tugging at her coat.

"You're Elena's sister," he said before she could speak, his voice rough as gravel but warm at the edges. He leaned against the doorframe, arms crossed, a faint smile tugging at his lips. "Saw it in your gait—same determined stride."

Clara's heart stuttered, surprise mingling with a surge of recognition. "You knew her?"

Thomas nodded, stepping aside to let her in. The farmhouse was sparse but lived-in, its walls lined with faded photos—of a family long gone, Clara guessed—and shelves of books yellowed by time. "She came to me years back, when the virus was still new. She came asking why I wasn't sick, took my blood, chased answers. We never found them, but she didn't quit."

A faint smile from Clara, brittle but genuine, and she sank into a worn chair at his kitchen table. "That was Elena. She never stopped fighting."

Thomas settled across from her, his hands clasped on the scarred wood. "She told me about you once. Said you'd carry it on, with those gray eyes like hers."

The words landed like a gift and a burden, stirring the ember of hope Clara had almost forgotten. Maya's face flashed in her mind—those gray eyes, so like Elena's, peering up at her with a trust that felt both precious and fragile. "Do you think there's still a chance?" she asked, leaning forward, her voice trembling with urgency. "A way to save the men who are left—to stop this?"

Thomas's gaze drifted to the window, where the fields stretched toward a horizon swallowed by dusk. His expression darkened, shadows pooling in the lines of his face. "I don't know," he admitted, his voice low. "I've seen too many go—friends, family, strangers. The virus doesn't tire. But if there's a way, you've got her fire in you. That's more than most have left."

Clara left the farmhouse as the first stars pierced the sky, her mind a whirlwind of possibilities. Thomas hadn't given her a cure, hadn't handed her the key to unravel the virus's grip. But he'd given her something else—a thread to follow, a connection to Elena's relentless spirit. She didn't know if she could replicate his immunity, didn't know if the sperm banks held enough to rebuild what was lost. But she knew she had to try—not just for the world, but for Maya, who deserved more than a life shadowed by absence. The world was running out of time, and the weight of Elena's legacy had shifted in her hands—no longer a crushing load, but a torch passed from sister to sister, a call to rise and fight.

As she drove back through the city's empty streets, the silence pressed against her, thick and oppressive. Buildings loomed like tombstones, their windows dark, their stories extinguished. The men were vanishing, and with them, a piece of humanity itself—an equilibrium of voices, a tapestry of lives, unraveling thread by thread. The fall of the Y chromosome wasn't just a crisis of science; it was the end of an epoch, a requiem for a world that would never return.

Clara's hands tightened on the wheel, her jaw set against the tide of doubt. She wasn't sure she was ready for what lay ahead—ready to lead, to hope, to bear the legacy of a fight she hadn't won. But as Maya's small, determined face flickered in her mind, those gray eyes so like Elena's, she knew one thing with a clarity that cut through the dark: she couldn't stop. Not now. Not ever. She'd promised Elena she'd protect her daughter, and she'd promised herself she'd find a way to save what remained.

The lab waited for her, a fortress of flickering lights and unanswered questions. And in its quiet depths, with Maya's future as her lodestar, Clara would search—for answers, for miracles, for a world her niece could inherit.

6

The Echoes of Absence

The air in the abandoned grocery store hung thick with dust, a stale shroud that clung to Clara Hayes's lungs as she moved between the skeletal remains of shelves long stripped bare. Her flashlight carved a narrow beam through the dimness, its light catching on cobwebs and the glint of shattered glass, relics of a world that had once bustled with life. Behind her, Maya trailed close, her small fingers gripping the hem of Clara's weathered coat with a tenacity born of instinct. At five years old, she knew the rules—etched into her young mind through repetition and the quiet urgency of Clara's voice: *Stay quiet. Stay close. Don't touch anything.* The world beyond the enclave was a tapestry of dangers, its threads woven from scarcity and decay, but even here, in this hollowed-out husk of civilization, the silence pressed down like a physical weight, heavy with the absence of what once was.

"Auntie," Maya whispered, her voice so soft it barely stirred the stillness, "is this where Mama got the apples?"

Clara froze mid-step, the innocent question slicing through her like a shard of ice. Elena's memory loomed large in moments like these, a ghost summoned by her daughter's curiosity. Five years had passed since Elena's death—five years since she'd bled out in a makeshift clinic, the last of her strength spent bringing Maya into a world already crumbling. There had been no doctors by then, only a handful of volunteers armed with faded textbooks and a dwindling cache of bandages, their hands trembling as they tried to staunch a hemorrhage they couldn't stop. Clara had been there, kneeling by the cot, her sister's blood staining her palms as Elena managed one fleeting smile at her newborn before the light faded from her gray eyes. Now, Maya knew her mother only through the stories Clara wove—fragile threads of a patchwork quilt stitched from half-remembered moments and the love she couldn't let go.

"No, sweetheart," Clara said softly, lowering herself to one knee to meet Maya's gaze. The girl's eyes, wide and piercing like Elena's, shimmered with a quiet trust that pierced Clara's heart. "The apples are all gone now. But we'll find something else, okay?"

Maya nodded, her thumb slipping to her mouth—a stubborn habit Clara hadn't managed to break, despite her gentle coaxing. Those eyes darted to the empty shelves, scanning the shadows as if she might will something into being. Clara hated these scavenging trips, the necessity of them a bitter pill she swallowed with every outing. The enclave's rations were stretched thin, the community's stores dwindling as the virus's aftermath choked out supply chains. What little remained was hoarded, rationed, fought over in hushed tones behind closed doors. But for Maya—for the child who deserved more than hunger and dust—Clara ventured out, flashlight in hand and dread in her chest.

By 2045, the male population had plummeted to fewer than a million worldwide, a statistic that echoed through the enclave like a death knell. Boys born after the virus's emergence were rare miracles, their fragile lives snuffed out in infancy by cancers that struck with the ferocity of wildfire—leukemia blooming in tiny bones, tumors strangling lungs that had barely learned to breathe. Governments had fractured into regional councils, led by women who'd stepped into the void with grim determination, their focus honed to the essentials: securing food, purifying water, guarding the sperm banks that held humanity's last, flickering chance at a future. But even those banks were faltering, their cryogenic systems reliant on a power grid that stuttered and failed with increasing frequency.

Clara's community—a cluster of repurposed office buildings in downtown Sydney—stood as one of Australia's last bastions, a fragile hub of survival carved from the city's bones. Women filled every role now: farmers coaxing meager harvests from rooftop gardens, engineers patching together solar arrays with scavenged parts, soldiers patrolling the perimeter with rifles slung over their shoulders. But the absence of men was a wound that never closed, a silent ache woven into the fabric of daily life. Maya had never known a world with fathers or brothers, her understanding shaped by Clara's stories and the emptiness that surrounded her. Clara, though, remembered—vividly, painfully—the clamor of crowded bars thick with laughter, the calloused hands of construction workers lifting beams, the gruff patience of her own father as he'd taught her to tweak a carburetor under the hood of their old truck. Now, the streets lay quiet, their echoes swallowed by time.

Back at their apartment—a cramped corner of a former accounting firm—Clara tucked Maya into bed, the girl's small frame dwarfed by a threadbare blanket. Maya clutched her ragged stuffed rabbit, its fur worn to patches, its button eyes dangling by threads. The toy had been Elena's, salvaged from their childhood home before the collapse, a talisman Maya refused to sleep without. Clara brushed a strand of dark hair from the girl's forehead, her fingers lingering on the warmth of her skin.

"Tell me the story," Maya murmured, her eyelids fluttering as sleep tugged at her.

"Which one?" Clara asked, though she knew the answer, the ritual as familiar as breathing.

"The one where Mama saves the world."

Clara's throat tightened, the lie a necessary shield she'd crafted over countless nights. She smoothed Maya's hair and began, her voice steady despite the ache beneath it. "Your mama was a hero. She worked day and night to fight the bad germ, the one that made people sick. And your papa—he was there too, strong and brave, healing people who are sick in the hospital so Mama could keep going. They loved you more than anything, Maya."

"Did they love you too?" Maya's voice was a sleepy whisper, her thumb brushing the rabbit's ear.

Yes," Clara said, the word catching like a stone in her chest. "We are family, Maya. We all love each other."

Maya's breathing deepened, a soft rhythm that filled the small room, and Clara watched her for a long moment, memorizing the curve of her cheek, the flutter of her lashes. Then she rose, slipping out to the balcony where the night air bit at her cheeks, sharp and unforgiving. Below, the compound's perimeter lights flickered, casting jagged shadows across streets that stretched empty into the dark. She pulled a crumpled photo from her pocket—Elena, eight months pregnant, laughing in a sunlit lab, her hand resting on her swollen belly. The last photo they'd taken together, a snapshot of a moment when hope had still felt real. Clara's fingers traced Elena's face, the paper worn soft from too many touches.

"You'd know what to do," she whispered, her breath fogging in the chill. "You always did."

The next morning, Clara left Maya with Lina, a retired schoolteacher whose stern warmth had turned the enclave's daycare into a sanctuary for the handful of children left. Maya clutched her rabbit, her small face solemn as Clara kissed her forehead. "Be good for Lina, okay? I'll be back soon."

"Promise?" Maya's voice was small, her gray eyes searching.

"Promise," Clara said, forcing a smile she didn't feel.

The lab awaited her, a shell of its former glory, its once-gleaming halls now dim and cluttered with scavenged equipment. Half the machinery had been looted in the early chaos of the collapse, the other half jury-rigged to limp along on sporadic power. It was a far cry from the Sydney Institute's heyday, but it remained Clara's refuge, a tether to the scientist she'd been before the world unraveled.

Dr. Amina Okoye was already there, her slight frame hunched over a microscope, her once-vibrant curls dulled by streaks of gray. Her lab coat, stained with coffee and patched at the elbows, hung loose on her shoulders. "Still no progress," she said without looking up, her voice flat with exhaustion. "The latest samples are degrading faster than we can analyze them. Another batch lost."

Clara slumped into a chair, the metal cold against her back. The sperm banks were failing—not just here, but everywhere. Cryogenic storage demanded a steady power supply, a luxury eroded by blackouts that rolled through the enclave like storm clouds. Even if they stabilized the grid, the virus had evolved its assault, targeting male embryos in utero with ruthless precision. Women who conceived using the banked sperm—those precious vials guarded like relics—miscarried within weeks, their bodies rejecting pregnancies that dared to carry a Y chromosome. Each loss was a blow, a reminder that their last lifeline was slipping through their fingers.

"We're wasting time," Clara said, the words bitter on her tongue, sharp with a frustration she could no longer bury. "We need to pivot. Permanently."

Amina finally lifted her head, her dark eyes narrowing as they met Clara's. "Parthenogenesis."

It wasn't a question, but a gauntlet thrown between them. They'd circled this debate for months, their arguments a tangle of science and ethics. Parthenogenesis—virgin birth, a trick of nature seen in reptiles and insects—was a desperate leap, a genetic fantasy for humans. Yet whispers had reached them from California: a coalition of female scientists, armed with CRISPR edits and a reckless will, was experimenting to bypass the need for sperm entirely, to trigger reproduction from a single genome. It was radical, untested, a rewriting of humanity itself.

"It's the only way," Clara pressed, leaning forward, her hands gripping the edge of the table. "The banks won't last another decade. Even if they did, we can't risk another generation of boys dying in the womb. We have to... evolve."

Amina's gaze hardened, her fingers tightening around the microscope's focus knob. "And if we fail? If we create something we can't control?"

"Then we fail," Clara shot back, her voice trembling with conviction. "But at least we tried. At least we didn't sit here waiting for the end."

Amina held her stare, the silence stretching taut between them, heavy with the weight of their choices. Finally, she sighed, a sound that carried years of weariness. "We'll need more than what we have here. Equipment, power, data—it's a long shot even with the best conditions."

"Then we go where the conditions are better," Clara said, the seed of a decision taking root. "The California coalition—they've invited me to join them. They're pooling everything: resources, personnel, expertise. If parthenogenesis is going to work, it'll happen there."

Amina's brow furrowed, but she didn't argue. Instead, she turned back to her microscope, her silence a reluctant assent.

That afternoon, Clara took Maya to the community garden, a patchwork of dirt and hydroponic trays wedged onto the rooftop of their building. The wind carried the faint tang of compost and salt from the distant harbor, a rare breath of life in the city's stillness. Maya knelt beside a row of pea plants, her tiny hands brushing the leaves with a reverence that tugged at Clara's chest. She'd inherited Elena's curiosity, that relentless need to poke at the world until it yielded its secrets.

"Why do plants need water?" Maya asked, tilting her head, her hair spilling over her shoulder.

Clara sank to her knees beside her, a faint smile softening her exhaustion. "Same reason we do, love. To grow."

"But plants don't have mouths," Maya countered, her brow creasing in that earnest way that always reminded Clara of Elena.

"They drink through their roots," Clara explained, tracing a finger along the soil. "Like straws pulling water up from the ground."

Maya frowned, her small mind wrestling with the idea. "What happens if they don't drink?"

"They die," Clara said quietly, the words slipping out before she could soften them.

Maya's face crumpled, her lip trembling as she looked up. "Like Mama?"

The question hit Clara like a fist, stealing her breath. She pulled Maya into her lap, the girl's warmth a stark contrast to the cold wind whipping across the roof. "Oh, sweetheart," she murmured, pressing her cheek to Maya's hair. "Your mama didn't want to leave you. She fought so hard to stay—she loved you so much."

Maya buried her face in Clara's shoulder, her voice muffled against the fabric of her coat. "I don't want you to fight. I want you to stay."

Clara's arms tightened around her, a fierce ache blooming in her chest. "I'm not going anywhere, love. I promise you that."

But even as she spoke, the weight of that promise settled over her—a vow she wasn't sure she could keep, not with the road she was choosing.

That night, Clara stood before the enclave's council, the room a cramped bunker beneath the main building, its walls lined with cracked concrete and flickering fluorescent lights. The air was thick with the smell of stale coffee and the tension of too many hard decisions. Eight women sat around a scarred table, their faces etched with fatigue and resolve—Councilwoman Richter at the head, her steel-gray hair pulled tight, her judge's eyes sharp despite the years.

"The U.S. coalition has invited me to join their research," Clara said, her voice steady despite the tremor in her hands. She stood with her shoulders squared, Elena's journal a silent weight in her pocket. "They're pooling resources—equipment, data, personnel—everything we lack here. If we're going to crack parthenogenesis, if we're going to give humanity a future, it'll happen there."

Richter leaned forward, her fingers steepled, her gaze cutting through the dim light. "And if you go, what becomes of us? We're barely holding on as it is. We need every scientist, every pair of hands, right here."

Clara met her stare, unflinching. "You need a future, not just survival. Right now, we don't have one. If I go, there's a chance—a real chance—to change that."

Murmurs rippled through the council, voices clashing in a low hum of debate. Richter's jaw tightened, but she raised a hand for silence. "You're asking us to gamble our last resource on a theory. What if you don't come back? What if they fail?"

"Then we're no worse off than we are now," Clara said, her voice softening but firm. "But if they succeed—if I succeed—it's not just for us. It's for every enclave, every child like Maya who deserves more than this."

The vote stretched into the early hours, a seesaw of arguments and silences that left Clara's nerves raw. In the end, Richter relented, her voice heavy with resignation. "Go," she said, lines deepening around her mouth. "But if you find answers, you bring them back. For all of us."

Packing was a quiet ritual, completed in less than an hour under the flicker of a single bulb. Clara filled two backpacks—clothes patched with care, ration bars wrapped in foil, Elena's journal tucked beside a folded photo of her and Maya. She woke Maya before dawn, the girl's small form stirring beneath the blanket, her rabbit clutched tight.

"Where are we going?" Maya mumbled, rubbing sleep from her eyes as Clara eased her into a coat.

Clara knelt, buttoning the too-big garment with steady hands. "Somewhere new, sweetheart. Somewhere safe."

"Will there be other kids?" Maya's voice was thick with drowsiness, but her eyes searched Clara's face.

"Yes," Clara said, her throat tightening. "I hope so."

They slipped through the compound's gates as the first light brushed the horizon, streaks of pink bleeding into the gray. The air was sharp, carrying the faint salt of the harbor, and in the distance, a bird trilled—a solitary note Clara hadn't heard in years, fragile and defiant against the silence. She hoisted Maya onto her hip, the girl's weight a grounding anchor as they stepped onto the cracked road leading west.

Maya squeezed her hand, her small fingers warm against Clara's calloused palm. "Auntie?"

"Yes, love?"

"I'm scared."

Clara shifted her, pressing a kiss to her forehead as she adjusted the backpacks' straps. "Me too, dear. But we'll be brave together, okay?"

"Okay," Maya whispered, resting her head against Clara's shoulder.

The road ahead was a ribbon of uncertainty, winding through a landscape scarred by loss and littered with the bones of a world that no longer turned. Clara didn't know what waited in California—whether the coalition's experiments would yield salvation or collapse into another dead end. But as she walked, Maya's steady breathing soft against her neck, something stirred in her chest—a flicker of something she'd almost forgotten, buried beneath years of grief and struggle.

Hope. Tentative, fragile, but alive.

She tightened her grip on Maya and kept moving, step by step, toward a horizon that shimmered with the promise of something new.

7

The Ghosts of the Sky

The plane hummed softly as it sliced through the ink-black night, its engines a low, steady drone that vibrated through the metal frame. Inside, the cabin was bathed in a faint, bluish glow from the overhead lights, dimmed for the late hour, casting long shadows across the rows of empty seats. The air felt thick with stillness, the kind that amplified every small sound—the creak of a seat, the rustle of a blanket, the faint whistle of wind against the fuselage. Clara sat by the window, her forehead pressed against the cool, smooth glass, her breath fogging faintly with each exhale. Outside, an endless sea of stars stretched into the void, their cold light shimmering against the boundless dark. It was beautiful, in a desolate way, but it offered her no peace.

Beside her, Maya slept soundly, her small body curled into the curve of Clara's side. The girl's head rested heavily on Clara's shoulder, her dark hair spilling across the worn fabric of Clara's jacket. In her arms, she clutched her ragged stuffed rabbit, its once-white fur now a patchwork of gray stains and frayed seams, a relic of a safer, softer time. The rhythmic rise and fall of Maya's chest, the soft whistle of her breath, was a small anchor for Clara—a fragile tether to the present. But it wasn't enough to quiet the storm raging in her mind.

Memories of Elena clawed their way to the surface, unbidden and relentless, as they always did in moments like this—when the world outside fell silent and the noise within grew deafening. Clara's chest tightened as the past unfurled before her, vivid and inescapable.

It was 2040, the year the virus had begun its merciless acceleration, spreading like wildfire through the population, leaving chaos and despair in its wake. Clara and Elena had been in the lab late that night, as they so often were, surrounded by the hum of machinery and the sterile scent of antiseptic. The room was a cocoon of artificial light, their computer screens glowing with strings of data, casting eerie shadows across the walls. Papers littered the desk between them—scribbled notes, half-finished equations, coffee-stained charts—all evidence of their desperate race against time. Elena, heavily pregnant, sat across from Clara, her belly round and taut beneath her lab coat. Her movements were slower then, deliberate, but her mind remained a razor-sharp blade, cutting through the fog of exhaustion that hung over them both.

"What if we're looking at this all wrong?" Elena had said suddenly, her voice piercing the quiet. She leaned back in her chair, one hand resting on her stomach, the other tapping absently against the armrest.

Clara looked up from her notes, her pen pausing mid-sentence. "What do you mean?"

Elena's gaze was distant, her brow furrowed in thought. "We've been trying to fix the Y chromosome, to stop the virus from shredding it apart. Years of patching and prodding and praying it holds. But what if we're wasting our time? What if we bypass it altogether? Rewrite the genetic code so it doesn't even need the Y chromosome to function."

Clara blinked, setting her pen down. "You're talking about parthenogenesis. In humans."

"Not exactly," Elena replied, her eyes snapping back to Clara's, sparkling with that familiar blend of excitement and defiance. "More like... editing the blueprint. Rebuilding the system from the ground up. If we can't save the Y chromosome—if it's too far gone—maybe we can create a workaround. A new pathway for reproduction, one the virus can't touch."

Clara let out a short, incredulous laugh, though it carried no real mirth. "You're insane, you know that? This isn't some sci-fi novel we're writing here."

"It's not fiction if we make it real," Elena shot back, her grin wide and unapologetic. She leaned forward, resting her elbows on the desk, her enthusiasm infectious despite the absurdity of it all. But then her expression softened, and she placed both hands gently over her stomach, her fingers tracing small circles. "I just... I want to make sure this little one has a future. A real one. Not just survival, but a chance to live."

Clara's throat tightened at the words. She reached across the cluttered desk, her hand finding Elena's and squeezing it gently. "We'll figure it out," she said, her voice firm despite the uncertainty gnawing at her. "Together."

The memory twisted and shifted, sharpening into a different scene, one etched so deeply into Clara's soul that it felt like a wound that would never heal. It was the night Elena went into labor, months later, when the world had already begun to crumble around them. They were in the clinic, a hastily converted space in the research facility, its walls stark and cold. The air was heavy with the sharp sting of antiseptic and the undercurrent of fear that clung to everything in those days. Elena lay on the narrow bed, her face pale and slick with sweat, her breathing shallow and labored. Machines beeped steadily beside her, their screens flashing numbers Clara couldn't bear to look at. Despite the pain, Elena's voice remained steady, cutting through the chaos.

"Clara," she said, her hand gripping Clara's with surprising strength, her fingers trembling but unyielding. "Promise me something."

"Anything," Clara whispered, her voice breaking as she knelt beside the bed, her free hand brushing damp strands of hair from Elena's forehead.

"If something happens to me... if I don't make it..." Elena's eyes locked onto Clara's, fierce and unwavering despite the exhaustion clouding them. "You'll take care of her. You'll protect her, no matter what."

Clara nodded, tears spilling hot and fast down her cheeks. "I promise," she choked out, the words tasting like ash.

Elena managed a faint smile, her grip loosening slightly as her strength began to fade. Her eyes fluttered closed for a moment before opening again, softer this time. "Good," she murmured. "Because you're the only one I trust to keep her safe."

The plane shuddered violently, hitting a pocket of turbulence that snapped Clara back to the present. Her breath caught, and she pressed a trembling hand to her face, wiping away the tears that had gathered on her cheeks. Across the aisle, a flight attendant—a young woman with tired eyes and a practiced smile—glanced at her, offering a fleeting look of sympathy before turning away. Clara ignored it, shifting her gaze back to the window, where the stars still burned coldly against the night sky.

The memories refused to relent, each one slicing deeper than the last. Elena had always been the light in their partnership, the one who could find humor even in the bleakest moments. Clara's mind drifted to a quieter memory, one that felt like a lifetime ago. They'd been working late in the lab, their coffee long gone cold, the fluorescent lights buzzing overhead. Elena had suddenly straightened in her chair, stretched dramatically, and then—without warning—launched into a terrible, off-key rendition of a pop song from their teenage years. Her voice cracked on every high note, her arms flailing in an exaggerated dance move that knocked over a stack of files. Clara had burst out laughing, so hard she'd fumbled her mug and sent cold coffee splashing across the desk. Elena had cackled, pointing at the mess.

"You're such a klutz," she'd teased, her grin wide and mischievous. "Good thing you're the brains of this operation."

"And what does that make you?" Clara had retorted, still giggling as she grabbed a handful of napkins to mop up the spill.

"The beauty, obviously," Elena had said, striking a mock pose before dissolving into laughter again.

The sound of their shared joy had echoed through the empty lab, a rare moment of lightness in a world growing darker by the day.

But that light had been snuffed out too soon. Elena's death had come like a thief in the night, swift and merciless—a complication during labor that no one could have foreseen. Clara had been there, helpless, as the doctors worked frantically and failed. She'd held Maya for the first time just hours later, the tiny, squirming bundle of life that was all that remained of her sister. In that moment, staring into the newborn's wide, uncomprehending eyes, Clara had made a silent vow to keep her safe, to honor the promise she'd made.

Now, on the plane, Clara's breath hitched painfully, and she pressed a hand to her mouth to stifle the sob threatening to escape. Maya stirred beside her, mumbling incoherently in her sleep, but didn't wake. Clara closed her eyes, letting the tears fall freely down her face, hot and silent.

"I'm trying, Elena," she whispered, her voice so faint it was nearly lost beneath the hum of the engines. "I'm trying so hard to keep my promise."

But the weight of that promise pressed down on her like a physical thing, heavy and unyielding. The world beyond the plane was unraveling—societies collapsing, resources dwindling, hope fading—and Clara wasn't sure she had the strength to hold their small piece of it together.

The plane tilted slightly, beginning its descent, and the first glimmers of California's lights appeared below, twinkling like fallen stars against the dark coastline. Clara wiped her face with the sleeve of her jacket, drawing a deep, shaky breath to steady herself. She couldn't afford to fall apart—not now, not when Maya depended on her.

The landing gear whirred as the plane touched down, the jolt reverberating through the cabin. Clara glanced at her niece, still asleep, her small face serene and untouched by the burdens Clara carried. For a fleeting moment, she saw Elena in her—the same sharp cheekbones, the same quiet resilience that had defined her sister even in her final moments.

"We're here, darling," Clara murmured, reaching out to brush a stray strand of hair from Maya's forehead. "We're going to make this right."

The words felt like a prayer, fragile and uncertain, as she gathered their meager belongings and prepared to step off the plane. The air outside was cool and sharp, tinged with the salt of the Pacific, and as Clara took her first steps into the unknown, she couldn't shake the sensation that Elena's ghost lingered close—walking beside her, whispering words of encouragement laced with quiet warnings.

The road ahead stretched into shadow, its end hidden from view. But Clara would walk it, step by trembling step. For Elena, whose dreams still echoed in her mind. For Maya, whose future rested in her hands. And for the fragile hope of a world they all deserved, one she refused to let slip away.

8

A New World

The research complex in California defied every expectation Clara Hayes had carried across the Pacific. Nestled in the rolling hills outside San Francisco, it rose like a vision from a lost future—a sprawling fortress of glass and steel, its gleaming surfaces catching the golden light of late afternoon. High fences encircled it, their razor wire glinting faintly, while armed guards patrolled the perimeter with a quiet, mechanical precision. The government had carved this place from the chaos of 2045, offering Clara a sanctuary within its walls: a small apartment with stark white walls, a narrow bed, and a window framing the undulating hills and the distant, shimmering edge of the Pacific Ocean. It was meant to be a haven, a cocoon where she could focus on her work, insulated from the crumbling world beyond. But as Clara stepped from the dust-streaked car that had ferried them from the coast, Maya's small hand clasped tight in hers, a shiver of unease rippled through her.

The complex was too quiet, its stillness a stark contrast to the clamor of Sydney she'd left behind. The air carried a faint tang of disinfectant, sharp and clinical, and the only sound was the low, persistent hum of generators buried somewhere beneath the earth. Gone were the chaotic streets of her youth—the honk of horns, the chatter of crowds, the pulse of a city alive with motion. Here, silence reigned, a sterile void that pressed against her ears and settled into her bones. Maya's grip tightened, her five-year-old fingers digging into Clara's palm as she peered up at the towering structure, her gray eyes—so like Elena's—wide with a mix of awe and trepidation.

The government had granted them a month to settle in, a generosity that felt almost surreal after years of scraping by on rationed hours and dwindling hope. Those first days blurred into a haze of bureaucracy—paperwork stacked in neat piles, security clearances that required retinal scans and clipped questions, introductions to faces that blurred together in her exhaustion. Everyone seemed to know her name before she spoke it: Dr. Clara Hayes, Elena's sister, the geneticist who'd survived the virus's worst and now bore the mantle of humanity's salvation. Their hushed whispers and sidelong glances followed her through the corridors, a weight of expectation that clung to her like damp cloth, suffocating in its quiet intensity.

Maya, at least, found her footing with a child's resilience. The complex housed a small school for the researchers' children—a rare pocket of warmth amid the steel and glass—and Clara enrolled her on their second day. The classroom was a burst of color, its walls plastered with hand-drawn pictures and faded posters of animals long vanished from the wild. Maya had hesitated at the threshold, her small frame pressed against Clara's leg, her rabbit tucked under one arm. But Mrs. Alvarez, the teacher—a wiry woman with a gentle smile and a braid of silver-shot hair—knelt before her, offering a soft word and a brightly painted wooden block.

"She'll be fine," Mrs. Alvarez assured Clara, resting a hand on Maya's shoulder as the girl clutched the block with tentative curiosity. "We'll take good care of her. She's not the only one starting fresh here."

Clara nodded, her throat tight with a knot she couldn't swallow. Letting Maya out of her sight, even for a few hours, felt like a jagged betrayal of the promise she'd whispered to Elena five years ago—to keep her daughter safe, to shield her from a world that devoured innocence. But she couldn't cocoon Maya forever, couldn't let fear dictate the boundaries of her life. She forced a smile, ruffled Maya's hair, and left her there, the echo of her small voice trailing behind as Clara stepped back into the sterile quiet.

The research complex was a marvel, a testament to a technology that had once promised boundless horizons. Its hallways shimmered with holographic displays, their glowing screens casting real-time maps of the virus's spread—red tendrils snaking across continents, numbers ticking downward as the male population shrank to a whisper. The labs were pristine, their counters lined with equipment Clara had only dreamed of in Sydney's crumbling facilities: gene sequencers humming with precision, CRISPR arrays glowing with potential, microscopes that peered into the very threads of life. Yet for all its gleaming promise, the complex felt hollow, its vastness underscoring the absence of those who'd once filled it. The virus had scythed through more than half the world's population, and the researchers who remained were a thin, weary thread stretched across a gaping void. Clara wandered the halls late at night, her footsteps echoing off polished floors, the silence a weight that pressed against her ribs and shadowed her every thought.

One evening, as she sat in the cafeteria—a cavernous space of white tables and flickering lights—she picked at a plate of synthetic protein and reconstituted vegetables, the food tasteless despite its engineered nutrition. The room was nearly empty, save for a few scattered figures hunched over their trays, their murmurs swallowed by the stillness. A shadow fell across her table, and Clara looked up to see a woman standing there—tall and lean, her sharp features framed by a cropped sweep of dark hair, her hazel eyes glinting with a no-nonsense clarity.

"Dr. Hayes," the woman said, extending a hand with a grip firm and cool. "Dr. Emily Carter. I'm heading the parthenogenesis initiative. Welcome to the team."

Clara shook her hand, summoning a smile that felt brittle on her lips. "Thank you. It's... impressive."

Dr. Carter arched an eyebrow, settling into the seat across from her without invitation. "But?"

Clara hesitated, then let the truth slip free, unguarded in the face of Carter's directness. "But it feels like a tomb. Where is everyone?"

Carter's expression darkened, her fingers tightening around the edge of her tray. "Gone," she said, her voice low and clipped. "Dead, mostly. Or too afraid to leave their bunkers and basements. The virus didn't just take the men, Dr. Hayes. It took our hope. What you see here is what's left: the stubborn, the desperate, the ones who can't let go." She leaned back, her gaze piercing. "You're one of us now."

The words lingered, a quiet challenge that sank into Clara's bones. She nodded, unsure how to respond, and Carter rose with a curt nod, leaving her to the solitude of her meal.

On weekends, Clara carved out time for Maya, a fragile tether to the life beyond the lab's walls. The complex was ringed by miles of untouched wilderness—pine-scented hills rolling toward the horizon, their slopes dotted with wildflowers that defied the world's decay. They took to walking the trails, the crisp California air a balm after the complex's sterile chill. Maya skipped ahead, her small boots crunching on pine needles, her laughter a rare, bright note against the quiet. Clara followed, her chest loosening with each step, the weight of her work easing in the presence of her niece's unburdened joy.

One Saturday, they ventured into San Francisco, a pilgrimage to a city that had once pulsed with life. The drive was a silent descent through abandoned suburbs, their lawns overgrown, their windows dark. The Golden Gate Bridge loomed as they approached, its rust-red towers rising stark against a sky heavy with gray clouds, a monument to a past that felt like myth. The streets were a ghostly tableau—cars rusted in place, storefronts gaping with shattered glass, the few people they passed hurrying by with masked faces and wary eyes, their footsteps swallowed by the stillness.

Maya clung to Clara's hand, her curiosity warring with the unease that shadowed her small frame. "Where is everyone, Auntie?" she asked, her voice soft as they paused on a sidewalk.

Clara crouched beside her, searching for words simple enough for a five-year-old yet gentle enough to shield her. "They're... staying inside, love. To stay safe from the bad germ."

Maya nodded, her brow furrowing as she glanced around, her rabbit dangling from one hand. "Are they scared?"

"Sometimes," Clara admitted, brushing a strand of hair from Maya's face. "But we're here together, and that makes us brave."

They wandered to a small park, its playground a relic of neglect—swings rusted to stillness, slides buried under weeds. Maya broke free, her hesitance melting as she scrambled onto a swing, its chains creaking under her weight. Clara pushed her, the rhythmic squeak of metal cutting through the silence, and for a moment, the world shrank to the two of them— Maya's laughter, the sway of the swing, the fleeting illusion of normalcy. Clara's throat tightened, a lump rising as she watched her niece's small legs kick at the air. This was the world Maya would inherit—empty streets, silent cities, a legacy of fear and loss. But in that laughter, Clara glimpsed something else: a spark of defiance, a chance to build anew.

As the month drew to a close, Clara surrendered herself to the work, the parthenogenesis initiative a daunting mountain she scaled one step at a time. The lab became her second skin, its walls a canvas of whiteboards scrawled with equations and genetic maps, its air humming with the soft whir of machinery. Dr. Carter was a relentless guide, her sharp mind cutting through ambiguity with surgical precision, her demands pushing Clara to beyond of her knowledge.

"We're not just rewriting the genetic code," Carter said one evening, her voice low as they stood before a holographic model of a DNA strand, its double helix pulsing with light. The lab was dim, the other researchers gone, leaving only the glow of screens and the murmur of cooling units. "We're rewriting the future. And that starts with you."

Clara nodded, the weight of Carter's words settling over her like a mantle she wasn't sure she could bear. She thought of Elena—of the late nights they'd spent hunched over microscopes, their voices overlapping with ideas, their dreams of a cure a shared fire that had burned bright until it couldn't. Now, that fire was hers alone to tend, to stoke into something greater. For Elena. For Maya. For the world they'd both vowed to save.

Late one night, as the complex slept, Clara sat alone in the lab, her chair creaking beneath her as she scrolled through old photos on her phone. The screen cast a faint glow across her face, illuminating the lines etched by years of strain. There was Elena, her smile radiant, her eyes alight with hope as she stood in a sunlit lab, one hand resting on her pregnant belly. There was Maya as a newborn, her tiny hand curled around Clara's finger, her face scrunched in sleep. And there was Sydney—its harbor glittering under a sky unmarred by loss, its streets alive with a pulse that had long since faded. The images blurred as tears welled, hot and unbidden, spilling down her cheeks to drip onto the desk.

"I'm trying, Elena," she whispered into the silence, her voice breaking as she pressed a hand to the screen, as if she could reach through time to touch her sister's face. "I'm trying to keep my promise."

The lab stretched empty around her, its sterile expanse a mirror to the hollow ache in her chest. The road ahead was a shadowed path—long, uncertain, paved with risks she couldn't yet name. But Clara would walk it, step by resolute step. For Elena, whose legacy burned in her blood. For Maya, whose future hung in the balance of every choice she made. For the promise of a new world, fragile and unformed, but within reach if she dared to grasp it.

She wiped her eyes, straightened her spine, and turned back to the data glowing on the screen before her. The work wasn't done—not tonight, not ever. And neither was she.

9

A Spark in the Silence

Months had slipped by since Clara Hayes arrived at the California research complex, their passage marked by a rhythm that had settled into her bones like a quiet metronome. Her days unfurled in the lab, hunched over screens and samples, her nights folded into the small apartment where Maya's soft breathing filled the stillness, and her weekends drifted through the empty trails or the ghostly streets of San Francisco. The parthenogenesis project had swallowed her whole, a consuming vortex of equations and embryos that left little space for anything beyond its relentless pull. It was her tether to Elena's legacy, her shield against the void, her fragile bridge to a future she could scarcely envision. Yet within this mechanical cadence, cracks of unexpected light began to pierce the gray.

It began on a Tuesday morning, in the small coffee shop tucked into a corner of the complex—a utilitarian nook of steel counters and humming dispensers, its air thick with the faintly synthetic scent of roasted beans. Clara stood in line, her mind already tangled in the day's experiments—gene edits, delivery vectors, the stubborn resistance of mouse embryos—when she shifted her weight and bumped into the person behind her. Her elbow jostled a cup, sending a splash of dark liquid arcing through the air.

"Oh, sorry," she said, the words tumbling out as she stepped back, heat rising to her cheeks.

"No worries," came the reply, warm and unruffled, a voice that cut through her distraction like a steady note. "You're not the first person to spill coffee on me, and you probably won't be the last."

Clara glanced up, startled, and met a pair of hazel eyes crinkling at the corners with an easy smile. He was tall, his frame lean beneath a faded jacket, his dark hair tousled and his scruffy beard flecked with gray. He held up his hand, now splattered with coffee, and grinned—a lopsided, disarming expression that softened the sterile edges of the moment.

"I'm really sorry," she stammered, fumbling for a napkin from the dispenser, her fingers clumsy with embarrassment. "I wasn't paying attention."

"It's fine," he said, taking the napkin with a casual grace and wiping his hand. "I'm Alex, by the way. Tech wing—AI development mostly. Born and raised right here in California."

"Clara," she replied, extending her hand automatically. His grip was warm, steady, though she caught a faint tremor in it. "Genetics."

"Ah, so you're one of the miracle workers," Alex said, his tone teasing but laced with a genuine note of respect. "Trying to save the world and all that?"

Clara laughed—a nervous exhale that surprised her with its lightness, a sound she hadn't heard from herself in too long. "Something like that. More like trying not to break it worse."

They stood there, the line shuffling forward, and the awkwardness of the moment softened into something gentler. Alex had a way of looking at her—not as Elena's shadow, not as the scientist bearing humanity's last hope, but as Clara, plain and present. It was a gaze that peeled back the layers she'd armored herself with, and she realized, with a quiet ache, how much she'd missed being seen.

"So, Clara," Alex said, breaking the pause with a playful tilt of his head, "do you always spill coffee on strangers, or is this a special occasion?"

She smiled despite herself, a real one this time, tugging at the corners of her mouth. "Only on Tuesdays. Keeps things interesting."

"Good to know," he said, his grin widening. "I'll steer clear of you on Tuesdays then"

They both laughed, a shared ripple of sound that echoed faintly in the near-empty shop, and for a fleeting moment, the weight of the world—of the virus, the losses, the endless fight—lifted, leaving a sliver of air she could breathe.

Back in the lab, the parthenogenesis project marched forward, its progress a slow crawl through a mire of setbacks and faint promises. Early experiments with simpler organisms—worms, fish—had yielded fragile successes, embryos sparking to life without a whisper of male DNA. But mammals were a steeper cliff, their complexity a wall that defied every tool in Clara's arsenal. The lab was a hive of controlled chaos: whiteboards scrawled with looping equations, screens flickering with genetic maps, the soft hum of centrifuges spinning late into the night. Dr. Emily Carter stood at its heart, her sharp mind a compass guiding their faltering steps.

"We're close," Carter said one afternoon, her voice clipped as they hovered over a holographic model of a mouse embryo, its delicate cells pulsing in digital amber. The lab's lights cast stark shadows across her angular face, deepening the lines etched by years of strain. "But close is meaningless if we can't make it work in vivo. We need viability, Clara—not just a spark, but a flame."

Clara nodded, her eyes tracing the embryo's fragile structure, its promise snuffed out in every trial by day three. "We're missing something," she murmured, her fingers tapping absently against the console. "Maybe it's the gene sequence—too unstable—or the delivery method's off. I don't know yet."

Carter's hand landed on her shoulder, firm but not unkind, a rare gesture from a woman who guarded her warmth like a scarce resource. "You'll figure it out. You always do. That's why you're here."

The confidence should have bolstered her, but doubt gnawed at Clara's edges. The pressure was a rising tide—every failed trial a stone added to the pile on her chest, each one a betrayal of Elena's dream, Maya's future, the fragile hope she'd carried across oceans. She forced a tight smile and turned back to the data, burying her uncertainty beneath analysis.

A few days later, fate nudged her toward Alex again, this time in the complex's library—a quiet warren of shelves and dim light, its air heavy with the musty scent of old paper and the faint buzz of digital archives. Clara was hunting a rare journal on genetic editing, her fingers trailing over cracked spines, when a familiar voice broke her focus.

"Looking for something?"

She turned to find Alex leaning against a shelf, a stack of books cradled in his arms, that same easy smile lighting his face. He wore a faded sweater now, its sleeves rolled to his elbows, revealing forearms dusted with dark hair and faint scars she hadn't noticed before.

"Just some research," she said, holding up the journal—its cover a faded blue, its pages yellowed with age. "Trying to crack the code, as they say."

"Mind if I join you?" he asked, nodding toward the empty chair across the table where she'd set her notes.

Clara hesitated, the instinct to retreat warring with a quiet pull she couldn't name. "Sure," she said finally, sliding the journal onto the table as he settled in.

They spent the next hour talking, the conversation unfurling like a slow bloom. It drifted from her work—parthenogenesis, the stubborn embryos—to his: AI systems modeling survival scenarios, preserving knowledge in a fading world. Alex was sharp and funny, his wit dancing around her exhaustion. He spoke with his hands, gestures animating his words, though a faint tremor betrayed them now and then—a relic of survival, he'd confess later.

"So, what's it like working on AI in the middle of all this?" Clara asked, gesturing to the library's empty rows, its silence a testament to the absent voices that once filled it.

"Lonely," Alex admitted, his smile fading into something softer, unguarded. "I grew up here—California—raised by my dad after my mom took off when I was a kid. Single father, tough as nails, taught me everything worth knowing. Then the virus hit, and he was gone—just like that. Took everything I had left." He paused, a shadow crossing his face, his voice dropping. "Turns out I was immune—lucky me. They made me a test subject for months after he died, poking and prodding me weekly until my hands shook. Took a toll on my health—still does. So I opted out, figured I'd live what's left of me on my terms, not theirs."

Clara's breath caught, the weight of his words settling over her. "I'm sorry," she said softly, her hand twitching toward his before she pulled it back. "That's... a lot to carry."

He shrugged, a small, tired gesture, but his eyes held hers with a quiet strength. "We all carry something, right? Most days, it's just me and the algorithms now, teaching them to hold what we can't. There's hope in it—like planting seeds for a future we won't see."

Clara frowned, resting her chin on her hand. "That's a little bleak, don't you think?"

"Maybe," he said, shrugging one shoulder, his eyes glinting with a quiet defiance. "But it's also kind of beautiful, in a way. Like we're planting seeds for a future we won't see—something bigger than us."

The words stirred a memory—of Elena, her voice hoarse with determination as they pored over data in Sydney, dreaming of a cure that would outlive them. "I guess I can see that," Clara said quietly, her fingers tracing the edge of the journal. "Leaving a legacy, even if it's not what we planned."

Alex leaned forward, his gaze softening as it met hers. "You're not alone in this, Clara," he said, his voice low, steady. "Whatever you're working on, whatever weight you're carrying—you don't have to shoulder it all by yourself."

The sincerity caught her off-guard, a gentle breach in the walls she'd built around her heart. Her breath hitched, and for a moment, she couldn't find words. "Thank you," she managed finally, her voice barely a whisper, the gratitude raw and unguarded.

As the weeks unfurled, Clara found herself seeking out Alex's presence—a quiet anticipation threading through her days. They met for coffee in the shop, the ritual evolving into a shared pause amid the storm. They traded books—her genetics texts for his novels of forgotten worlds—each exchange a bridge between their solitary orbits. One weekend, they took to the trails together, Maya skipping ahead with her stuffed rabbit dangling from one hand, her laughter a bright thread woven into the pine-scented air. Alex tossed a pebble for her to chase, his grin wide as she darted after it, and Clara watched them, a warmth blooming in her chest she hadn't felt in years.

It wasn't grand—a spark, not a fire—but it was enough, a fragile connection tethering her to a world that often felt cold and hollow.

Meanwhile, the parthenogenesis project crept forward, its gains measured in painstaking increments. Clara and her team had coaxed embryonic development in mice without fertilization—a faint pulse of life sparked by edited genes—but the embryos faltered, their delicate cells collapsing by day four. It was progress, a whisper of possibility, but it fell short of the breakthrough they needed. The lab buzzed with quiet urgency, its nights stretching long as Clara and Carter dissected each failure, searching for the missing piece.

"We're getting closer," Carter said one evening, her voice taut as they stood before a screen displaying the latest results. The lab was a shadowed cocoon, its lights dimmed, the other researchers gone home. The data glowed in stark lines—viability rates up by two percent, survival past day three a flickering hope. "But we need a leap, Clara, not a step."

Clara nodded, her mind racing through a labyrinth of possibilities—enzyme tweaks, RNA scaffolds, a radical shift in approach. She thought of Alex, of his quiet faith in legacies, his belief that even small acts could ripple outward. Maybe he was right—maybe they didn't need to save the world in one grand stroke. Maybe it was enough to keep pushing, to plant seeds in the dark.

That night, as the complex slumbered, Clara sat in her apartment, the faint glow of a lamp casting soft shadows across the room. Maya slept in the next bed, her small form curled around her rabbit, her breathing a steady rhythm that anchored Clara's restless thoughts. She pulled Elena's journal from her bag, its leather worn smooth by time, and flipped through its pages—notes, sketches, a chronicle of her sister's fight. The words blurred as exhaustion tugged at her, but she lingered on a single line, scrawled in Elena's hurried hand: *Keep going, even when it's hard. For her.*

Clara closed the journal, her gaze drifting to Maya, then out the window where the hills stretched dark and silent under a star-pricked sky. She allowed herself to dream—not of a cure blazing across the horizon, nor a breakthrough carved in stone, but of something simpler: a future where loss didn't define every breath. She thought of Alex—his laughter sharp and bright, the tremor in his hands a badge of endurance, the way he saw her beyond her failures. It was a small thing, this spark he'd kindled—a flicker of warmth in a cold expanse—but it was enough.

For the first time in years, Clara felt hope stir—not just for the parthenogenesis project, not just for a world remade, but for herself. She rose, tucked the blanket tighter around Maya, and returned to her desk, a faint smile tugging at her lips as she opened her laptop. The silence wasn't empty anymore—it hummed with possibility, fragile and alive. And Clara leaned into it, ready to chase the spark as far as it would take her.

10

A New Chapter

The weeks at the California research complex spun into months, a quiet current that carried Clara Hayes through a life she hadn't dared to imagine. Alex had slipped into her days like a steady tide, his easy laughter and unassuming optimism threading through the fabric of her routine until they felt as essential as breath. What had begun as a tentative spark—a chance encounter over spilled coffee—had deepened into something richer, a lifeline that pulled her from the undertow of years spent merely enduring. It wasn't just survival anymore; it was the faint stirrings of living, a sensation so foreign it left her dizzy with its weight.

One evening, as the golden haze of dusk filtered through the apartment's narrow window, Clara sat on the worn couch with Maya nestled beside her. The girl's small frame curled against her, eyes fixed on the flickering screen where an old cartoon played—a relic of a world before the virus, its colors faded but its joy intact. Clara's fingers absently traced circles on Maya's shoulder, the rhythm a quiet anchor as her mind churned. Alex had become a fixture in their lives, his presence a gentle constant that softened the edges of their days. Maya had taken to him with a child's unguarded trust, her initial shyness dissolving under his playful teasing and endless patience for her games. But

Clara needed to know—needed to hear it from Maya's lips—before she let this shift become permanent.

"Maya," she said, pausing the cartoon with a click of the remote, the sudden silence sharp in the small room. "Can I ask you something?"

Maya tilted her head up, her gray eyes—Elena's eyes—wide with curiosity, a faint smudge of peanut butter lingering at the corner of her mouth from their makeshift dinner. "What is it, Auntie?"

Clara took a deep breath, her pulse quickening as she searched for the right words. "You know Alex, right? The man we've been spending time with?"

Maya nodded, a small smile tugging at her lips, her rabbit clutched against her chest. "He's funny. And he lets me win at hide-and-seek—even when I hide in the same spot every time."

Clara chuckled, the sound a soft release of tension. "He does, doesn't he? Sneaky of him. Well, I was thinking..." She paused, her fingers tightening around the remote. "What if Alex started spending more time with us? Not just as a friend, but as... someone special to me. Would that be okay with you?"

Maya tilted her head, her dark hair spilling over one shoulder as she considered this, her small face scrunching in thought. "You mean like a boyfriend?" she asked, the word careful but bright, as if testing its shape.

Clara felt her cheeks flush, a warmth creeping up her neck. "Yes, like a boyfriend. But only if you're okay with it, love. You're the most important person to me, and I need to know what you think."

Maya was quiet for a long moment, her gaze drifting to the paused screen where a cartoon duck grinned mid-quack. Then she nodded, decisive and sure. "I like Alex. He makes you smile. And he's nice to me."

Clara's heart swelled, a tender ache blooming in her chest as she pulled Maya into a hug, the girl's warmth seeping into her. "He is nice to you, isn't he? The best kind of nice."

Maya grinned, squirming free to beam up at her. "Can we tell him he can be your boyfriend?"

Clara laughed, a full, unguarded sound that echoed off the apartment's bare walls. "We'll see, darling. We'll see?"

After that conversation, Alex's presence grew roots in their lives, anchoring them in ways Clara hadn't anticipated. He joined them for dinners cobbled together from the complex's rations—synthetic proteins and dehydrated vegetables turned into makeshift feasts with his knack for seasoning and storytelling. He sat cross-legged on the floor with Maya, helping her trace clumsy letters for her homework, his patience unwavering as she grumbled about the letter 'G.' He even taught her chess, though she quickly tired of the rules and invented "chess tag," chasing him around the apartment with a knight in hand, giggling as he feigned defeat. Clara watched them, her heart caught between gratitude and a fragile disbelief. It had been years—decades, it felt—since she'd dared to dream of a life beyond the lab, beyond the virus's shadow. Now, here it was, unfolding in small, quiet moments she hadn't known she could still claim.

One weekend, Alex proposed a rare outing—a trip to the beach, a sliver of coastline spared by the collapse, its sands still kissed by the Pacific's restless waves. The three of them piled into a borrowed electric jeep, the hum of its motor a soft counterpoint to Maya's chatter as they wound through the hills. The air grew salty and sharp as they descended, the ocean stretching before them in a restless expanse of gray-blue, its horizon unbroken by ships or sails. They walked along the shore, Maya darting ahead to pluck seashells from the tide's edge, her small hands cradling treasures of pink and pearl. Clara and Alex trailed behind, their footsteps sinking into the damp sand, their hands brushing now and then—a tentative dance of closeness she didn't pull away from.

"You know," Alex said, his voice soft against the crash of waves, "I never thought I'd get to do something like this again. Just... be with people. Be happy."

Clara glanced at him, the wind tugging strands of his dark hair across his forehead, his hazel eyes fixed on the water. "What do you mean?"

He shrugged, kicking at a pebble half-buried in the sand. "After the virus hit, I locked myself away—figuratively, mostly. Lost my brother, my dad, most of my friends. I didn't see the point in trying to connect with anyone after that. It felt... safer to just exist, you know? But then I met you and Maya, and..." He trailed off, a faint smile curving his lips. "It's like you woke something up in me. Reminded me there's still something worth holding onto."

Clara's throat tightened, his words echoing a truth she'd buried deep. "I feel the same way," she said, her voice barely audible over the surf. "I didn't realize how much I'd shut down until you showed up."

They walked in companionable silence, the rhythm of the waves filling the space between them, a steady pulse that matched the beat of her thoughts. Then Alex stopped, turning to face her, his expression open and unguarded. "Clara, I... I really care about you. About both of you. I just want you to know I'm here—however you need me, for as long as you'll have me."

Her breath caught, and she reached for his hand, her fingers slipping into his with a certainty that surprised her. His palm was warm, rough at the edges, and she squeezed it gently. "Thank you, Alex. That means more than you know."

Ahead, Maya squealed as a wave chased her up the shore, her laughter a bright thread stitching the moment together. Clara and Alex smiled, their hands still linked, and followed her, the ocean stretching vast and wild before them.

One evening, as the sun dipped below the hills, painting the sky in streaks of amber and violet, they sat on Clara's balcony—a narrow slab of concrete overlooking the complex's quiet sprawl. Maya was inside, sprawled on the couch with her rabbit, the cartoon's tinny soundtrack drifting faintly through the open door. Alex leaned against the railing, a mug of tea cradled in his hands, his gaze distant as the last light faded.

"There's something I've been meaning to tell you," he said, his voice low, almost lost in the evening breeze. "About why I'm immune."

Clara turned to him, her curiosity sharpening. "You don't have to—"

"No, I want to," he interrupted, setting the mug down with a soft clink. "I've been tested a dozen times—blood, tissue, the works. They can't find anything unusual in my DNA. No markers, no anomalies. It's like... I just got lucky."

She frowned, her scientific mind spinning into motion, sifting through possibilities like grains of sand. "There has to be a reason. Something subtle—maybe an environmental factor, or a mutation we haven't mapped yet..."

Alex shook his head, a rueful smile tugging at his lips. "I've thought about it—trust me, I've turned it over a thousand times. But the truth is, I don't know. And honestly, I'm not sure I want to."

Clara studied him, her curiosity warring with a quiet respect for the shadows in his eyes. "Why not?"

He sighed, running a hand through his hair, the gesture weary and familiar. "Because if it's just random—if there's no reason I made it when so many didn't—then what's the point? Why me, when my dad's gone and everyone I grew up with? If it's just luck, it feels... meaningless."

Her heart ached for him, a mirror to her own unspoken questions—why Elena, why Daniel, why not her? She reached for his hand, her fingers threading through his, grounding them both. "I don't know why, Alex," she said, her voice firm despite the tremor beneath it. "I don't have the answers. But I know you're here now, and that matters—to me, to Maya, to this fight. You're not meaningless."

He looked at her, his hazel eyes searching hers, a flicker of something—gratitude, relief—passing through them. "Does it?" he asked, softer now, almost a plea.

"Yes," she said, squeezing his hand with a fierceness she felt in her bones. "It does."

That conversation lingered in Clara's mind, a seed planted in restless soil. That night, as she lay in bed, the hum of the complex's generators a faint lullaby through the walls, her thoughts drifted to Alex's work in AI development. If biology alone couldn't unlock the secrets of immunity—or the breakthrough they needed for parthenogenesis—perhaps technology could bridge the gap. The idea took root, restless and bright, keeping sleep at bay until dawn streaked the sky.

The next morning, she found Alex in the tech wing, a cavernous space of blinking servers and glowing screens, the air sharp with the scent of ozone and metal. He was bent over a console, his brow furrowed as he typed, but he straightened when she approached, a smile breaking through his focus.

"Hey, you," he said, leaning back in his chair. "What brings you to my corner of the chaos?"

"What if we combined our work?" Clara blurted, her excitement spilling over as the idea crystallized. "Your AI systems—they could analyze the genetic data faster than any of us could hope to. We've got terabytes of sequences, mutations, variables we can't parse by hand. What if your algorithms could find patterns, connections we've missed?"

Alex's eyes lit up, a spark of recognition flashing across his face. "That's... actually brilliant," he said, standing to pace a tight circle, his hands gesturing as his mind raced. "My team's been tweaking a new algorithm—deep learning, adaptive, built to sift through massive datasets and spot correlations humans overlook. It's designed for survival modeling, but it could handle this. It could work."

Clara grinned, her pulse quickening with possibility. "So, what do you say? Want to help me save the world?"

He laughed—a full, bright sound that echoed off the server racks—and pulled her into a hug, his arms warm and solid around her. "I thought you'd never ask. Let's do this."

Over the next few weeks, Clara and Alex wove their worlds together, a fusion of biology and code that hummed with potential. The tech wing became a second lab, its screens alive with scrolling data as Alex's algorithm digested the genetic archives—samples from immune survivors like him, embryonic failures from the parthenogenesis trials, decades of viral mutations. Clara worked beside him, her expertise guiding the parameters, refining the questions they fed into the system. The results came swiftly, like a tide turning: patterns emerged—subtle shifts in gene expression, overlooked protein interactions, a faint thread of hope stitched into the chaos.

One evening, as dusk settled over the complex, they sat in the genetics lab, the glow of a monitor casting their faces in blue light. The latest findings sprawled before them—viability rates up by five percent, a cluster of genes flagged as potential stabilizers. Clara's breath caught, her voice trembling with a surge of hope. "This could be it, Alex. This could be the breakthrough we've been waiting for."

He smiled, his hand resting on her shoulder, a steady warmth against her racing pulse. "You're amazing, you know that? This—we—couldn't have gotten here without you."

Clara shook her head, her cheeks flushing as she met his gaze. "It's not just me. It's us—all of us. You, Carter, the team, Maya..." Her voice softened, a quiet awe threading through it. "We're doing this together."

She glanced around the lab, its walls a testament to their shared fight—whiteboards streaked with markers, coffee cups stacked in precarious towers, the faint buzz of machines that never slept. In the corner, Alex had set up a makeshift table for Maya, where she now sat with him, giggling as he balanced a pencil on his nose, her rabbit perched beside a scattering of crayons. Dr. Carter stood nearby, her stern face softened by a rare smile as she reviewed a printout, her voice a low murmur to another researcher. These women, this man, this child—they'd become her family, a constellation of light in a sky that had been dark too long.

The road ahead stretched long and shadowed, its challenges a mountain yet to be climbed. The parthenogenesis project teetered on the edge of possibility, its success still uncertain, and the virus loomed beyond the complex's walls, a specter that refused to fade. But for the first time in years, Clara felt a shift—a sense that they might, against all odds, have a chance. Not just to survive, but to build something new, something lasting.

She leaned into Alex's touch, her hand finding his, and let the hope bloom, fragile but fierce, in the silence they'd reclaimed together.

11

A World Reborn

The world had changed in ways no one could have foreseen, its transformation both profound and disorienting. The collapse of the Y chromosome, a genetic unraveling that had once seemed like a distant hypothesis, had not only rewritten humanity's biological destiny but had also triggered a seismic shift in the systems and structures that had anchored society for millennia. What emerged from the ashes was a world caught in a perpetual state of flux—a fragile tapestry woven from threads of hope and despair, conflict and cooperation, as humanity grappled with the daunting task of adapting to its new reality.

In the wake of the crisis, smaller nations, their populations dwindling and economies buckling under the strain, began to dissolve their borders in quiet, pragmatic surrenders. Once fiercely guarded lines on maps—etched with the blood and pride of generations—lost their meaning in the face of a shared existential threat. Peaceful mergers became commonplace, born not out of conquest but necessity. The European Union, once a fragile alliance of sovereign states, swelled as it absorbed nations that had long resisted its embrace, their leaders recognizing that unity offered the only path to survival. In Africa, regional coalitions sprang up like lifelines, pooling scarce resources, scientific expertise, and manpower to confront the cascading challenges of food shortages, crumbling infrastructure, and rampant disease. Even in the Americas, where nationalism had once burned bright as a beacon of identity, a reluctant acknowledgment took root: no single nation could weather this storm alone.

Yet not every corner of the world bent willingly to this new order. In pockets where the old ways clung desperately to life, men who had once thrived under patriarchal systems lashed out, their rage a cocktail of fear, grief, and fading power. Riots flared in cities where the old guard dug in their heels, refusing to yield to the inevitable. Clara had seen the footage—grainy streams of shouting men hurling Molotov cocktails into abandoned storefronts, their voices hoarse with defiance as they chanted slogans from a bygone era. The streets they fought to claim were eerily empty, littered with the debris of a world that no longer existed. But as the male population continued its relentless decline—each year marked by fewer births, more deaths—these rebellions withered. Their leaders, hollowed out by the virus or broken by the futility of their cause, faded into obscurity, leaving behind only echoes of their anger.

In their absence, women rose to fill the void. Governments that had once been bastions of male dominance transformed almost overnight, their corridors of power now echoing with the voices of women. Presidents, prime ministers, and councilors emerged, their leadership shaped by a pragmatic focus on collaboration, sustainability, and the long game. It wasn't a utopia—old rivalries still simmered, and new power struggles flared—but the shift was tectonic. Where men had often built legacies on competition, conquest, and the flexing of strength, women leaned toward community, resilience, and the painstaking work of repair. Clara had watched it unfold with a mix of awe and unease, wondering if the world could truly hold together under such fragile new foundations.

One of the most immediate crises was the plummeting birth rate, a quiet catastrophe that loomed over every nation. Governments, desperate to stem the tide, launched sweeping campaigns—billboards plastered with smiling mothers, radio ads promising financial incentives, glossy brochures outlining support systems for those willing to bear children. But the promises rang hollow for many. The virus's shadow hung heavy, its ability to claim sons before they could even draw breath a wound too fresh to heal. Clara had seen the fear firsthand, etched into the faces of women at community meetings in the sprawling residential complex where she and Maya lived.

"It's not just about losing a child," one woman had said, her voice trembling as she stood in the dimly lit meeting hall, her hands twisting a frayed handkerchief. "It's the pain of hoping for a future—of pouring everything into a dream that might never come." Her words had hung in the air, met with murmurs of agreement from the crowd, their collective grief a palpable thing.

Clara had felt the weight of that sentiment ripple through her own chest, a mirror to her own buried fears. Across the globe, women who had once envisioned bustling households filled with laughter now hesitated, their faith in tomorrow shattered by loss after loss. Yet, amidst the pervasive dread, glimmers of defiance emerged. In some communities, women forged new paths, banding together to raise children collectively—networks of aunts, sisters, and friends weaving a safety net that defied the old boundaries of family. Clara had visited one such commune, a sprawling compound on the outskirts of the city, where children darted between solar-powered homes, their laughter a fragile but fierce rebuttal to the despair outside.

Energy, too, became a battleground where women's influence shone. With fossil fuel reserves nearly exhausted and aging infrastructure crumbling into rust, the world turned its gaze to renewables. Solar farms sprouted across sun-scorched plains, their panels glinting like mirrors under the relentless sky. Wind turbines rose along coastlines and hilltops, their blades slicing the air with a rhythmic whoosh. Women engineers, scientists, and laborers—many of whom had been overlooked in the old world—spearheaded these projects, their hands shaping a future powered by sun and wind. Progress was agonizingly slow, hampered by shortages of materials, skilled workers, and time, but each turbine erected, each panel installed, felt like a small victory against the encroaching dark.

Clara carried these changes with her as she worked tirelessly in the lab, her mind a whirlwind of data and possibility. The breakthrough she and Alex had achieved—harnessing AI to sift through mountains of genetic data and uncover hidden patterns—had cracked open a door to a solution, but the path forward was a labyrinth of obstacles. Late nights blurred into early mornings, the lab's sterile glow her constant companion as she pored over sequences, ran simulations, and chased the elusive thread that might save them all.

One evening, as the sky outside darkened to a bruised purple, Alex found her hunched over her workstation, the holographic display casting flickering light across her tired face. He slid a steaming cup of coffee onto the desk beside her, the faint aroma of roasted beans cutting through the sterile air. "You've been at this for hours," he said, his voice gentle but firm. "Take a break, Clara."

She sighed, rubbing her eyes with the heels of her hands before leaning back in her chair, the cracked leather creaking under her weight. "I can't. Not yet. We're so close, Alex—I can feel it, like it's just out of reach." Her fingers tightened around the coffee mug, its warmth seeping into her palms.

He nodded, settling into the chair across from her, his own exhaustion evident in the shadows beneath his eyes. "I know," he said, his tone steady. "But you're no good to anyone if you burn yourself out. Not to Maya, not to the team, not to this." He gestured vaguely at the glowing data swirling between them.

Clara managed a faint smile, lifting the mug to her lips and taking a sip. The coffee was bitter, strong—exactly what she needed. "When did you get so wise?" she asked, a teasing lilt creeping into her voice despite her fatigue.

Alex grinned, leaning back with a mock shrug. "I've always been wise. You just never noticed because you're too busy saving the world."

She chuckled softly, the sound a rare release of tension, and for a while they sat in companionable silence. The lab hummed around them—computers whirring, cooling fans buzzing, the distant drip of a leaky faucet in the corner. Then Clara's gaze drifted to the holographic DNA strand hovering above the table, its elegant spirals a mesmerizing dance of life and potential. "Do you ever think about what the world will be like if we succeed?" she asked, her voice barely above a whisper. "If we actually find a way to bypass the Y chromosome?"

Alex followed her gaze, his expression sobering as he considered the question. He was quiet for a long moment, his fingers drumming absently against the armrest. "I think it'll be a world where people can hope again," he said finally, his words deliberate. "Where they can look at their kids—girls, boys, whatever comes next—and dream of a future without that constant, gnawing fear."

Clara nodded, her throat tightening with the weight of his words. "That's what I want," she murmured, her eyes tracing the glowing helix. "For Maya. For Elena's memory. For everyone who's still holding on."

The weeks that followed were a blur of small victories and quiet setbacks. Outside the lab, the world continued its uneven metamorphosis. The riots that had once scorched cities dwindled into silence, replaced by a tentative peace stitched together with compromise and necessity. Renewable energy projects gained traction, their successes—new solar grids powering entire towns, wind farms lighting up remote villages—spreading like wildfire through whispered stories and crackling broadcasts. In the lab, Clara and her team edged closer to their goal, each painstaking step a flare of hope in a world that had grown accustomed to despair.

One crisp afternoon, Clara stepped onto the balcony of her modest apartment, the air sharp with the scent of pine and distant salt from the coast. The sun dipped toward the horizon, painting the hills in shades of amber and gold, and she leaned against the railing, letting the breeze tug at her hair. For the first time in years, a flicker of something unfamiliar stirred in her chest—optimism, fragile but undeniable. The road ahead stretched long and treacherous, its end shrouded in uncertainty. The challenges—scientific, societal, personal—loomed as vast and immovable as ever. But as the last rays of sunlight slipped below the hills, Clara allowed herself to believe, just for a moment, that they might actually have a chance to remake the world.

She closed her eyes, the wind carrying the faint sound of Maya's laughter from inside, and whispered a silent promise to keep fighting—for her niece, for the future, for a rebirth worth believing in.

12

The Edge of Possibility

The lab lay cloaked in a stillness that felt alive, its quiet hum a heartbeat threading through the sterile air. Holographic displays cast a soft, ethereal glow across the room, their swirling patterns of light pulsing with data streams, while the occasional beep of Alex's AI system punctuated the silence like a metronome counting down to something monumental. Clara Hayes sat at the heart of it, her chair creaking faintly beneath her as she stared at the floating model of a DNA strand hovering above the table. Its double helix shimmered in amber and blue, a fragile lattice of hope and risk that held the weight of years—years of loss, of relentless searching, of a dream she'd inherited from Elena. The breakthrough she'd chased through sleepless nights and shattered trials was finally within reach, but it was a tenuous thread, stretched taut over a chasm of uncertainty.

The idea had struck her in the small hours, a jolt that yanked her from the edge of sleep as she lay staring at the apartment's cracked ceiling, Maya's steady breathing a soft anchor in the dark. For years, they'd fought the virus—*Chromovirus-X*—as an enemy, a relentless predator dismantling the Y chromosome with surgical precision. But what if they stopped resisting its nature? What if, instead of battling its destructive power, they harnessed it, bending its ability to rewrite

DNA into a tool for survival? The thought was a lightning strike, wild and untested, igniting her mind with a possibility she couldn't shake.

The next morning, she stood before Alex and the team in the lab, her voice steady despite the adrenaline thrumming through her veins. The room was a hive of worn equipment and flickering screens, its walls scarred with equations and coffee stains, a testament to their collective endurance. "We've been trying to cure the virus," she began, her hands clasped to still their trembling, "to stop it from shredding the Y chromosome. But what if we've been looking at it wrong? What if we stop seeing it as the enemy and start using it? What if we take its ability to manipulate DNA and turn it into our advantage?"

The air thickened with silence, her words settling over the team like a heavy fog. Faces turned toward her—Dr. Carter's sharp features etched with skepticism, Amina's dark eyes narrowing in thought, the younger researchers exchanging wary glances. Then Alex spoke, his voice cutting through the hush with a cautious excitement that mirrored her own. "You're talking about weaponizing the virus—not to destroy, but to create. Using it to separate the X chromosome and pair it with another, building a new reproductive pathway from scratch."

Clara nodded, her pulse quickening as the idea took shape in the space between them. "Exactly. The virus is already a master at rewriting genetic code—it's why it's so lethal. If we can control that process, guide it, we might bypass the need for the Y chromosome entirely. Turn its strength into ours."

The room held its breath, the weight of her proposal sinking into every corner. It was a radical leap, a defiance of nature's rules that teetered on the edge of science fiction. But it was also their most audacious shot—a gambit born of desperation and daring, a chance to wrest survival from the jaws of extinction.

Alex's AI system became their cornerstone, a marvel of code and computation that hummed with a life of its own. It could sift through billions of genetic sequences in hours, its algorithms weaving patterns from chaos with a precision no human mind could rival. Clara and the team fed it their arsenal—decades of data on the virus's mutations, reams of human genomic maps, fragile successes from parthenogenesis trials in fish and reptiles. The screens glowed with its labor, streams of numbers and helixes cascading in endless loops, a digital oracle parsing their fate.

The results flickered onto the display late one evening, the lab dim and hushed, its air thick with the scent of burnt coffee and ozone. Clara stood before the team, her voice tight as she read the projections aloud. "The AI estimates a success rate of 8.7%—low, but it's the highest we've ever seen. It's not a guarantee, but it's a foothold."

"It's not much," she admitted during a team meeting the next day, the holographic model spinning slowly above the table, its light casting shadows across their faces. "But it's something—a crack in the wall. Right now, something is better than the nothing we've been staring at."

Dr. Carter leaned forward, her arms crossed, her gaze piercing. "It's a long shot, Clara. We're betting on a whisper when we need a shout."

"I know," Clara said, meeting her stare. "But we've run out of safe bets. This is what we've got."

A murmur rippled through the room, a current of resolve threading through the doubt. The team nodded, their determination a steel thread unbroken by the odds. They plunged into the work—running simulations that stretched into the small hours, tweaking variables as the AI modeled every conceivable mutation of the virus, its potential effects on human DNA a kaleidoscope of possibilities. It was grueling, a marathon of patience and precision, each iteration a test of their endurance. Clara moved among them, her voice a steady guide through the haze, refusing to let exhaustion claim their momentum.

The day of the first live experiment dawned gray and heavy, the lab buzzing with a tension that crackled like static. Clara stood at the center, her hands trembling faintly as she prepared the sample—a cluster of human cells suspended in a sterile vial, their fate a microcosm of humanity's own. The team gathered around her, their breaths held, eyes locked on the holographic display where real-time data pulsed in jagged lines. Amina adjusted the microscope, her fingers deft despite the shadows under her eyes, while Carter hovered near the console, her silence a coiled spring.

"Initiating sequence," Clara said, her voice cutting through the stillness, steady despite the knot of anxiety twisting in her chest.

The AI took over, its interface glowing as it guided the virus into the sample, a conductor orchestrating a symphony of molecular chaos. The process unfolded in agonizing slowness, each step a dance of calibration—adjusting vectors, monitoring replication, coaxing the virus to bend to their will. Clara's heart thudded against her ribs, her gaze darting between the display and the vial, her mind racing through every contingency she'd memorized over sleepless nights. The team stood as statues, their collective breath a held note, the weight of years pressing down on this single moment.

Then, at last, the AI chimed—a soft, clear tone signaling completion. The room stilled, the silence so absolute it seemed to hum. Clara leaned over the console, her fingers flying across the keys as she pulled up the analysis, her breath shallow with anticipation.

"It worked," she whispered, the words trembling as they left her lips. "The virus separated the X chromosome and fused it with another. The sample's viable—stable cell division, no degradation."

The room erupted, a dam breaking as cheers and gasps shattered the tension. Amina clapped her hands over her mouth, tears glinting in her eyes, while Carter let out a rare, sharp laugh, her fist pounding the table. Researchers embraced, their voices overlapping in a cacophony of relief and disbelief. Clara swayed, her knees buckling as the enormity sank in, a wave of exhilaration and exhaustion crashing over her. She gripped the edge of the table, steadying herself, her vision blurring with unshed tears.

But the triumph was fleeting, a spark in a storm. The sample was a proof of concept—a single flame in a vast darkness. The true test loomed ahead: replicating the process in a living organism, bridging the gap from petri dish to life. The cheers faded into a sober quiet as the team exchanged glances, the unspoken question hanging heavy: *Could they do it again?*

That night, the research complex threw a small celebration, a fragile burst of joy in a world that rarely paused to breathe. The cafeteria, typically a stark expanse of white tables and fluorescent glare, had been transformed—string lights strung haphazardly across the ceiling, casting a warm glow; makeshift decorations of colored paper and scavenged fabric draped over chairs; a table laden with rare treats—crackers, dried fruit, a precious bottle of wine rationed from the stores. A few researchers had unearthed instruments—a battered guitar, a violin with a chipped bow—and their tentative notes wove through the chatter, a melody that felt like a memory of better days.

Clara stood near the window, a glass of wine cradled in her hands, its faint bite a grounding sting against her lips. She watched the scene unfold—Maya twirling with a cluster of children, her dark hair flying as she laughed, her joy a bright thread in the tapestry of the night. Across the room, Alex leaned against a table, deep in conversation with Dr. Carter, his hands gesturing as he spoke, but his hazel eyes kept drifting to Clara, a small smile tugging at his lips each time their gazes met.

After a while, he wove through the crowd, two glasses of wine in hand, the light catching the amber liquid as he approached. "You look like you could use a refill," he said, handing her one with a grin.

Clara smiled, swapping her empty glass for the full one. "Thanks. I think I've earned it today."

"You definitely have," Alex said, clinking his glass against hers, the soft chime a quiet toast. "To the woman who might have just saved humanity."

She laughed, though a shadow of sadness threaded through it, tempering the warmth in her chest. "Let's not get ahead of ourselves. One viable sample doesn't mean salvation. We're still a long way from anything certain."

"Maybe," he said, his tone softening as he leaned against the window beside her, his shoulder brushing hers. "But it's a start. That's worth celebrating, even if it's just for tonight."

They stood in companionable silence, the hum of the room wrapping around them—the clink of glasses, the strum of the guitar, Maya's giggle as she spun too fast and stumbled into another child. Then Clara spoke, her voice low, almost lost in the noise. "Do you ever think about what this means, Alex? If we pull this off... there'll be no more men. Not now, not ever. We're carving half of humanity out of the future."

He hesitated, his usual ease faltering as he turned the glass in his hands, staring into its depths. "I've thought about it—more than I'd like to admit. It keeps me up some nights. But what choice do we have? The virus is erasing them anyway—me, the others, every boy born who doesn't make it past a year. At least this way, we're choosing survival. We're giving people a shot at something beyond this."

Clara's gaze drifted to the crowd, her mind churning with a storm of questions. "Survival at what cost, though? It's not just men we're losing—it's diversity, a whole spectrum of what makes us human. The way men laugh, fight, love, build—it's all going to fade. What does that do to us? To who we become?"

Alex turned to face her, his expression grave, the lines around his eyes deepening in the soft light. "I don't know," he admitted, his voice rough with honesty. "I don't have the answers—nobody does. But we're not erasing men, Clara. The virus did that, piece by piece, before we even understood what was happening. We're just... adapting, trying to hold onto something when everything else is slipping away. Making sure there's still *us* left to wrestle with these questions."

She swallowed hard, her throat tight with the weight of it—the truth in his words warring with the ache of loss she couldn't shake. "It feels like a betrayal," she said, her voice cracking. "Like we're letting go of something irreplaceable, something we were supposed to protect."

"Maybe," he said quietly, his gaze steady on hers. "But maybe we're also creating something new—something that honors what we've lost by refusing to let it bury us. It's not perfect, Clara. It's messy and broken and uncertain. But it's life."

Her eyes brimmed with tears, the room blurring as she looked at him, his face a lifeline in the storm of her doubts. "What if we're wrong?" she whispered, the question a raw plea.

Alex reached for her hand, his fingers threading through hers, warm and solid. "Then we'll face that, too—together. But right now, this is the only path we've got. And Maya deserves to walk it, to grow up in a world that doesn't just end."

The weight of his words settled over her, heavy but grounding, a tether pulling her back from the edge. He was right—the alternative was a slow fade into nothingness, a surrender she couldn't accept. She squeezed his hand, a silent acknowledgment, and let the music swell around them, its notes weaving through the laughter and chatter.

The celebration stretched into the night, the cafeteria alive with a fragile joy that felt borrowed but precious. Clara danced with Maya, twirling her until they both collapsed in giggles, the girl's small hands clutching hers. Alex joined them, spinning Maya in a clumsy waltz as she shrieked with delight, and for a moment, the lab, the virus, the weight of their choices fell away, leaving only this—a flicker of light in a long darkness.

As the weeks unfurled, Clara and the team pressed forward, refining the process with a relentless focus. The AI churned through new simulations, its predictions sharpening as they adjusted variables—enzyme triggers, viral load, cellular stability. Success rates crept upward—9.2%, then 10.4%—incremental gains that felt like miracles against the backdrop of past failures. Each live trial was a crucible, a test of nerve and hope, and though some samples faltered, others held, their cells dividing with a stubborn vitality that whispered of possibility.

Every setback was a gut punch, a reminder of the stakes etched into every breath they took. Every victory was a beacon, fragile but fierce, lighting the path ahead. Clara moved through it all, her hands steady, her voice a compass for the team, her heart buoyed by the laughter of Maya's play and the quiet strength of Alex's presence.

The road remained long, its horizon shadowed by questions they couldn't yet answer—could they scale this to humans, preserve humanity's essence, navigate the ethical abyss they'd stepped into? But for the first time in a decade, Clara let herself believe they might succeed. For Elena, whose fire still burned in her veins. For Maya, whose future was the heartbeat of every choice she made. For the world they all deserved, teetering on the edge of possibility, waiting to be born.

13

Homecoming

The plane touched down in Sydney after a long, restless flight, and Clara stepped onto the tarmac, blinking against the glare of the late afternoon sun. Four years of trials had slipped by since she'd last stood here, and the city pulsed with a strange duality—familiar yet distant, like a half-remembered dream. The air hung heavy with the scent of eucalyptus and the faint, briny edge of saltwater, so different from the dry, thin chill of California she'd grown accustomed to. Maya skipped ahead, her small sneakers kicking up dust, her voice bright with excitement as she pointed at everything she recognized. Alex trailed behind, their bags slung over his shoulders, his eyes sweeping the terminal with a quiet, thoughtful curiosity. Clara paused, taking a slow, deep breath. The weight of the past few years settled across her shoulders—not crushing, but steady, a reminder of how far she'd come. She'd left Sydney a different person, uncertain and driven by a singular, desperate hope. Now, she was back to share what that hope had become, both for herself and for the world.

Their first stop was the research institute where Clara had cut her teeth before leaving for the U.S. The building loomed ahead, its glass façade catching the sunlight in sharp, dazzling streaks, just as she remembered. Inside, the hallways buzzed with life—computers humming, voices overlapping, the faint clatter of equipment being shifted.

Most of the faces were new, younger researchers with eager eyes, but the rhythm of the place felt unchanged. Then came a familiar voice cutting through the din: "Clara!" Dr. Priya Sharma, her dark hair pulled into a loose braid, rushed forward, enveloping Clara in a hug that smelled faintly of jasmine and antiseptic. "I can't believe you're really here."

Clara laughed, returning the embrace with equal warmth. "It's good to be back. I didn't realize how much I missed this chaos."

Priya pulled away, her sharp gaze scanning Clara's face. "You look... different. Lighter, somehow. Happier." Her tone carried a question, and Clara's smile softened as she glanced over at Alex and Maya, who were now peering at a glowing lab display with one of the junior researchers. "A lot's changed," she said simply.

Priya's brow arched, her curiosity piqued as she followed Clara's line of sight. "And who's the tall one with the bags?"

"That's Alex," Clara said, a flush creeping up her neck. "He's... well, he's part of why I'm happier."

Priya's grin widened, a teasing glint in her eyes. "Oh, I'm going to need the full story on that. But first—tell me about this breakthrough. The rumors have been flying, and I need the details straight from you."

Later that day, Clara stood at the front of a packed conference room, the air thick with anticipation. The seats were filled with familiar faces—old mentors, former lab partners, friends who'd seen her through late nights and failed experiments—mixed with newcomers who'd only heard her name in passing. She adjusted the projector, steadying herself as she began. "Four years ago, I left Sydney with one goal: to find a way to save humanity from the virus tearing through us," she said, her voice clear despite the knot in her chest. "Today, I'm here to tell you we've taken the first real step toward that." She launched into the science, her words measured but alive with purpose. Holographic models flickered to life above the table—spiraling strands of DNA, the virus's structure unraveling and reconfiguring, X chromosomes split and fused in ways once thought impossible. She explained how her team had turned the virus's own mechanisms against it, a disease repurposed into a cure. The room held its breath, the gravity of her achievement sinking in. When she finished, silence hung for a beat—then applause thundered through, loud and unrestrained. Priya stood first, tears glinting in her eyes as she clapped. "Clara, this is... this is beyond incredible, you've outdone us all" she said, voice thick. "You've given us hope when we'd almost forgotten what it felt like."

The next morning dawned bright, the sky a vivid blue streaked with wispy clouds. Clara, Alex, and Maya drove through the winding streets toward the cemetery where Elena rested. The landscape rolled by—sprawling parks, houses with sun-bleached roofs, the distant shimmer of the harbor—and Clara let the familiarity seep into her bones. At the cemetery, the air was warm, laced with the sweet chirp of birds and the faint, rhythmic crash of waves from the cliffs nearby. Clara knelt before Elena's headstone, its gray surface weathered but polished, her fingers brushing the carved letters of her sister's name. "Hey, sis," she murmured, her throat tightening. "I'm back."

Maya stood close, clutching her stuffed rabbit, its floppy ears brushing her chin. "Is this where Mama is?" she asked, her voice small and solemn.

Clara nodded, wrapping an arm around her daughter and pulling her into a gentle hug. "Yes, darling. This is where she rests." She pressed a kiss to Maya's hair, breathing in the faint scent of shampoo and salt from their morning at the hotel pool.

Alex lingered a few steps back, hands in his pockets, his presence steady but unobtrusive. Clara glanced at him, her chest aching with a tangle of grief and gratitude. "Elena," she said softly, turning back to the stone, "I want you to meet Alex. He's been a rock these past few years—more than I could've asked for. And he's so good with Maya, you'd love him for that alone." She paused, picturing Elena's teasing smile, the way she'd have sized Alex up with a playful jab before pulling him into the fold. "I wish you could've met him for real."

They stayed there longer than Clara had planned, the silence stretching out, heavy with things she couldn't say aloud. She traced the headstone again, remembering Elena's voice, her laugh, the way she'd always pushed Clara to keep going. Eventually, she stood, brushing dirt from her knees, the motion grounding her. "Let's go home," she said, taking Maya's hand, her voice steadier than she felt.

The rest of the trip unfolded in a warm, hectic blur. Clara showed Alex and Maya the Sydney she'd once known—the harbor's glittering expanse, where ferries cut smooth paths through the water; the beaches with their golden sands and relentless waves; the cramped little café where she and Elena used to linger over coffee and scones, debating everything from science to the best way to dodge seagulls. Maya soaked it all in, her delight spilling over as she dragged Alex through her old neighborhood, pointing out the park where she'd learned to ride a bike, the corner store with the best ice creams. Clara watched them, her heart swelling at how easily Alex fit into this piece of her past—patiently listening to Maya's chatter, asking questions about the city with genuine interest.

One evening, as the three of them sat on a quiet beach, the sun melting into the horizon in a blaze of red and gold, Clara turned to Alex. The sand was cool beneath her, the air soft with the hum of distant waves. "Thank you," she said, her voice barely above a whisper. "For coming with me. For being here through all of this."

Alex's hand found hers, his fingers warm and sure as they laced through hers. He smiled, the kind that reached his eyes and softened the lines of his face. "There's nowhere else I'd rather be."

Clara leaned into him, her shoulder brushing his, feeling the steadiness of him beside her. The horizon stretched out endless and open, a promise of days still to come. The road ahead wasn't finished—there were hurdles left to clear, questions her breakthrough hadn't yet answered. But sitting there, with Maya giggling as she traced shapes in the sand and Alex's quiet strength anchoring her, Clara felt a certainty she hadn't known in years. She was home—not just in Sydney, but in this moment, this life she'd built from the ashes of loss. For Elena, whose memory still guided her. For Maya, whose future she'd fight to protect. For the hope they all deserved, fragile but growing, like a seed finally breaking through the soil.

14

The Echoes of Childhood

The Sydney beach lay hushed under the fading day, its waves slipping gently onto the shore as Clara settled into the cool sand, knees drawn to her chest. The sun hovered low, spilling a wash of orange and pink across the sky, while the air carried the sharp, briny bite of the sea. Down the shoreline, Maya darted after seagulls, her squeals piercing the quiet, and Alex stood nearby, hands in his pockets, watching her with a faint, indulgent smile. Clara hadn't come to join them—she'd come to sit, to think, to let the tide of Elena's memory rise and fall over her like the water at her feet.

She hadn't let herself linger in those memories for years. The grief had been too jagged, too close, a wound she'd learned to step around rather than touch. But today, on this stretch of sand where they'd spent so many childhood afternoons, the past felt less like a threat. The beach hadn't changed much—the same jagged rocks jutted from the dunes, the same gulls wheeled overhead, their cries sharp against the murmur of the surf. Sitting here, Clara felt ready, or as ready as she'd ever be, to let Elena back in.

They'd been bound tight as kids, she and Elena, despite the five years between them. Elena had a gift for spinning the ordinary into something grand, her optimism a light Clara couldn't help but follow. One summer day—she must've been eight, Elena thirteen—they'd poured hours into a sandcastle that rose like a fortress, its towers sculpted with driftwood sticks and shells for decoration. Elena had planted herself atop it, declaring herself queen of their gritty empire, her hair wild with salt and wind. Clara, already skeptical and precise, had crouched beside it, peering at the tiny crabs skittering through the moat they'd dug.

"What if the crabs are the real rulers?" she'd asked, her small brow creased. "What if they're just letting us think we're in charge?"

Elena had thrown her head back, laughing that bright, unguarded laugh of hers. "Then we'll have to bargain with them. Offer a treaty—say, a handful of seaweed snacks in exchange for the castle."

Clara had huffed, pretending to be annoyed, but the grin tugging at her lips betrayed her. Elena could do that—crack through her seriousness like sunlight through clouds. They'd spent the rest of the afternoon debating crab politics, Elena spinning wild tales while Clara insisted on "evidence" for every twist.

The ocean had always been their playground, its mysteries a shared obsession. They'd perch on the sand for hours, legs tucked beneath them, staring out at the waves as if they could peel back the surface. "What if whales have a secret kingdom down there?" Elena had asked one hazy afternoon, her voice soft with awe. "A whole world—schools where they teach whale songs, libraries carved into coral, palaces made of sunken ships."

Clara had smirked, kicking at the sand. "If they're that smart, where's the proof? Shouldn't we see something—underwater cities, whale monuments?"

Elena's eyes had gleamed. "Maybe they're masters of disguise. Or maybe they're hiding it because they know we'd show up with nets and ruin everything."

That idea took root, blooming into weeks of invention. Elena sketched whales draped in seaweed crowns, wielding scepters of bone, while Clara puzzled over the details—how sound traveled underwater, what materials could withstand the pressure, how a whale city might glow with bioluminescent light. They'd spread their drawings across the kitchen table, arguing and laughing until their mother shooed them outside. Those days shimmered in Clara's mind, bright and fragile, but they carried a sting too. When had they drifted from this beach? Had it been Elena's college years, when she'd moved an hour north? Or earlier, when Clara's own world shrank to textbooks and lab notes, leaving no room for their games? Time had blurred the edges, and grief softened what remained.

As they grew, their bond bent into something sharper—a rivalry, playful at first, then laced with quiet stakes. Science pulled them both in, and they'd spar over who could unravel a puzzle first. One muggy evening, sprawled on the porch with lemonade sweating in their glasses, Elena had grinned. "Bet I can figure out why the sky's blue before you."

Clara had shot back, "Too easy. Rayleigh scattering—blue wavelengths scatter more because they're shorter. Done."

Elena leaned closer, mischief in her eyes. "Sure, but why does it scatter like that? What's the real trick?"

Clara had opened her mouth, then snapped it shut, stumped. "Okay, fine," she'd muttered. "You win this round." Elena's triumph had been a burst of laughter, though Clara retaliated by disappearing into a physics book for hours, determined to even the score. Those clashes had fueled them, pushing Clara to dig deeper, think harder—always chasing Elena's spark.

Now, alone on the beach, the weight of those years settled over her. The dunes stretched out, shadowed and familiar, and the waves whispered against the shore like an old song. She missed Elena's laughter, the way it filled a room, the way her curiosity turned questions into quests. She missed how Elena saw her—not just the studious younger sister, but someone capable of wonder, someone worth believing in even when Clara's confidence faltered. The grief hadn't dulled; it sat heavy in her chest, an ache she'd carried since the day Elena was gone. But here, cradled by the sand and the sea, it felt less like a burden. The memories—of sandcastles, whale kingdoms, late-night debates—wove through the pain, softening its bite with warmth.

The sun sank fully below the horizon, plunging the sky into a deep lavender. Clara stood, brushing sand from her jeans, the grains clinging stubbornly to her palms. Maya and Alex were walking back toward her, Maya's energy finally waning, her small figure dwarfed by Alex's steady stride. Their silhouettes stood out sharp against the last threads of light.

"Ready to go?" Alex asked, his voice low and gentle, as if he sensed the weight of her silence.

Clara nodded, reaching for Maya's sandy hand. "Yeah. Let's head home."

They started toward the car, the crunch of shells underfoot mingling with the rhythm of the waves. Halfway there, Clara paused, glancing back at the beach. The tide was rising now, smoothing the sand where she'd sat, erasing the shallow imprint of her presence. For a heartbeat, she imagined Elena there—cross-legged on the shore, sketchpad balanced on her knees, her hair whipping in the wind as she laughed at some private joke.

"I miss you, sis," Clara whispered, the words swallowed by the sea's endless murmur.

She turned away, Maya's hand warm in hers, and felt a flicker of something new—peace, faint but real, threading through the tangle of loss and memory. Elena was gone, but she wasn't erased. She lived in the questions Clara still asked, the curiosity she still chased, the quiet strength she'd learned to carry. The grief would stay, stitched into her, but so would the love—and that, Clara realized as they reached the car, was enough.

15

Seeds of Tomorrow

Seven years had stretched out since Clara's breakthrough, a span of time that felt both fleeting and eternal, as though the world had been caught in a slow dance with its own redemption. The planet moved forward like a river carving its path—deliberate, unhurried, reshaping the landscape while leaving the scars of its past etched deep into the earth. Cities, once chaotic with the clamor of ambition, now stood quieter, their rhythms tempered into something steady and deliberate. Humanity had learned to breathe again, a collective inhale after decades of holding its breath. The male population had withered to a fragile million, a shadow of what it once was, most lost to the creeping hands of age or the silent, relentless toll of a virus that had long since exhausted its rage. Yet life clung on, fragile but fierce, cradled by the hum of automation and the unyielding resolve of those who refused to let the story end.

Automation had woven itself into the fabric of existence, an unseen pulse driving civilization forward where human hands faltered. Solar-powered drones painted streaks across the skies, their wings glinting as they ferried medical supplies to remote mountain villages nestled in the Himalayas or delivered packets of hardy seeds to the reclaimed farmlands of the Sahel. In the American Northwest, vast vertical farms rose like glass cathedrals, their AI-curated systems coaxing harvests so bountiful that surplus grain was loaded onto cargo ships bound for drought-ravaged corners of Africa and Asia. Hunger, that ancient specter that had haunted humanity for millennia, had been driven back into the shadows, its grip loosened by ingenuity and cooperation. Governments, once splintered by the petty squabbles of war and pride, now turned their gaze inward, pouring resources into ambitious restorations—reforesting the Amazon's scarred edges, filtering the choked waters of the Pacific, transforming abandoned factories into buzzing hubs of renewable energy. The United States, battered but unbroken, took a bold step, open-sourcing its AI logistics algorithms to any nation willing to set survival above sovereignty, a gesture that sparked a quiet, global alliance of necessity.

But progress was a painstaking crawl, measured not in triumphant leaps but in the smallest of inches. The world's population tilted heavily toward the aged, their numbers dwarfing the young, their faces lined with the wisdom of survival and the weariness of loss. In small towns and sprawling cities alike, retirement homes had become unexpected bastions of knowledge, doubling as makeshift schools where silver-haired grandmothers taught the next generation—girls and a scattering of boys born before the virus's peak—the arts of coding, hydroponics, and resilience. These children, wide-eyed and curious, would never know a world filled with fathers or brothers, their understanding of "family" shaped by the women who raised them and the faded photographs on mantelpieces.

For women of childbearing age, the future loomed as a paradox, a tangle of hope and dread. Clinics across the globe had stockpiled donor sperm, carefully preserved from the last surviving men, a genetic archive of a vanishing era. Yet the queues remained sparse. The grief of losing sons—surrendered to the virus in its merciless early waves—or the terror of bringing another into a world where they might wither before crawling kept many from stepping forward. The ache of such loss was a wound too raw to risk reopening. In Jakarta, 28-year-old Riana sat on the steps of a clinic, her hands idle in her lap, her voice a quiet echo of millions: "I can't love someone that way again. Not when the world still feels like a graveyard, every corner holding a ghost." Her infant son had been among the first claimed, his tiny chest stilling as she sang him lullabies, and the memory anchored her to a refusal that was both shield and shackle.

Others, though, clung to the old ways, seeking fragile unions with the dwindling men who remained. These relationships bloomed like wildflowers in cracked pavement—beautiful, fleeting, and shadowed by inevitability. Every touch carried the weight of a countdown, every kiss a quiet farewell. In rural Scotland, a woman named Eilidh tended a small garden with her partner, a man whose cough had begun to deepen, his frame thinning despite her best efforts. Their laughter was real, but it was laced with the knowledge that time was a thief they could not outrun.

Then came the news from Oslo, a whisper that grew into a roar.

A team of scientists, building on the fragile threads of Clara's research, had ventured into the impossible and emerged victorious: a viable zygote crafted through parthenogenesis, born from a single egg and a modified somatic cell. No sperm. No Y chromosome. No lurking virus waiting to claim its due. Nine months later, under the sterile glow of a Norwegian lab, a healthy girl named Lina took her first breath, her genetic code a shimmering mosaic of her mother's strength and the ingenuity of those who dared to rewrite life's rules. She was flawless—ten fingers, ten toes, a cry that split the silence—and she was theirs, humanity's first step into a future untainted by the past.

The announcement ignited the world. From the dusty town squares of Nairobi to the rain-slicked streets of São Paulo, holograms flickered to life, broadcasting Lina's first wails in a loop that felt like a heartbeat. Strangers locked eyes and embraced, their tears mingling with laughter. Elders, their hands trembling with age, wept openly, clutching one another as though they could anchor this moment forever. For the first time in decades, the word *future* shed its weight of uncertainty, slipping from a desperate prayer into a tangible promise, something to hold and nurture.

Clara watched the footage from her lab in California, the screens casting a soft glow across her face. Alex stood beside her, his hand resting on her shoulder, a steady warmth against the storm of her thoughts. "She's proof," he murmured, his voice thick with awe. "Proof we can outgrow the damage, that we're more than what we've lost." Clara nodded, but her gaze lingered on Lina's tiny features, the curve of her cheeks stirring a memory she couldn't shake. *This was your dream too, Elena*, she thought, the ghost of her beloved sister's smile flickering in the infant's face. *A world that doesn't just survive—it evolves, reaching beyond the ruins.*

The world did not mend itself in an instant. Cities still bore the jagged cracks of collapse—empty skyscrapers looming like sentinels of a lost age, streets silent where crowds once thronged. Nights carried the echoes of grief, the voices of those who remembered "before" rising in quiet songs or whispered stories. Yet the chaos that had once threatened to swallow everything had softened to a murmur, a background hum beneath the sounds of renewal. Communities turned parking lots into gardens, their soil rich with composted dreams. Artists scaled crumbling walls, painting murals of emerald forests and sapphire seas over the gray of concrete. In Sydney, Clara's childhood beach—once a graveyard of plastic and driftwood—now teemed with life, its sands crisscrossed by the trails of hatchling sea turtles. Volunteers, young and old, knelt in the dusk, cheering the tiny creatures toward the waves, their voices a chorus of fragile hope.

Maya, now 16, was among them, her face windburned and radiant as she knelt beside a turtle no bigger than her palm. "They're like us," she told Clara over a flickering video call, her grin fierce against the backdrop of the ocean. "They adapt. They don't look back. They just keep going, even when the odds are stacked against them." Clara smiled, the pride in her chest warring with a pang of longing for the girl Maya had been—the child who'd once clung to her hand, asking why the world had to break.

Before leaving Sydney for good, Clara made one last pilgrimage to Elena's grave. The headstone stood weathered by salt and time, its edges softened under the shade of a gnarled eucalyptus tree. She knelt, placing a seashell beside it—a smooth, ivory relic from the beach where they'd once sprawled in the sand, spinning tales of whale kingdoms and starlit seas. "We did it," she whispered, her fingers brushing the stone. "Not perfect. Not whole. But... alive." The wind stirred the leaves above, a rustling sigh, and for a fleeting heartbeat, Clara swore she heard Elena's laugh—bright, unyielding, threaded with the certainty that even the darkest oceans hid miracles beneath their depths.

That night, Clara sat on her porch in California, the air thick with the scent of jasmine and the winking glow of fireflies. Alex joined her, balancing two mugs of tea, the steam curling upward like a prayer. He settled beside her, the wooden boards creaking under his weight. "What now?" he asked, his voice soft but searching.

She sipped her tea, the warmth seeping into her bones as she watched the stars pierce the twilight, sharp and defiant. "Now we keep teaching the world to want tomorrow," she said. "To believe it's worth fighting for, even when it hurts."

The road ahead stretched long and shadowed, its edges jagged with wounds that time alone couldn't heal. But in a clinic in Oslo, a newborn girl had redefined what *possible* could mean, her existence a spark in the dark. And somewhere, in a quiet apartment bathed in lamplight, a woman who had sworn never to love again sat cradling her friend's parthenogenesis consent forms. Her fingers trembled as she traced the lines, her heart a hesitant bud stirring in the thaw, daring to imagine a child—a daughter—who might carry her forward.

The future was not kind, not yet. It was raw and unpolished, a canvas streaked with pain and promise. But it was theirs, shaped by hands that refused to let go, by voices that still sang through the silence. And in that fragile, stubborn persistence, it was enough.

16

The Fractured Horizon

The laboratory thrummed with a quiet, relentless energy, its sterile air pierced by the faint hum of machinery and the cool, ethereal glow of holograms that danced above the workstations. Clara stood at her console, her fingers hovering over the controls as she fine-tuned the gene-editing parameters yet again. She had lost count of how many iterations she'd run—hundreds, maybe thousands—each adjustment a tiny step toward perfection. Parthenogenesis wasn't just a theory anymore; it was a lifeline. Across the globe, a sprawling network of clinics buzzed with activity, reporting a steady stream of healthy births week after week. Little girls with double X chromosomes entered the world, their futures bright and untainted by the virus that had once threatened to erase humanity's tomorrow. It was a triumph, a beacon of hope stitched together by science and sheer will. And yet, as Clara's gaze drifted to the cluttered chaos of her desk—strewn with gene maps, aging biomarkers, and scribbled notes on yellowing paper—a shadow lingered. This was a story of victory, yes, but beneath it, a quieter, more jagged truth gnawed at her, one she wasn't sure the world could bear to hear.

Across the room, Alex hunched over a microscope, his silhouette framed by the soft light filtering through the lab's tall windows. In his 40s, he carried the weight of time more visibly now. Strands of silver wove through his dark hair, catching the light like threads of frost, and his shoulders bore a subtle stoop that hadn't been there a year ago. His hands, once so quick and sure, moved with the deliberate steadiness of experience, though Clara could see the faint hesitation, the creeping slowness that betrayed his fatigue. She watched him in silence, her chest tightening as if squeezed by an invisible hand. He's aging twice as fast, she thought, the words looping through her mind like a relentless echo. The latest scans had stripped away any lingering denial: his telomeres were fraying at an alarming rate, his mitochondrial function decaying, his body racing toward an endpoint that loomed closer with every breath. The immune men—those rare few who'd survived the virus's initial wrath—weren't truly spared. They'd been given a reprieve, not a pardon, and now they faced a slow, merciless unraveling, a farewell stretched out across years instead of months.

A few years ago, Clara and Alex had dared to dream beyond the lab's cold walls. A naturally conceived pregnancy had sparked in a fleeting moment of reckless hope, a fragile ember they'd nurtured in secret. For eight precious weeks, Clara had let herself imagine a child—a little soul with Alex's warm, rumbling laugh and the fierce curiosity she'd once seen in Elena, her lost sister. She'd pictured tiny hands and bright eyes, a life that could defy the chaos they'd inherited. Then came the ultrasound, the grainy image flickering on the screen like a cruel mirage: a Y chromosome, delicate and doomed, already buckling under the virus's dormant strain. The termination that followed was swift, mechanical, a procedure stripped of warmth or ceremony. Alex had sat beside her, his hand wrapped around hers, his grip steady even as his face remained a mask of quiet strength. He hadn't shed a tear. Clara, though, hadn't stopped crying—not outwardly, perhaps, but inside, where the grief pooled deep and silent, a wound that refused to close. Now, as she stood in the lab, her finger traced the edge of a cold steel countertop, lingering on a faint scratch etched into its surface—one of Maya's careless marks from years past. Alex's voice drifted back to her from the night before, soft and heavy in the darkness: "What if we're just delaying the inevitable?" She hadn't answered, feigning sleep to escape the question she couldn't face.

"Clara?" The voice jolted her back to the present, sharp and clear. She blinked, refocusing as Dr. Nia Patel stepped into the doorway, her young face bright with purpose. Nia, Clara's sharpest protege, clutched a data pad tightly, her dark eyes flickering with a mix of excitement and hesitation. "The Nairobi team just sent their latest results. Their success rate's climbed to 68%." Clara took the pad, her gaze skimming the figures with practiced efficiency. Healthy births. No detectable defects. No Y chromosomes to falter and fail. "Good," she said, her voice clipped but steady. "Add it to the global database." Nia shifted her weight, lingering as if tethered by an unspoken thought. "They're also asking... well, everyone's asking if you'll join the Geneva summit. They want you to keynote." Clara's eyes flicked involuntarily to Alex, who was now scribbling notes across the room, his hand trembling just enough to notice. "Tell them I'm occupied," she replied, turning back to the console. Nia pressed gently, "They'll keep asking. You're the face of this." The face. The architect. The woman who'd dragged humanity back from the brink but couldn't save the man she loved. "Let them wait," Clara snapped, the edge in her tone cutting deeper than she'd meant. Nia nodded once, retreating with the soft hiss of the lab doors closing behind her.

When the lab finally emptied, the silence settling like dust, Clara's fingers danced across the console to unlock a hidden partition—encrypted files glowing faintly under the codename *Project Lazarus*. This was her secret, her forbidden defiance. While the world toasted the success of parthenogenesis, she'd diverted resources into a desperate side venture: splicing telomerase boosters with viral vectors, a long shot to halt—or even reverse—Alex's cellular collapse. The early tests on lab mice had flickered with promise, their tiny bodies showing signs of rejuvenation under the microscope. But human trials? The thought alone carried the weight of taboo—unethical, illegal, a gamble born of love and dread. "You're working late," Alex's voice broke through, soft but startling. She slammed the hologram shut, her pulse spiking as she turned to find him in the doorway, his smile worn thin at the edges. "Just reviewing data," she lied, the words tasting bitter. He stepped closer, his gaze lingering on the console as if he could sense the truth humming beneath its surface. "You don't have to fix everything, you know," he said, his tone gentle but piercing. *But I do*, she thought, the words screaming silently in her chest. *For you. For the son we lost.*

That weekend, they drove to the Pacific Sanctuary, a windswept coastal enclave where the last immune men had gathered—a place that had once been a sun-drenched resort, now transformed into a quiet hospice clinging to the cliffs. Middle-aged men dotted the courtyards, their laughter faint as they moved chess pieces across weathered boards, their faces etched with a weary acceptance. "Why here?" Alex asked as they walked a narrow path along the bluffs, the sea crashing below. "I need to understand what's happening to you," Clara replied, her voice almost lost to the wind. "To all of you." Dr. Elias Marlow met them in his office, his 59 years carved into the lines of his face and the mottled skin of his hands. He pulled up genomic scans with a flick of his wrist, the data stark against the screen. "It's not just aging," he said, his voice sharp despite his frailty. "The virus altered us. Made us... compatible with its goals. We're not immune, Clara. We're incubators." Alex's posture stiffened beside her. "Meaning what?" he pressed. Elias's eyes darkened. "Meaning our bodies tolerated the virus because they mirrored its purpose—to phase out the Y chromosome. Now that it's succeeded, we're redundant. Evolution's dead ends." Clara's nails bit into her palms, drawing tiny crescents of pain. "There has to be a countermeasure," she insisted. "A way to—" "To cheat evolution?" Elias cut in, a bitter chuckle escaping him. "You've already done that. Let the rest of us go."

That night, back in the lab, Clara's hands trembled as she injected the first telomerase cocktail into a lab mouse, its small body twitching faintly under the needle. By dawn, the results glowed on her screen:

cellular rejuvenation, a spark of life rekindled. By noon, the mouse lay still, its tiny chest unmoving. She stared at the lifeless form, her vision swimming as exhaustion and despair blurred the edges of her world. *Too fast. Too unstable.* Alex found her there hours later, her forehead pressed against the cool lab table, her breath shallow. He didn't speak, just knelt beside her and wrapped his arms around her, his warmth seeping into her bones. His heartbeat pulsed against her back, fragile and fleeting, a rhythm she couldn't bear to lose. "I can't lose you," she whispered, the words breaking free at last. "You won't," he murmured, the lie soft and steady against her ear.

The Geneva summit invitation sat unanswered on her desk, its text glowing faintly: *Keynote: The Future of Human Reproduction.* Clara closed her eyes, the memory of the ultrasound flooding back—the grainy silence, the way Alex had kissed her hair afterward and whispered, "We'll try again," as if hope could rewrite fate. She opened a new file, her fingers steady as she typed: *Project Lazarus: Phase Two.* The world could wait. For now, she'd fight the clock ticking in Alex's cells, chasing a miracle on the fractured horizon of their shared tomorrow.

17

Echoes and Edges

The attic fan hummed a low, persistent tune, its blades slicing through the stagnant air and sending dust motes spiraling into shafts of late afternoon light. Maya knelt on the creaking floorboards, her hands buried in a cardboard box marked *ELENA—OLD STUFF* in faded Sharpie. The label was a lie, or at least a half-truth. Clara had always waved it off as "just junk," her voice tight with dismissal whenever Maya pressed her about it. But junk didn't warrant a fireproof safe, its lock long since broken by Maya's teenage curiosity and a hairpin she'd pilfered from Juniper's toolkit. The box smelled of time—mothballs and yellowed paper—and Maya's pulse quickened as her fingers grazed something solid amid the softness of old fabric.

It was a pocketknife, its blade folded neatly into an ivory handle carved with a tiny whale, its edges worn smooth by years of handling. She turned it over in her palm, marveling at its weight, before setting it aside to dig deeper. Beneath a tangle of faded ribbons, she found a journal, its cover frayed at the corners, its pages curling like they'd been kissed by damp sea air. She opened it, and her breath snagged in her throat. The first page bore a sketch—two girls on a windswept beach, one tall and beaming with a gap-toothed grin, the other small and glaring at the world with furrowed brows. *Me & My Sister, 2035,*

Elena had written in her unmistakable looping script, the ink still bold despite the passage of a decade.

"You weren't supposed to find that."

Maya's head snapped up. Clara stood framed in the attic doorway, her lab coat streaked with the bluish smear of bioreactor gel, her hair pulled back in a messy bun that betrayed a long day in the lab. At 16, Maya carried traces of her mother in her wild curls and the quick, cutting edge of her wit, but Elena's wide, unguarded smile was a ghost that lived only in photographs now, a memory Maya chased through the stories Clara rationed like precious drops of water.

"Why'd you hide it?" Maya asked, holding the journal aloft like evidence in a trial.

Clara didn't answer right away. She stepped into the attic, the floor groaning under her weight, and sank down beside Maya with a sigh that sounded older than her 40 years. "Your mom..." she began, then paused, her fingers brushing the edge of the box as if testing its reality. "She'd have wanted you to see it when you were ready."

Maya's eyes narrowed. "I'm 16, not 5."

Clara's mouth quirked, a flicker of amusement breaking through her fatigue. "Age isn't readiness, kid."

It was such a Clara thing to say—measured, maddeningly logical—that Maya couldn't help rolling her eyes. But she didn't argue. Instead, she flipped the journal open again, letting the pages fall where they would. Elena's handwriting spilled across them, jagged and alive, pulling Maya into a world she'd only glimpsed in fragments before.

One entry caught her eye, dated June 2037:

Clara's "curing" my kombucha again. Swears my SCOBY's contaminated. Joke's on her—I'm brewing a probiotic to survive her cooking.

Maya let out a loud snort, the sound echoing in the attic's stillness. "You tried to kill her kombucha?"

Clara's lips twitched, a reluctant smile tugging at the corners. "She retaliated by dumping chili flakes in mine. Said I needed to 'spice up my rigid worldview.' I choked on it for a week."

Maya laughed, the kind of laugh that bubbled up from deep in her chest, and turned the page. The journal was a treasure map of Elena's life, each entry a coordinate marking the woman Maya longed to understand. At 19, Elena had bluffed her way into a biotech conference, posing as a grad student with forged credentials to grill a keynote speaker on the ethics of gene editing—her questions so sharp the guy had stammered through his rebuttal. At 22, she'd been hauled off in handcuffs for spray-painting endangered sea turtles across the grimy walls of a coal plant, calling it "artistic civil disobedience" in the police report Clara still kept in a drawer somewhere. There was the night she'd dragged a protesting Clara to a queer poetry slam in a dimly lit basement bar, where Clara—awkward, stiff Clara—had stumbled into her first girlfriend, a poet with a penchant for metaphors and a disdain for schedules.

"Wait," Maya said, jabbing a finger at the page. "You dated a poet?"

Clara's cheeks flushed a faint pink, and she rubbed the back of her neck. "Briefly. She called me a 'walking flowchart.' Said I lacked 'lyrical spontaneity.' It fizzled out in three months."

Maya grinned, wide and wicked. "So, Mom was the fun one."

"She was..." Clara's voice softened, her gaze drifting to the journal. She reached out, her finger tracing a sketch of their old lab—two desks cluttered with pipettes and petri dishes, a window cracked open to let in the salt tang of the ocean. "Relentless. Even when it hurt her. Even when it broke us."

The attic grew quiet, the fan's drone filling the space between them. Maya closed the journal, her thumb brushing the whale on the pocketknife. She didn't push Clara further—not yet. But the weight of Elena's words lingered, a thread she couldn't let go of.

Later that evening, in the garage-turned-lab she shared with Juniper, Maya hunched over her microscope, the cool glass of the eyepiece pressing against her brow. A slide of telomere sequences glowed under the lens, fragile chains of DNA unraveling like a story with no ending. Behind her, Juniper's laptop hummed, its screen alive with the latest iteration of an algorithm designed to map genetic decay in girls born of parthenogenesis, a desperate bid for survival in a world where the old rules of biology had crumbled. Juniper leaned over Maya's shoulder, her nose ring catching the light, her dark braid swinging as she squinted at the data.

"Your aunt's gonna freak if she finds out you're hacking her database," Juniper said, her nose ring glinting as she leaned over Maya's shoulder.

Maya didn't look up. "She's too busy freaking out about *this*" She tapped the journal, now splayed open on the workbench to a page of Elena's furious notes on gene-drive ethics. "They knew narrowing the gene pool would screw us eventually. They knew, but they did it anyway."

Juniper shrugged, her pragmatism as unshakeable as ever. "Survival first, right? Fix the mess later."

"Survival's not enough," Maya shot back. She swiveled her chair to face the monitor, pulling up her latest project: a CRISPR sequence glowing in crisp blue lines, a patchwork fix for the autoimmune flaws snaking through their generation like cracks in a dam. "Mom didn't risk everything—her freedom, her life—just so we could stumble along half-broken."

Juniper raised an eyebrow but didn't argue.

It was past midnight when Clara stormed into the garage, the door banging against the wall. The lab was awash in the sterile glow of DNA models spinning onscreen, and Clara's shadow fell long and sharp across the floor.

"You're using my viral vectors?" She clutched the journal in one hand, and her voice was a blade, honed by exhaustion and something deeper - betrayal, maybe, or fear.

Maya stood, meeting her aunt's glare with one of her own. "You're using them to save Alex. Why's it different when I try to save everyone else?"

Clara's breath hitched, her grip on the journal tightening. "That's not the same."

"Because he's family?" Maya pressed, stepping closer.

"Because he's dying!" Clara's shout tore through the room, raw and jagged, and for a moment, the air seemed to fracture around them. Juniper muttered something about coffee and slipped out, the door clicking shut behind her with a sound like a full stop.

Maya didn't flinch. "Mom wouldn't have hidden this," she said, her voice steady despite the ache in her chest. "She'd have fought for solutions, not just —"

"Don't invoke her." Clara's words cracked, splintering with grief. "You didn't see her at the end. How much it *cost* her to hope"

The argument dissolved into silence, heavy and unresolved. Clara turned away, her shoulders slumped, and left the garage without another word. Maya stared at the empty doorway, her hands clenched into fists.

At dawn, Maya found the pocketknife waiting on her desk, its whale carving glinting in the soft light. A scrap of paper lay beneath it, Clara's precise handwriting scrawled across it:

She'd want you to have this. Be relentless. But kinder than we were. —Aunt C

Downstairs, the kitchen smelled of burnt toast and coffee. Clara and Alex sat at the table, their heads bent close over a tablet displaying reams of data. Alex's laugh lines crinkled as he ribbed Clara about her culinary failures, his voice warm despite the gray threading his hair. He's aging, Maya thought, her chest tightening. And she's racing a clock she can't outrun.

She slipped the knife into her pocket, its weight a tether to Elena's defiance, and returned to her room. Her laptop screen flickered to life, the *CRISPR-XX*: *Phase One* file blinking like a challenge. She opened it, her fingers hovering over the keys, ready to write the next line in a story Elena had left unfinished.

That night, Clara dreamt of the beach. She and Elena were young again—25 and 30—standing ankle-deep in the surf, the wind whipping their hair into tangles. They were arguing, as they always had, their voices rising over the crash of waves.

"You can't fix the world alone," Elena said, her eyes bright with that infuriating, unbreakable fire.

"Watch me," Clara snapped, kicking at the water.

Elena laughed, loud and wild, and tossed a shell into the churning sea. "Someday, you'll need to let Maya to throw the first stone."

Clara woke as her throat tight. The journal lay open on her nightstand, its pages ruffled by some unseen breeze. In the margin, a new sketch caught her eye—two whales breaching, their tails entwined, drawn in Maya's steady hand. It wasn't Elena's work, but it carried her echo, bold and unapologetic, reaching across the years.

18

The Fractured Promise

The air in the lab was thick, oppressive, saturated with the sharp bite of disinfectant that mingled uneasily with an undercurrent of despair. It clung to Clara's skin, seeped into her lungs, as she sat hunched over her workstation, her posture a testament to exhaustion. Her eyes, rimmed red from nights spent wrestling with sleeplessness, darted across the holographic display flickering before her. Her fingers, trembling with a mix of fatigue and desperation, danced over the controls, tweaking the viral vector parameters yet again—perhaps for the hundredth time, perhaps more. She'd lost count. *Project Lazarus* shimmered in the air above her desk, its twisted double helix a haunting amalgam of telomerase boosters and the ghostly remnants of *Chromovirus-X*. It glowed faintly, a dim, pulsating light that reminded her of a star on the verge of collapse. Beside it, the AI's latest simulation churned out its relentless verdict in bold, crimson text: *NO VIABLE PATH FORWARD. RECALIBRATE OR TERMINATE.*

"Recalibrate," Clara muttered under her breath, her voice a brittle rasp. She slammed her fist onto the desk, the sound reverberating through the sterile room. The equipment rattled faintly, but the hologram didn't waver. "Recalibrate."

Behind her, the lab door hissed open with a pneumatic sigh, cutting through the suffocating quiet. Alex stood framed in the doorway, his silhouette stark against the harsh fluorescent light spilling in from the corridor. In one hand, he cradled a thermos of soup, the steam curling faintly upward; in the other, he carried the weight of his own deteriorating body. He'd lost weight in recent weeks—too much weight. His collarbone jutted sharply beneath the thin fabric of his shirt, a cruel reminder of the virus eating away at him. His face, pale and drawn under the lab's unforgiving glow, betrayed a quiet resignation.

"You missed dinner again," he said, his voice soft but edged with concern.

Clara didn't turn to face him. Her gaze remained locked on the hologram, as if staring hard enough might will it into yielding a solution. "I'm close," she said, the words more a mantra than a response.

"Clara." His tone tightened, a thread of frustration weaving through it. "It's 2 a.m."

"I said I'm close." Her reply was sharper this time, a defensive snap that hung in the air.

A tense silence stretched between them, fragile and heavy. Then, with a sudden clatter, the thermos hit the table. Clara flinched at the sound, her eyes finally flicking toward him. Alex's gaze wasn't on her—it was fixed on the hologram, his expression darkening as he read the text hovering there: *Project Lazarus: Subject A1 – Telomere Degradation Reversal (FAILED).*

"What the hell is this?" His voice was low, dangerous, a tremor of betrayal lurking beneath the surface.

Clara's chest tightened, a spike of panic surging through her. "It's nothing," she said quickly, too quickly. "A side project."

"A side project?" Alex's laugh was harsh, brittle, devoid of humor. He stepped closer, the light from the hologram painting his face in eerie, shifting hues. "You're trying to reverse aging. Using *my* DNA."

She swiveled in her chair, its screech against the floor jarring in the stillness. "It's not just aging," she shot back, her voice rising. "It's the virus. It's rewriting your cells, Alex. You're—"

"Dying," he cut in, his words flat and final. "I know." He took another step toward her, close enough now that she could see the cracks in his composure, the way his voice fractured on the edges. "But you don't get to turn me into another one of your experiments. Not without asking me first."

Clara surged to her feet, the hologram casting jagged shadows across her face, accentuating the hollows beneath her eyes. "I couldn't tell you!" she shouted, the words tearing free from some deep, wounded place inside her. "You'd have said no. You'd have given up!"

"Given up?" Alex's hand brushed the flickering simulation, the red light staining his skin like blood. His voice trembled with a mix of anger and exhaustion. "I've watched you tear yourself apart for months, Clara. You think I don't know what's in those syringes? What's coursing through my veins right now?"

Her composure shattered completely then, a dam breaking under the weight of too much loss, too much fear. "I lost her!" she cried, her voice raw and ragged. "Elena—she was all I had! Our parents left us alone in that hospital when their plane went down, and I was *three*, Alex. Three years old. She raised me. She taught me how to fight, how to survive. And now you—" Her voice broke, splintering into a sob she couldn't suppress. "You're all I have left. I can't... I can't lose you too."

The confession hung between them, jagged and bleeding, a wound laid bare. Alex stared at her, his anger melting away, replaced by something softer, sadder—pity, perhaps, or love too worn to fight anymore. He reached for her, his hand hesitant, but she flinched back, retreating from his touch as if it burned.

"You don't understand," she whispered, her voice barely audible now. "When they died, Elena held me in that hospital for hours. No one came for us, Alex. No one ever came. It was just us—always just us. And then she was gone, and now you're slipping away too, and I—" She choked on the words, her hands curling into fists at her sides.

"I'm here," he said, his voice a quiet anchor in the storm of her grief. "Right now, Clara. I'm still here."

She crumpled then, her strength giving out as her back slid down the edge of the lab bench. She hit the floor with a soft thud, her knees drawn up, her face buried in her hands. Alex knelt beside her, wincing as his joints protested, but he ignored the pain. He always did, for her.

"You think I want to go?" he murmured, his thumb brushing a tear from her cheek, leaving a faint streak of warmth against her cold skin. "You think I don't lie awake every night, terrified of leaving you alone in this world?"

Clara's breath hitched, a shuddering gasp that shook her whole frame. "Then let me fix this," she pleaded, her voice small and desperate. "Let me save you."

"You can't." He pressed his forehead to hers, his breath warm against her skin, grounding her even as his words broke her heart. "Not everything is a problem you can solve, Clara. Not this."

They stayed like that for what felt like hours, locked in a fragile embrace as the lab's windows slowly bled gray with the first hints of dawn. Alex's arms encircled her, steady despite his frailty, while Clara pressed her face into the crook of his neck, breathing him in as if she could hold onto him through sheer will alone. Above them, the hologram pulsed on, its red warning a silent sentinel bearing witness to their unraveling.

"Promise me something," Alex said eventually, his voice rough with emotion, worn thin by the night. "When it's time... let me go. No more serums. No more simulations. Just let me go."

Clara closed her eyes, and in the darkness behind her lids, she heard Elena's voice—soft, steady, a memory that cut deeper than any blade: *"You can't save everyone, little sister. Not even me."*

"I promise," she whispered, the lie slipping from her lips as easily as a breath, as heavy as the silence that followed.

19

Tides of Change

The private jet's engines hummed smoothly beneath Clara's feet as she sat stiffly in the plush leather seat, a blindfold snug against her eyes. She'd been shrouded in darkness since they boarded, Alex's steady hand resting on her knee to keep her from sneaking a peek. The flight felt endless, the low drone of the engines blending with the faint churn of her own thoughts. When the pilot's voice finally crackled through the cabin speakers with a clipped, "We're descending," Maya's fingers were quick to untie the knot.

"Surprise!" Maya's voice rang out, brimming with a glee so rare it jolted Clara even before her vision adjusted.

Clara blinked against the flood of light streaming through the jet's wide windows. Below, emerald cliffs plunged into turquoise waves, waterfalls cascading like silver threads down volcanic slopes. The island of Kauai stretched beneath them, wild and verdant, its raw beauty stealing her breath.

"Hawaii?" Clara turned to Alex, her voice laced with disbelief. His grin was boyish, unrestrained—the kind she hadn't seen since their first meet.

"How did you—?"

"Stole your lab access codes to freeze your schedule," Maya cut in, her tone teasing as she leaned forward from the seat across the aisle.

"Oh, and Juniper hacked the university payroll to fund it. Kidding!" She dodged Clara's playful swat, her laughter bright against the jet's subtle hum.

Alex squeezed Clara's hand, his calloused fingers warm against hers. "You haven't taken a day off since... well, ever. Not really."

Clara opened her mouth to protest, but the words faltered, dissolving into the quiet rumble of the descent. In the silence, Elena's voice slipped through the cracks of her memory: *"Burnout's just failure with a time delay, Clara."* Her sister's words, sharp yet gentle, lingered like a ghost. Elena—gone sixteen years now, lost to the brutal miracle of Maya's birth—had always known how to pierce Clara's defenses. And here was Maya, her daughter, pulling the same trick.

They landed smoothly on a private airstrip near a beachfront villa, its wooden decks adorned with crimson hibiscus petals that danced in the salty breeze. For three days, time seemed to unravel, loosening the knots Clara hadn't realized she'd tied around herself. They snorkeled through coral labyrinths, Alex marveling at the darting parrotfish while Maya mimicked their neon hues with exaggerated gestures, her laughter echoing over the water. They devoured shave ice dripping with lilikoi syrup, the tart sweetness staining their lips, and Clara felt her lab-pale skin begin to freckle under the relentless sun. At night, they sprawled on the sand, watching green sea turtles lumber ashore to nest, their ancient rituals a quiet counterpoint to the chaos Clara usually chased in her lab.

On the fourth morning, she woke to empty rooms, the sheets cool where Alex and Maya should have been. She found Maya alone on the beach, her bare toes buried in the sand, a notebook balanced on her knees. The ocean stretched before her, infinite and restless.

"Since when do you draw?" Clara asked, lowering herself onto the sand beside her niece.

Maya shrugged, her pencil pausing mid-stroke. "Juniper says it helps her code better. Thought I'd give it a shot."

Clara peered at the page. Bioluminescent jellyfish floated across it, their tendrils curling into intricate double helixes, precise yet whimsical. The sketch was more than art—it was a blueprint.

"It's... a project," Maya said, her voice dipping into shyness, a rare crack in her usual bravado. "Nanobots modeled on jellyfish mucus. They could deliver CRISPR edits without viral vectors. Less invasive, cleaner."

Clara stared at her, the implications blooming in her mind. "You're sixteen."

"So were you when you published your first paper," Maya shot back, a smirk tugging at her lips. But her eyes softened, searching Clara's face. "Mom would've loved this. She hated needles, remember?"

Clara's throat tightened. She did remember—Elena fainting during her first blood draw at school, her sheepish grin afterward as she clutched Clara's arm for balance. That memory, sharp as a scalpel, cut deeper now with Maya's earnest gaze on her.

"Your Mom and Dad would be proud of you," Clara said, her voice barely above a whisper. "I'm proud of you, too"

Maya leaned into her, her shoulder pressing against Clara's. "I miss you, you know. Even when you're right there."

The confession hung fragile between them, carried on the sigh of the waves. Clara wrapped an arm around her, pulling her close. "I'm here now," she murmured, and for once, she meant it.

That evening, over a spread of kalua pork and mango salsa, Maya dropped a bombshell that shattered the easy rhythm of their meal.

"So, Juniper and I are... you know. Dating."

Alex choked on his mai tai, coughing into his napkin. Clara froze, a forkful of rice suspended halfway to her mouth, the grains trembling slightly.

Maya rolled her eyes, leaning back in her chair. "Come on, it's not like you didn't see it coming. We've been lab partners for a year."

"I— We—" Clara stammered, then burst into laughter, the sound surprising even herself. "Sorry, I'm just... old."

"Ancient," Maya agreed, her grin wicked. "But seriously, you're cool with it?"

Clara reached across the table, squeezing Maya's hand. "Juniper's brilliant. And she makes you happy. That's all that matters."

Alex raised his glass, still recovering from his coughing fit. "To Juniper! May she survive the Hayes women's combined intensity."

Maya groaned, burying her face in her hands. "You're both embarrassing."

Later, as they walked along the shore under a moon that turned the waves to liquid silver, Maya's steps slowed. Clara matched her pace, sensing the shift in her niece's mood.

"Aunt Clara..." Maya began, scuffing her sandal in the sand. "I applied to universities. MIT, Stanford, Caltech, Sydney Bio. I'll graduate early—next spring."

Clara stopped, the word *early* ringing in her ears. "But you're only sixteen."

"I finished my coursework. They're fast-tracking me." Maya's voice was steady, but her fingers twisted nervously at her sides. "I'm scared to leave you alone."

The word *alone* landed like a stone in Clara's chest, stirring echoes of sterile hospital rooms and the hollow silence of Elena's absence. She forced a smile, though it felt brittle. "You think I survived your mom's chili-flake kombucha experiments just to crumble without you?"

Maya didn't laugh. Her eyes, so like Elena's, held steady. "After Mom died, you shut down. I don't want... I don't want you to shut down again."

Clara pulled her into a fierce hug, burying her face in Maya's wind-tangled hair. "You're not Elena," she whispered. "And I'm not that person anymore."

On their final night, they hiked to a secluded cove, the trail lined with fragrant plumeria that perfumed the air. The sunset spilled molten gold across the sky, igniting the horizon as they settled on the rocky shore. Alex snapped photos—Maya caught mid-laugh, her head thrown back; Clara with her hair whipping wildly in the breeze; their silhouettes etched against the boundless ocean. The images felt like promises, fragile yet tangible.

As the stars began to prick the darkening sky, Clara sat alone at the water's edge, the tide lapping at her bare feet. Alex joined her, his presence a quiet comfort as he rested a hand on her back.

"You okay?" he asked, his voice soft against the murmur of the waves.

She nodded, though her chest ached. "Maya's leaving. And I... I don't know how to let go."

He pressed a kiss to her temple, his lips warm against her skin. "You don't have to. She'll always come back."

Clara leaned into him, the weight of his words settling over her. For the first time in years—since Elena's death, since the endless nights in the lab trying to outrun grief—the future felt less like a ticking clock and more like an open sea. She tilted her head to meet his gaze, the starlight catching in his eyes, and something long-buried stirred within her.

"Alex," she began, her voice trembling with a vulnerability she rarely allowed. "What if... what if we tried again? To have a kid, I mean. Together."

He stilled, his hand tightening slightly on her back. For a moment, she feared she'd misread him, that the old wounds—her hesitation after Elena's death and previous miscarriage, the years she'd poured into raising Maya instead—had built too high a wall. But then his face softened, a smile breaking through the lines etched by time and worry.

"Clara," he said, his voice rough with emotion and a hint of excitement, "I've been waiting for you to say that for so long."

She laughed, a shaky sound that mingled with the crash of the waves, and pressed her forehead to his. The idea of it—a child of their own, a new beginning—felt daunting, fragile, yet impossibly right. With Maya stepping into her own future, perhaps it was time for Clara to reclaim a piece of hers too.

20

The Burden of Tomorrow

The private jet touched down on the California tarmac just as the sun sank below the horizon, igniting the sky in a blaze of orange and purple that spilled across the sprawling city below. Clara sat by the window, her forehead pressed lightly against the cool glass, her breath fogging faintly with each exhale. The vacation in Hawaii had been a rare gift—an unexpected pause in the relentless storm of their lives. For the first time in years, clarity had washed over her, not because the tangled questions of her work had unraveled, but because she'd finally allowed herself to stop running long enough to feel the air in her lungs. Those fleeting days with Alex and Maya had stripped away the noise, leaving only what mattered: the fragile, fierce love that tethered them together and the future they were clawing to protect.

As the jet taxied toward the gate, Clara's gaze shifted to Alex, slumped in the seat beside her, his chest rising and falling in the shallow rhythm of sleep. The lines etched into his face—deepened by years of quiet worry—softened now, giving him an almost boyish look that tugged at her chest. She reached over, her fingers trembling slightly as she brushed a strand of silver hair from his forehead. Love and fear twisted together in her heart, sharp and inseparable. He was slipping, his body betraying him in ways neither of them could outsmart, and she knew it. But for now, he was here, warm and solid beside her, and she clung to that like a lifeline.

Across the aisle, Maya sat hunched over her tablet, her fingers dancing across the screen with a focus Clara recognized all too well. The glow illuminated her niece's face, casting shadows over the sharp angles that echoed Elena's features. Clara's lips curved into a faint smile, pride swelling until it pressed against her ribs. Maya was blossoming into something extraordinary—a scientist with a mind as relentless as her mother's, driven by the same insatiable curiosity that had once lit up Elena's eyes. Sixteen years ago, Elena had left her behind in a flood of blood and silence, and Clara had stepped into the void, raising Maya as her own. Now, watching her, Clara saw the future taking shape—a future she'd fought for, bled for, but one she knew she'd soon have to release into Maya's hands.

The jet shuddered to a stop, and the cabin lights flickered on, pulling Clara back to the present. She unbuckled her seatbelt, her movements mechanical, as the weight of reality began to creep in again. Hawaii had been a reprieve, but the lab, the research, the looming questions—they were all waiting. As they disembarked, the cool California air hit her skin, sharp with the scent of jet fuel and asphalt, and she braced herself for the return to the grind.

Back at the lab the next morning, Clara's office felt smaller, the walls pressing in as she stared at the invitation on her desk. The letters glaring at her: *Keynote: The Future of Human Reproduction, Geneva Summit*. She'd let it sit there for weeks, untouched, its presence a silent accusation. The idea of standing before the world—scientists, policymakers, strangers—to defend the path they'd carved with parthenogenesis had knotted her stomach with doubt. Could she face their scrutiny, their questions, when she wasn't even sure of the answers herself? But the clarity from Hawaii lingered, a quiet ember in her chest. She picked up the invitation, her fingers tracing the edges, and after a long, steadying breath, she typed her response: *I accept*.

The summit was months away, a distant horizon that gave her time to prepare. Yet the questions it summoned were already clawing at her mind, insistent and unyielding. Parthenogenesis had been their lifeline—a fragile thread dangled to a species teetering on collapse after the virus had ravaged the male population. It allowed women to conceive without men, a scientific miracle born of desperation. But it was imperfect, riddled with risks that gnawed at her: reduced genetic diversity, the specter of inherited diseases, the unknown consequences of a world without Y chromosomes. Each doubt was a weight she carried, a reminder of the lives hanging on her choices. She couldn't dodge them anymore—not after seeing the hope in Maya's eyes, the trust in Alex's quiet strength.

In the weeks leading up to the summit, Clara threw herself into the work with a ferocity that startled even her team. She pored over data late into the night, her desk a chaos of research papers and coffee cups, consulting experts from Tokyo to Stockholm via flickering holo-calls. The risks were stark, undeniable—genetic bottlenecks that could weaken humanity's resilience, mutations that might lurk undetected for generations. She scribbled notes in the margins of reports, her handwriting growing erratic as time passed, driven by the need to confront every flaw head-on. This wasn't just science; it was a reckoning with the future she'd helped forge.

One evening, as the lab lights buzzed overhead and the sky outside darkened to ink, Maya's knock broke through the haze. The door creaked open, and her niece stepped inside, her brows furrowed with concern. "Aunt Clara, you've been in here forever. You need to stop."

Clara glanced up, her eyes burning from strain, but her resolve unyielding. "I can't, Maya. There's too much riding on this. The summit—people are counting on me to know what's next, and I... I'm not sure I do."

Maya shut the door behind her and crossed the room, her sneakers silent on the tile. She dropped into the chair across from Clara, her gaze steady. "You don't have to have it all figured out. No one does. But you're the one who's been fighting for this, who's given people something to believe in. That's what counts."

Clara exhaled, leaning back in her chair, the springs creaking under her weight. "Hope's not enough, Maya. Not when the stakes are this high. What if we're building a future that collapses under its own flaws?"

Maya's expression hardened, a flicker of Elena's stubborn fire in her eyes. "Then we keep going. We fix it. Science isn't about perfection—it's about pushing forward, figuring it out as we go. You taught me that."

Clara's lips twitched into a tired smile, warmth blooming through her exhaustion. "When did you get so smart?"

Maya grinned, a flash of mischief breaking the tension. "Raised by the best."

The day of the Geneva Summit arrived like a storm rolling in—heavy, inevitable. Clara stood backstage, her pulse hammering as she peeked through the curtain at the packed auditorium. Scientists in crisp suits, policymakers with stern faces, journalists tapping at tablets—their collective anticipation pressed against her like a physical force. She smoothed her blazer, her palms damp, and whispered to herself: *For hope. For them.* When her name echoed through the speakers, she stepped into the spotlight, the glare momentarily blinding her. She took a deep breath, the air cool in her lungs, and began.

"Ladies and gentlemen, thank you for being here today. We stand at a crossroads in human history, faced with a choice that will shape the future of our species. Parthenogenesis has given us a way forward, a chance to rebuild and thrive in the face of unimaginable loss. But it is not a perfect solution, and we must be honest about the risks."

She paused, her gaze sweeping across the audience. "Reduced genetic diversity, the potential for inherited diseases, the long-term consequences of a population without men—these are real concerns, and they cannot be ignored. But I believe that the path we have chosen, while imperfect, offers hope. It gives people the choice to bring new life into the world, to continue our species, and to build a future that honors the sacrifices of those who came before us."

The silence in the room was thick, every gaze locked on her. Clara's chest tightened under their scrutiny, but she pressed on, her words carrying the weight of sixteen years without Elena, of every sleepless night spent raising Maya. "I don't have all the answers—no one does. What I do know is that fear can't stop us. We must keep adapting, innovating, facing what comes with courage. The future of reproduction isn't just science—it's resilience, it's defiance, it's the heartbeat of humanity refusing to fade."

When she finished, the applause roared through the auditorium, a wave that crashed over her as she stepped off the stage. Her legs trembled, but her mind felt lighter. She'd spoken her truth—raw, unpolished—and it was enough.

That evening, in their hotel room overlooking Geneva's shimmering lights, Clara sat by the window, a glass of untouched wine in her hand. The summit had been a triumph, but the questions lingered, circling like moths around a flame. She thought of Maya's brilliance, Alex's quiet faith, the fragile hope they were all holding onto. Parthenogenesis was a beginning, not an end—a cracked foundation they'd have to shore up together.

The door clicked open, and Alex stepped inside, balancing a tray with two steaming cups of tea. "Figured you'd need this more than the wine," he said, his voice a gentle anchor as he set the tray down and handed her a cup.

Clara took it, the warmth seeping into her hands as she murmured, "Thank you. For everything."

He settled beside her, his shoulder brushing hers. "You were incredible today. I've never been prouder."

Her lips curved faintly, gratitude swelling in her chest. "I couldn't have done it without you, Alex. You've been my rock—more than I've ever deserved."

He took her hand, his touch steadying her. "You've always deserved it, Clara. You're the strongest person I've ever known."

They sat in silence, the city lights twinkling below like scattered stars. Clara rested her head against his shoulder, her mind still churning with the day's echoes. "Do you think we're doing the right thing?" she asked, her voice barely audible. "With parthenogenesis, I mean. What if we're creating more problems than we're solving?"

Alex sighed, his thumb tracing circles on the back of her hand. "I don't know," he admitted. "But I do know that you've given people hope. And sometimes, that's enough to keep going."

Clara closed her eyes, letting his words sink in. "I just... I don't want to fail them. I don't want to fail *you*."

Alex turned to her, his expression serious but gentle. "You're not failing anyone, Clara. You're doing the best you can with what you have. And that's all anyone can ask of you."

Tears welled in Clara's eyes, but she blinked them away. "I'm scared, Alex," she confessed. "Scared of what's coming. Scared of losing you. Scared of not being enough."

He pulled her into his arms, holding her tightly. "I'm scared too," he murmured into her hair. "But we're in this together. No matter what happens, we'll face it together."

Clara sank into him, the familiar scent of him grounding her as she let the weight slip from her shoulders. In his arms, the world felt less brutal, less impossible. Her thoughts drifted to Maya—the girl she'd raised from a newborn's wail, the spark of Elena's legacy. "Do you think she'll be okay?" she asked, her voice muffled against his shirt.

Alex smiled, his hand resting on her back. "Maya's going to change the world, Clara. She's got your brilliance and Elena's fire. There's nothing she can't do."

Clara nodded, a quiet peace settling over her. The road ahead was jagged, shadowed with unknowns, but she wasn't alone on it. For Elena, for Maya, for Alex—and for the future they'd dared to imagine—she'd keep going.

21

New Beginnings

The months slipped by in a quiet blur, a fragile rhythm of routines threading through the shifting seasons. Beyond the walls of Clara's home, the world lumbered forward, grappling with the jagged edges of its new reality—a humanity reshaped by loss and stitched together with science. But inside, time felt softer, more tentative, as if holding its breath. Maya had claimed the garage as her domain, transforming it into a makeshift lab where the hum of her computer mingled with the faint clatter of tools. Her latest obsession, *CRISPR-XX*, consumed her—a bold project blending computer simulations with experimental gene editing to bolster human genetics against the cracks left by the virus. It was ambitious, audacious even, but progress crawled, stymied by the lack of cutting-edge equipment and funding. Still, Maya pressed on, her jaw set with a determination Clara recognized all too well—a mirror of Elena's unyielding spirit, the sister she'd lost to the brutal miracle of Maya's birth.

Clara watched her niece from a distance, her heart a tangle of pride and unease. Maya's brilliance shone like a beacon, her mind a whirlwind of ideas that could reshape biology itself. Yet the intensity of her focus on *CRISPR-XX* gnawed at Clara's edges. The project danced on a razor's line—its potential to heal shadowed by risks that blurred into ethical gray. Clara knew the dangers of pushing too far, too fast; she'd seen it in her own work, *Project Lazarus*. But she also knew she couldn't leash Maya's curiosity. It was the same fire that had driven Elena to unravel mysteries through her research, the same spark that had fueled Clara's own breakthroughs. To dim it would be to betray them both.

One crisp spring morning, the three of them gathered around the kitchen table, sunlight spilling through the windows in golden ribbons that warmed the worn oak. Maya's laptop sat open before her, her fingers hovering over the keys with a nervous energy that crackled in the air. Clara, four months pregnant, rested a hand on the gentle curve of her belly, feeling the faint whisper of life beneath her skin. Alex leaned against the counter, cradling a steaming mug of coffee, his eyes crinkling with warmth as he watched them. The scene felt mundane yet sacred, a snapshot of a family teetering between endings and beginnings.

"Ready?" Maya asked, her voice tight with anticipation, her gaze flicking to Clara.

Clara nodded, her chest swelling with a pride so fierce it ached. "Go ahead."

Maya clicked open the first email, her eyes darting across the screen. "MIT... accepted!" Her voice broke into a grin, bright and unguarded, as she turned the laptop to show them.

Alex let out a whoop, slamming his mug down with a clatter that sloshed coffee onto the counter. "That's my girl!"

Clara reached over and squeezed Maya's hand, her own smile wide but tinged with a bittersweet ache. "I'm so proud of you, Maya."

The next email unfurled more triumph: Stanford, a full-ride scholarship, lauding her "exceptional talent and boundless potential." Maya read the letter aloud, her voice trembling with a mix of disbelief and joy, the words tumbling out as if she needed to hear them to believe them. "They're offering me a spot in their bioengineering honors program," she finished, looking up at Clara and Alex with eyes that shimmered like Elena's once had.

"I can't believe it," she breathed, her hands pressing against the table. "This is everything I've been working for."

Clara's heart swelled until it pressed against her ribs, but beneath the joy, a bittersweet tide rose. Maya's acceptances were a victory, a testament to her grit and genius—but they also marked the beginning of her leaving. Soon, she'd step into a world beyond their little orbit, a future that didn't orbit around the home Clara had built to shield her after Elena's death. She'd always known this day would come—Maya was never hers to keep forever—but the reality of it carved a hollow space in her chest.

As they celebrated with laughter and Alex's off-key rendition of "Sweet Caroline" (substituting "Maya" for the chorus), Clara's thoughts drifted to the life stirring inside her. The pregnancy had blindsided them—a fragile miracle born from the ashes of their parthenogenesis research. Using a refined technique, they'd fused Clara's egg with a cell from Alex, crafting a healthy female embryo in a lab dish before implanting it. It was a leap forward, a bridge between their past work and a future where humanity might reclaim what it had lost. But it was uncharted territory, shadowed by uncertainties—would the child inherit unseen flaws? Could their science hold against nature's unpredictability? Clara and Alex had chosen silence for now, guarding this tender hope like a flame in a storm, savoring it before the world's scrutiny could weigh in.

She pressed her palm against her belly, feeling a flutter like a secret shared. Watching Maya's face glow with dreams of MIT and Stanford, guilt flickered through her. Maya was on the cusp of her own life, and Clara didn't want the baby's arrival to dim her light or anchor her with new obligations—not when she'd spent sixteen years pouring everything into raising her niece.

That evening, as the house settled into a hush and the sky deepened to indigo, Clara found Maya in the garage. Her niece was hunched over her laptop, the screen's glow casting stark shadows across the cluttered workbench—scattered notes, tangled wires, a half-empty mug of tea gone cold. The air smelled of solder and ambition.

"Hey," Clara said softly, leaning against the doorway, her silhouette framed by the dim hall light. "Mind if I join you?"

Maya glanced up, her tense expression easing into a small smile. "Sure."

Clara stepped inside, her gaze drifting over the chaos of Maya's workspace—diagrams of DNA strands pinned to a corkboard, equations scribbled in marker on a whiteboard. She sank onto a stool beside her, resting a hand on Maya's shoulder. "Still working on *CRISPR-XX*?"

Maya nodded, her fingers tapping restlessly against the keyboard. "Yeah. I'm so close—I can feel it—but I don't have the gear to test it properly. It's like I'm building a rocket with a screwdriver."

Clara's lips quirked into a smile. "You'll get there. Look at what you've already done—MIT, Stanford. That's incredible, Maya."

Maya's smile was faint, her eyes drifting somewhere beyond the screen. "I just… I want to make a difference, you know? Like you and Mom did."

The mention of Elena pierced Clara, sharp and familiar, conjuring the ghost of her sister—her infectious laugh, her fierce debates over late-night coffee, the way she'd faded in that hospital bed as Maya's cries filled the room. Clara swallowed the ache and cupped Maya's face in her hands, her touch steady. "You already are, Maya. You're going to change the world in ways I can't even imagine and more."

Maya's gaze locked with hers, serious and searching. "What if I'm not ready? What if I mess it all up?"

Clara reached out and cupped Maya's face in her hands, her touch gentle but firm. "You're ready, Maya. And even if you stumble, you'll get back up. That's what we do. That's who we are."

Tears glistened in Maya's eyes, but she blinked them back, her jaw tightening with resolve. "I'm going to miss you," she whispered, the words fragile in the quiet. "Both of you."

Clara pulled her into a fierce hug, her own tears spilling as she pressed her cheek against Maya's hair. "I'm going to miss you too, sweetheart. But this is your time. Your future. And I couldn't be prouder of the woman you've become."

They stayed like that for a long moment, the hum of the laptop a soft undercurrent to their shared silence. When they finally pulled apart, the air felt lighter, threaded with a tender understanding. They talked deep into the night—about Maya's dreams of cracking *CRISPR-XX*, the universities vying for her mind, the sprawling possibilities ahead. Clara shared her hopes for the baby, her voice softening as she spoke of the tiny life she and Alex had dared to create—a girl, a new thread in their tapestry. It was bittersweet, this collision of endings and beginnings, but it bound them closer, a lifeline woven from love and loss.

As the hours stretched, Clara's hand rested on her belly, the faint kicks a quiet drumbeat beneath her skin. Alex joined them eventually, his presence steady as he leaned in the doorway, listening with a gentle smile. The road ahead loomed—Maya's departure for college, the baby's arrival, the relentless march of their work to mend a fractured world. It was daunting, uncertain, a path shadowed by questions they couldn't yet answer. But in that garage, surrounded by the clutter of Maya's dreams and the warmth of Alex's gaze, Clara felt something she hadn't in years: peace. The world remained broken, its scars deep and raw, but with these two—her family, her anchors—she believed they could piece it back together, one fragile, defiant step at a time.

22

A Quiet Goodbye

The weeks spun by in a dizzying rush, a cascade of anticipation and meticulous planning that swept through their lives like a gust of autumn wind. It began with the campus visits, a journey that carried them first to MIT—a sprawling tapestry of history and innovation stretched across Cambridge's gray streets. The campus thrummed with the restless energy of brilliant minds, its red-brick buildings standing sentinel over cutting-edge labs where the air buzzed with possibility. Maya led the way, her sneakers scuffing the pavement, her eyes wide and gleaming with a wonder that bordered on reverence as she peered through glass walls at robotic arms weaving precise patterns under stark lights. "This place is amazing," she breathed, her voice hushed with awe. "Look at that lab—it's like something out of a sci-fi movie."

Clara followed a few steps behind, her hand nestled in Alex's, their pace deliberate—not from weariness, but from the quiet weight of witnessing Maya inch toward her future. "It's incredible, Maya," Clara said, her smile bright but tinged with a tender ache that she buried deep. "You'd thrive here." The words rang true, but beneath them lingered an unspoken sorrow—the thought of Maya three thousand miles away, her laughter echoing through distant halls instead of their home. She swallowed it down, unwilling to cast a shadow over Maya's joy, but Alex felt the tremor in her grip. His fingers tightened around hers, a silent thread of reassurance stitching through her unease.

Next came Stanford, a sun-warmed haven that felt worlds apart from MIT's urban pulse. Palm trees swayed lazily over the quad, their fronds casting dappled shadows across Spanish-style arches bathed in golden light. Maya's face softened as they wandered through, her steps lighter, her excitement a quiet hum beneath her words. "This feels like home," she murmured, pausing by a sandstone bench where students sprawled with books and laptops, the air thick with the scent of eucalyptus. Clara's chest loosened, a wave of relief rippling through her. Stanford was closer—less than a day's drive from their California refuge—and Maya's choice to stay near felt like a lifeline, a tether she hadn't dared hope for. "It's a great school, and we'll be around if you need anything," Clara said, her voice warm with approval.

Maya grinned, though a flicker of sadness shadowed her eyes. "Yeah, it's not too far. We'll make it work." Her decision to choose Stanford had been deliberate, drawn not just by its prestigious biotechnology program but by its proximity to home—a balance between the independence she craved and the roots she wasn't ready to uproot entirely. Yet there was a twist: Juniper, her girlfriend, had secured a spot at UC Berkeley's renowned mechanical engineering program. The schools were an hour apart, a thin stretch of highway between them, but it loomed as a quiet challenge, a test of their bond that neither had fully voiced.

That evening, over a dinner of steaming takeout cartons strewn across the kitchen table, the conversation turned to Juniper's path. She sat beside Maya, her nose ring catching the lamplight as she twisted a chopstick between her fingers, her dark braid swaying with each tilt of her head. She'd chased Berkeley's mechanical engineering program with a tenacity that mirrored Maya's own—a dream forged in late-night sketches and grease-stained notebooks, her hands still faintly smudged from tinkering with a drone chassis that morning. Her acceptance was a triumph, a hard-won victory, but the distance—an hour's drive that felt both negligible and vast—hung between them like a taut wire. "I'm so proud of you, Juniper," Clara said, passing a carton of lo mein, her voice rich with sincerity. "Berkeley's program is one of the best anywhere. You're going to do amazing things there."

Juniper's smile was shy, her cheeks flushing as she glanced at Maya, who was nudging rice around her plate with a distracted fork. "Thanks, Dr. Hayes. It's just... I wish we could've landed at the same school, you know?" Her words carried a wistful ache, the kind that comes from tasting a dream while feeling its edges fray.

Maya's hand slid across the table, finding Juniper's and squeezing gently. "We'll figure it out," she said, her tone firm but soft, her thumb tracing a small arc over Juniper's knuckles. "It's not that far—an hour's nothing. We've got weekends, breaks, all of it." Her resolve was a shield, but Clara caught the flicker of uncertainty beneath it—the same push-and-pull she'd known herself, balancing love against the relentless pull of ambition. She'd felt it after Elena's death, pouring her grief into raising Maya while her own dreams simmered on a back burner.

"You'll make it work," Clara said, her voice gentle but steady, weighted with the wisdom of years. "You're both fierce, and you'll be chasing what lights you up. That's the core of it." Her heart ached for them, but she believed it—they were young, resilient, bound by something deeper than distance could unravel. Juniper's lips quirked, a spark of her usual wry humor glinting through. "Guess I'll just build a teleporter then," she murmured, nudging Maya's shoulder with her own, coaxing a laugh that broke the table's quiet tension.

Back home, life settled into a fragile new rhythm, a quiet cadence stitched with the threads of change. Maya filled her days with preparation—packing boxes with a methodical care that belied her excitement, flipping through Stanford's course catalog with a mix of anticipation and nerves, her voice drifting through the house as she debated bioethics with Juniper over speakerphone, her laughter sharp with Juniper's dry retorts about "ethics versus duct tape." Clara, her pregnancy now rounding her frame, navigated her own shifting landscape, balancing her work on *Project Lazarus* with the slow swell of impending motherhood. The dance was delicate—hours in the lab poring over data, then home to rest as her body demanded—but a calm had settled over her, a stillness she hadn't grasped since the night Elena slipped away, leaving Maya's cries to fill the silence.

The baby—a girl they'd named Elena, a quiet nod to the sister and mother lost—felt like a fragile miracle, a spark of renewal amid their scars. Clara's pregnancy was a triumph of their science, born from a refined offshoot of parthenogenesis that fused her egg with Alex's cell, coaxing a healthy embryo into being—a fragile bridge to a future where humanity might heal. It was groundbreaking, a whisper of hope in a world still reeling from the virus, but it carried shadows too—uncertainties about the child's genetic stability, questions that lingered in the margins of every scan. Clara rested a hand on her belly, feeling the gentle kicks that pulsed beneath her skin, and let herself linger in the wonder, even as the scientist in her cataloged every risk.

Alex, her rock through every storm, took on more at home—cooking dinners with a lopsided grin, assembling the nursery crib with a focus that bordered on obsession, nudging Clara to rest when her eyes grew heavy. He poured himself into *Project Lazarus* too, his steady hands calibrating equipment even as the project stubbornly resisted them. The virus's grip on his cells held fast, defying their every breakthrough, and Clara saw the toll in the faint tremor of his fingers, the shadows pooling beneath his eyes. Yet the desperation that once clawed at her had softened, muted by the baby's presence—a lens that sharpened the now over the relentless chase of tomorrow.

One evening, as the sun dipped below the horizon and painted the sky in amber streaks, Clara and Alex sat on the porch, the air thick with the scent of blooming jasmine carried on a cool breeze. She leaned her head against his shoulder, her hand resting on her belly where little Elena's kicks fluttered like a secret code. The silence wrapped around them, a rare pause in the chaos of their lives. "Do you ever think about what her future will be like?" Clara asked, her voice barely above a whisper, as if the words might shatter the stillness.

Alex's smile was soft, his hand sliding over hers, warm and steady. "All the time. I think about the world we're leaving her—the challenges she'll face, but also the opportunities. She's going to grow up in a world that's so different from the one we knew."

Clara nodded, her thoughts drifting to Maya, poised on the cusp of her own path. "I just hope we've done enough to give her a chance. A real chance, not just survival."

He turned to her, his gaze serious but gentle, the kind that had steadied her through every dark night. "We've done everything we can, Clara. And we'll keep doing everything we can. That's all we can do."

Her sigh trembled with the weight of it—their fragile victories, the looming unknowns. "I just... I don't want her to grow up in a world defined by loss. I want her to know hope, love, and possibility."

Alex pressed a kiss to her forehead, his lips lingering there. "She will, Clara. Because you're her mother. Because we're us."

The day of Maya's departure dawned crisp and clear, the air sharp with the scent of dew as they loaded her car—boxes of journals, Elena's pocketknife, a worn lab coat, a photo from Hawaii of the three of them laughing on the beach. Juniper lingered near the trunk, her hands quick as she tucked a battered sketchbook—Maya's jellyfish doodles tangled with her own gear designs—between a duffel and a stack of textbooks, her quiet grin flashing as she caught Maya's eye. The goodbyes were a tangle of tears and tight embraces, Clara wrapping Maya in a hug so fierce it felt like holding onto time itself. "I'm so proud of you," she said, her voice breaking as she pulled back to meet her niece's eyes—the girl she'd raised from a newborn's wail, now a woman with Elena's fire blazing within her. "You're going to do incredible things."

Maya hugged her back, her tears spilling as she pressed her face into Clara's shoulder. "I'll miss you, Aunt Clara. But I'll visit all the time, I promise."

Juniper stepped forward then, her arms sliding around Maya in a quick, fierce embrace, her voice low but steady. "Don't slack on CRISPR-XX without me, okay? I'll sneak down when I can." Her lips brushed Maya's cheek, a fleeting anchor before she pulled back, her nose ring glinting as she blinked hard against the sheen in her eyes.

Alex stepped in, enveloping Maya in a bear hug that lifted her briefly off the ground. "Take care of yourself, kid," he said, his voice rough with emotion. "And don't forget to call."

Maya laughed through her tears, wiping her cheeks with her sleeve. "I won't. Love you all"

They stood in the driveway—Clara, Alex, Juniper—as her car rumbled to life, watching her wave through the window, her smile brave but trembling. Juniper lingered a beat longer, her hand raised as the taillights faded, then turned away, her shoulders hunching slightly as she headed back to her own packed car, bound for Berkeley. As Maya's taillights vanished down the street, Clara leaned into Alex, his arm sliding around her shoulders, anchoring her as her breath hitched. "She's going to be okay," he murmured, his voice a quiet balm.

Clara nodded, her hand resting on her belly where Elena stirred. "I know. And so will we."

That night, as the house settled into an unfamiliar hush, Clara lay in bed, the darkness soft around her. Her thoughts turned to the future—the baby's gentle kicks a promise beneath her skin, Maya's laughter echoing in her mind, Alex's warmth beside her. "We're going to give you the best life we can," she whispered to the little one, her fingers tracing the curve of her stomach. "No matter what it takes."

Alex stirred, his hand finding hers in the dark, his grip firm despite the faint tremor she felt. "We will," he murmured, his voice thick with sleep and resolve. "Together."

Clara's lips curved into a smile, her heart swelling with a love so deep it ached. The road ahead stretched long and shadowed—Maya's journey at Stanford, the baby's arrival, the fragile threads of their work holding a broken world together. It was daunting, uncertain, a path carved with questions they couldn't yet answer. But in that moment, with Alex's breath steady beside her and the promise of Elena growing within, Clara felt ready. For her sister's memory, for Maya's future, for Alex's unwavering presence, and for the fragile, fierce hope they all carried—she would face it all.

23

A Distant Thunder

The months since Maya's departure for Stanford had slipped by in a quiet, fragile cadence, the world beyond their walls softening into a hum of tentative normalcy. Clara's pregnancy had unfolded with a gentle rhythm, each week drawing her closer to the arrival of little Elena—named for the sister she'd lost sixteen years ago, the mother Maya had never known. The research facility, once a frenetic hive of innovation, had settled into a quieter pulse, its focus narrowed to refining the parthenogenesis process and wrestling with the persistent specter of reduced genetic diversity. Clara spent her days poring over data, her hand often drifting to her swollen belly, a faint smile tugging at her lips with each kick. The work was meticulous, urgent yet steady, and beneath its surface, a simmering tension coiled—unseen, unspoken, but growing.

Beyond the lab's sterile walls, a storm had been brewing among the scattered remnants of immune men—survivors of the virus that had ravaged the male population decades ago. Once a flicker of hope in a dying world, they'd grown disillusioned, their voices drowned out by a society that had pivoted entirely to parthenogenesis and the future of female reproduction. To them, it felt like erasure, a deliberate snuffing out of the Y chromosome, their existence reduced to a footnote in humanity's desperate rewrite. Among them was Thomas, a man Clara had met years before in the early days of the crisis—a wiry, sharp-eyed survivor whose quiet optimism had once buoyed her own. Now, that hope had curdled into bitterness, his faith in the world replaced by a simmering resentment. He and others like him had begun to gather in secret, their anger hardening into a plan—a desperate bid to reclaim a voice in a future that seemed intent on leaving them behind.

It was a Tuesday morning, crisp and unassuming, when the world fractured. Clara stood in the lab, her lab coat straining slightly over her belly as she reviewed a dataset with Alex and a handful of researchers. The screens glowed with genetic simulations, a quiet hum underscoring their murmured exchanges. Little Elena kicked gently, a soft ripple beneath Clara's skin, and she smiled, resting a hand there. "She's restless today," she said, her voice warm with a tenderness that felt foreign in the lab's sterile air.

Alex's grin softened the lines etched into his face, his eyes crinkling as he glanced at her. "She's just impatient to meet us—takes after her mom already."

The moment hung there, fragile and bright, a shard of light in their relentless pursuit—until it shattered. A deafening explosion tore through the building, the ground lurching beneath their feet as the lab's windows erupted inward, spraying glass like jagged rain. Clara stumbled, her hands flying to her belly in a primal instinct to shield the life within as Alex's arm shot out, steadying her before she could fall. "What the hell was that?" a researcher shouted, their voice cracking with panic as dust thickened the air.

Before anyone could answer, a second blast roared through, closer this time, shaking the walls and snuffing out the lights in a flicker of sparks. Darkness swallowed the room, smoke curling in acrid tendrils that clawed at their throats. "We need to get out!" Alex yelled, his voice cutting through the chaos as he pulled Clara toward the emergency exit, his grip firm on her arm. She staggered after him, her pulse hammering, her mind reeling with the sudden brutality of it all.

But the third explosion was a merciless hammer, its force collapsing the roof in a thunderous cascade of steel and concrete. The world tilted, debris raining down as Clara's legs gave out beneath her. Alex's shout was lost in the roar, his hand slipping from hers as she fell, the weight of the rubble pinning her beneath its jagged embrace. Her last thought was a jagged splinter of anguish—not for herself, but for the baby, for little Elena, the life she'd carried with such fragile hope. Her heart broke as the darkness claimed her, a silent scream swallowed by the void.

The news spread like wildfire across a stunned world: Clara Hayes, the scientist who had stitched hope into humanity's fraying seams, was dead. The research facility lay in smoldering ruins, a twisted skeleton of steel and ash that mocked the progress it had once cradled. The attack's brutality left the globe reeling, a collective gasp of disbelief as headlines flashed across screens—*Pioneer of Parthenogenesis Lost in Terrorist Bombing*. The quiet Tuesday had become a wound, raw and irrevocable.

Maya was in her Stanford dorm, hunched over a textbook, when her phone buzzed with Juniper's name. She answered with a distracted "Hey," but the voice on the other end wasn't Juniper's—it was a trembling classmate, stammering through the news. The phone slipped from her hand, clattering to the floor as her knees buckled, the world tilting beneath her. Juniper burst in moments later, dropping her bag to wrap Maya in her arms as sobs tore through her, raw and guttural, a grief too vast to contain. Clara—her aunt, her guardian, the woman who'd raised her from the ashes of Elena's death—was gone, and the void she left was a chasm Maya couldn't fathom.

Alex had survived, though survival felt like a cruel jest. Rescuers pulled him from the wreckage, his body battered—broken ribs, a fractured arm, a gash across his temple weeping blood—but it was his spirit that lay in tatters. He'd been pinned mere feet from Clara, helpless as the life drained from her, their unborn daughter lost with her. In the hospital, he sat motionless, staring at the sterile white wall, his mind trapped in a relentless loop of her final smile, her hand on her belly, the warmth of her voice. The loss was a blade lodged in his chest, twisting with every breath, and he wasn't sure he could bear its weight.

The bombing's shockwaves rippled outward, igniting a firestorm of reaction across the globe. The men's resistance group—calling themselves the Sons of Adam—claimed responsibility in a chilling manifesto blasted across encrypted channels. "We will not be erased," it declared, their words dripping with venom. "The future belongs to all of us, not just the daughters of Eve." They condemned the government and scientific elite for abandoning them, for betting humanity's survival on a world without men. The statement was a match struck in dry grass, sparking outrage and fear in equal measure. Protests flared in cities from London to Tokyo, crowds surging with signs demanding justice for Clara, their voices a roar against the violence—and a quieter, desperate plea for answers to the unrest festering beneath society's fragile surface. The government, already teetering under the strain of a reordered world, scrambled to respond, its promises of stability sounding hollow against the ashes of the lab.

Maya drifted through the days that followed, a ghost in her own skin, her grief a tidal wave that drowned every thought. She sat in her dorm, surrounded by Clara's old journals—pages of meticulous notes in her aunt's slanting script, dreams of a healed world sketched in ink. The leather spines felt like relics, a lifeline to the woman who'd shaped her, and as she traced the words, a spark flickered through the haze of her pain. "I won't let them win," she whispered, her voice trembling but resolute, the sound swallowed by the quiet room. "I won't let her death be for nothing."

Juniper sat beside her, her hand a steady weight on Maya's shoulder, her own eyes red-rimmed but fierce. "What are you going to do?" she asked, her voice soft but urgent.

Maya looked up, her gaze hardening into something unyielding, a fire kindled from the embers of her loss. "I'm going to finish what she started. I'm going to save this world."

A few weeks later, Alex was discharged from the hospital, his body patched together with bandages and steel pins, but his heart a gaping wound that no medicine could mend. He returned to the ruins of the lab, the air thick with the stench of charred metal and dust as he stood amid the debris. His fingers brushed a shard of glass, its edges glinting in the weak sunlight, and he clutched it until his palm bled, trembling as he held it aloft. "I'm so sorry, Clara," he whispered, his voice fracturing under the weight of his guilt. "I should've protected both of you."

He sank to his knees, the rubble biting into his legs as tears carved trails through the grime on his face. The grief was a living thing, clawing at him, threatening to drag him under—but even in its depths, a faint pulse of purpose stirred. Clara's legacy wasn't gone; it lived in Maya, in the fierce determination he'd seen in her eyes at the hospital, in the work they'd poured their lives into. He couldn't give up—not yet. For Clara, for the daughter they'd lost, for the girl he'd vowed to stand by, he'd find a way to keep going.

The world had shifted in an instant, its fragile hope shattered like the lab's crumpled walls. The attack had exposed the cracks beneath humanity's fragile recovery, the rage of the forsaken clashing against the promise of a new dawn. Yet amid the devastation, a stubborn resilience flickered. Maya, her grief forging her into something sharper, vowed to carry Clara's torch, her hands already itching to rebuild what had been torn apart. Alex, broken but unbowed, clung to the echoes of Clara's dreams, determined to honor her in whatever time he had left. Across the globe, countless others—scientists, survivors, ordinary people touched by Clara's vision—felt the same call, their resolve hardening in the face of loss.

The road ahead stretched long and treacherous, shadowed by violence and uncertainty, its end obscured in smoke. But they would face it—together, in fragments, with the strength Clara had instilled in them all. For her. For little Elena, lost before her first breath. For Maya, who carried their past into an uncharted future. And for the world they still dared to believe could be saved.

24

The Echoes of Legacy

The weeks after Clara's death melted into a haze, a gray blur that swallowed time and left Maya adrift. Stanford had granted her an indefinite leave of absence, a gesture of kindness that felt more like a lifeline she couldn't yet grasp. Returning to her dorm, to the hum of lectures and the sterile precision of labs, seemed unthinkable—how could she bury herself in equations or pipettes when the world had been torn open? How could she sit among peers chattering about midterms when the woman who'd been her compass, her rock, her family was gone? Clara had been more than an aunt; she'd been the one who'd stitched Maya's life together after Elena's death in childbirth seventeen years ago, raising her with a fierce, quiet love that shaped every step she'd taken. Now, that anchor was ripped away, leaving Maya untethered in a storm she didn't know how to weather.

It took weeks for her to muster the strength to return home, each day a battle against the weight pressing on her chest. When she finally stepped through the door, the house felt like a hollow shell—its familiar corners sharper, its air thick with an absence that clung to every surface. Alex sat in the living room, hunched in an armchair, his face pale and etched with lines that seemed carved overnight. His arm rested in a sling, a stark reminder of the bombing's toll, and his graying hair fell unkempt over his forehead. He looked up as Maya entered, his eyes hollowed by grief but softening at the sight of her, a flicker of warmth breaking through the shadows. "Maya," he said, his voice rough and fraying at the edges, thick with unspoken emotion. "I'm glad you're here."

She dropped her bag by the door, the thud echoing in the stillness, and crossed the room to sink into the chair across from him. For a long moment, they sat in silence—a heavy, suffocating quiet that pressed against her lungs, yet carried a strange comfort. It was a shared language, this wordless ache, a bridge between their broken pieces. They bore the same wound, the same jagged loss, and in that stillness, they weren't alone.

"I keep thinking she's going to walk through the door," Alex said at last, his voice splintering as he stared at the empty doorway. "Like it's all just a bad dream."

Maya nodded, her throat constricting as the familiar pang surged. "Me too. I keep reaching for my phone to call her, to tell her about something I read or an idea I had. And then I remember..." Her words faltered, crumbling into the air, and she dropped her gaze to her hands, clenched tight in her lap, knuckles whitening under the strain. Alex reached across the space between them, his hand settling over hers—warm, trembling, a fragile tether against the tide of their grief.

"She loved you so much, Maya," he said, his voice softening to a whisper, thick with tears he didn't shed. "You were her world—everything she fought for."

The words pierced her, and tears welled up, spilling over despite her efforts to hold them back. They streaked down her face, hot and relentless, and she swiped at them with a shaky hand. "I don't know how to do this without her," she admitted, her voice raw and small. "She was the strong one, the one who knew what to do. Without her I'm just... lost."

Alex's grip tightened, his fingers steady despite the tremor in them. "You're stronger than you think. And you're not alone. We'll get through this together."

She looked up at him, her vision blurred, his face a soft anchor in the storm. "I don't know if I can."

"You can," he said, his tone firm, cutting through her doubt like a blade. "You're her niece, Maya. You've got her fire, her heart. And she believed in you—more than anything. We can't stop now, not with everything she gave still at stake."

The silence stretched again, heavy but charged, and after a time, Alex rose with a wince, his injuries slowing his movements. He crossed to the bookshelf, his good hand fumbling behind a row of worn spines—Clara's favorite novels, their edges softened by years of her touch. He retrieved a small, ornate key, its brass glinting faintly in the dim light, and returned to hand it to Maya. "This is for you," he said, his voice steady despite the strain in his eyes. "It's the key to Clara's safe. She wanted you to have it."

Maya took it, her fingers trembling as she turned it over, the metal cool against her skin. "What's in it?" she asked, her voice barely above a whisper, curiosity threading through her sorrow.

"Everything," Alex replied, the word carrying a weight that settled deep. "Her journals, her research, her unfinished dreams—it's all there. She wanted you to have it when the time was right. She believed you will know what to do"

Her breath hitched, a sharp intake that caught in her chest. She stood, following Alex to the study where a small safe crouched in the corner, its presence unassuming yet suddenly monumental. Kneeling before it, her hands shook as she slid the key into the lock and turned it, the click reverberating in the quiet room. The door swung open, revealing a trove stacked within—leather-bound journals, folders thick with notes, a faded photo of Clara and Elena laughing in their early days, a scattering of keepsakes that whispered of her aunt's life. Maya reached for the top journal, her heart hammering as she opened it, Clara's precise handwriting spilling across the pages like a lifeline.

The notes were meticulous—sketches of DNA helices curling into elegant spirals, equations scrawled in margins, ideas for experiments that danced on the edge of brilliance. Tucked between the pages were fragments of Clara's soul: a reminder to call Maya about her latest project, a note to check on Alex's cough, a scribbled plea to herself to pause, to breathe. Maya's vision blurred as she read, Clara's voice ringing in her mind—sharp, warm, unwavering. "I can't believe she kept all this," she whispered, her fingers tracing the ink as if it could summon her aunt back.

Alex eased himself down beside her, his movements stiff with pain, his sling brushing the floor. His eyes swept over the safe's contents, lingering on the photo of Clara and Elena, their smiles a mirror of Maya's own. "She wanted you to have it," he said, his voice thick. "She believed in you, Maya—more than anyone."

Maya sat back on her heels, clutching the journal to her chest like a shield. For the first time since the bombing, a spark pierced the fog of her grief—not just sorrow, but a fierce, trembling resolve. "We have to finish what she started," she said, her voice steady despite the tears carving paths down her cheeks. "We can't let her work die with her."

Alex nodded, his jaw tightening with a determination that mirrored hers. "We will. Together."

She wiped her face with her sleeve, rising with the journal still in her grasp. "I'll start tonight—go through her notes, figure out where she left off. There's got to be something we can use."

Alex's hand found her shoulder, a grounding weight that steadied her racing pulse. "Take your time," he said, his tone gentle but firm. "And remember, you're not alone. We'll do this together."

That night, the kitchen table became her battlefield, Clara's journals spread out in a chaotic constellation under the soft glow of a single lamp. The house was silent save for the rustle of pages as Maya turned them, her fingers brushing the paper as if it held Clara's heartbeat. Her phone buzzed on the table—a text from Juniper flashing across the screen: *You've got this, M. Call if you need me.* Maya's lips twitched into a faint smile, the words a quiet anchor from Berkeley, tethering her to a strength beyond these walls. Each word, each sketch in Clara's journals felt like a whisper from her aunt—guiding her, urging her forward through the dark. As she read, a pattern emerged, a thread Clara had been weaving in her final months—an unfinished tapestry of research aimed at stabilizing genes broadly, not just for parthenogenesis but for the broader genetic fallout of the virus. It tackled the rising tide of diseases and mutations, the cracks left by a bottlenecked humanity, a bold vision to mend the damage at its root.

Her pulse quickened, the weight of it sinking in. "Alex, I think I found something."" she said, her voice trembling with a mix of awe and urgency. He'd been dozing in the chair beside her, his head tipped back, exhaustion etched into every line of his face. At her call, he stirred, blinking awake as he leaned forward. "What is it?"

She held up the journal, her eyes alight with a fire that hadn't burned since before the bombing. "She was working on something bigger—stabilizing genes, preventing the mutations and diseases that've been spreading since the virus hit. It's not just about the Y chromosome—it's about fixing the whole mess."

Alex's expression softened, a flicker of pride breaking through his weariness as he rested a hand on her shoulder. "Then let's get to work."

The hours bled into the night, Maya and Alex hunched over the table, piecing together Clara's fragments like archaeologists unearthing a lost city. The work was slow, painstaking—each note a puzzle piece, each equation a clue—but it lit a spark in Maya's chest, a purpose that cut through the grief like a blade. Clara's vision unfurled before them: a method to reinforce humanity's genetic foundation, to shore up the weaknesses that threatened its survival. It was ambitious, daunting, a lifeline dangling just out of reach—but it was hers, a legacy Maya could seize and carry forward.

"We'll need more equipment," Maya said, her mind racing with possibilities. "And a team. But I think we can do this. I think we can finish what she started."

Alex nodded, his eyes shining with a quiet, fierce pride. "She'd be proud of you, Maya. I know I am."

A faint smile tugged at her lips, her heart swelling with a bittersweet blend of sorrow and hope. The road ahead loomed long and treacherous—littered with obstacles, shadowed by loss, its end shrouded in uncertainty. But as she sat there, surrounded by Clara's words and Alex's steady presence, Maya felt a flicker of strength ignite within her. She was ready to face it—for Clara, who'd given her everything; for Alex, who refused to let her fall; and for the future they all still deserved, fragile and fierce in equal measure.

25

The Embers of Tomorrow

The world had spiraled into chaos once more, its fragile seams unraveling in the wake of Clara's death. Protests erupted like wildfires across cities—London's gray streets choked with marchers, New York's skyscrapers echoing with chants, Sydney's harborside swelling with voices that cracked the air with desperation. The air grew thick with anger and fear, the streets a patchwork of signs swaying in restless hands: *"Protect Our Future!" "Stop the Violence!" "Clara Hayes Lives On!"* The bombing of her lab had jolted humanity awake, a brutal reminder of how tenuous its hope had become. But it was no singular wound—weeks later, another attack struck, this time in Munich, targeting a German research facility dedicated to parthenogenesis. The building crumpled under a barrage of explosives, its scientists buried in the rubble, their work reduced to ash. The Sons of Adam, the shadowy coalition of immune men who'd claimed Clara's life, issued another chilling decree through encrypted channels: "*We will not fade into oblivion. The world will hear us.*" Their message was a sledgehammer, shattering the fragile peace Clara's breakthroughs had begun to weave, leaving humanity teetering on a precipice of uncertainty.

Amid this storm, Maya and Alex made the heavy choice to return to Sydney—a pilgrimage to lay the ash of Clara and the unspoken loss of the unborn Elena to rest, to tether her to the earth beside her sister,

Elena. The journey was a quiet, somber affair, the weight of their loss a constant companion pressing against their ribs. Sydney greeted them with a muted hush, its once-vibrant streets dulled by tension, its skyline cloaked in a haze that mirrored their grief. The city pulsed with a subdued resolve, its people gathering in pockets to mourn Clara—scientists in lab coats, students with tear-streaked faces, strangers who'd clung to her vision of a healed world. The air crackled with unspoken questions: *How do we go on? What happens now?*

The service unfolded in a small cemetery perched on a cliff above the ocean, its grassy expanse framed by windswept eucalyptus and the endless sweep of waves below. Three markers stood in a solemn row: Elena Hayes's grave, etched with *Beloved Sister and Mother*, now flanked by two new stones—one for Clara, *Clara Hayes, Light of Hope*, and beside it, a smaller one, heartbreakingly simple: *Elena Hayes, Our Unborn Star*. The sight of that third marker—a tribute to the child lost with Clara in the bombing—caught Maya off guard, her breath hitching as she traced the carved letters with her eyes. Maya clutches the whale-carved pocketknife—a keepsake from Elena's legacy—to her heart, symbolizing the passing of the torch from her aunt and mother to her. Colleagues from the Sydney Institute of Advanced Genomics gathered around, their faces a gallery of sorrow and admiration, their usual lab coats swapped for somber attire that fluttered in the sea breeze.

Dr. Priya Sharma, Clara's confidante from their early days at the institute, stepped forward, her eyes glistening as she clasped Maya's hands. "Maya," she said, her voice quavering with emotion, "your aunt was the bravest, most brilliant person I've ever known. She fought for a future she could see so clearly, every single day. And little Elena... she was part of that dream. We owe them both so much."

"Maya," Priya said, her voice trembling under the weight of her tears, "your aunt was one of the bravest, most brilliant souls I've ever known. She believed in a future worth fighting for, and she never stopped—every single day. We owe her more than we can ever repay."

Maya nodded, her throat constricting as emotion clawed its way up. “Thank you, Dr. Sharma,” she managed, her voice a fragile thread. “She always spoke so highly of you—said you were the one who kept her sane during those late-night breakthroughs. I just... I wish she could see how much she meant to everyone.”

Priya’s lips trembled into a faint smile, her hand brushing Maya’s arm. “She knew, in her way. And she’d be so proud of you.”

Another figure stepped forward—Dr. Synclair Nguyen, a wiry geneticist with sharp features softened by sorrow. She placed a steady hand on Maya’s shoulder, her voice low but firm. "Clara was more than a scientist; she was a beacon of hope. Her legacy lives on in you, Maya. We're all here to support you, whatever you need."

The words wrapped around her like a lifeline, bittersweet and heavy, threading comfort through the raw edges of her pain. She felt the crushing weight of Clara’s absence—and now little Elena’s too, a loss she hadn’t fully grasped until this moment—but also the strength of the community rallying around her. Colleagues lingered after the formal words, sharing hushed memories—Clara’s late-night debates fuelled by black coffee, her quiet awe at Elena’s first kicks, the way she’d fought tooth and nail for every breakthrough. Maya drank in each story, her chest aching with the dual loss of the aunt who’d raised her from Elena’s shadow and the cousin she’d never meet.

After the service, as the crowd thinned and the ocean’s song rose to fill the quiet, Maya and Alex drifted to the beach below—the same stretch of sand where Clara and Elena had spent countless afternoons in their youth. The waves rolled in with a steady crash, their rhythm a soothing balm against the jagged ache in their chests. They sank into the cool sand, side by side, the breeze weaving through their hair with the mingled scents of salt and seaweed. The horizon stretched endless before them, a canvas of blue meeting the fading light.

“Do you remember the stories she used to tell us about this place?” Maya asked after a long stillness, her voice soft, almost lost to the tide.

Alex's lips curved into a faint, wistful smile, his gaze fixed on the waves. "Yeah. She said this was where she and Elena would dream about the future. They'd talk about saving the world, even back then."

Maya's smile mirrored his, though it trembled under the weight of memory. "I miss her so much," she said, her voice cracking. "And I miss my mom, even though I never really knew her. It's like... they're both inside me, pieces I can feel but can't touch."

Alex turned to her, his eyes gentle but shadowed with his own grief. "They're always with you, Maya. In here." He placed a hand over his heart. "And in everything you do."

The words settled over her, warm and heavy, and they sat in silence, letting the waves speak for them. The sun dipped below the horizon, spilling orange and pink across the sky in a fleeting blaze that felt like a goodbye. For a moment, the chaos of the world receded—the protests, the bombings, the fractured future—and they were just two souls bound by loss, finding solace in the rhythm of the sea.

As twilight deepened, painting the beach in shades of indigo, Maya shifted, her gaze sharpening with a resolve that cut through her sorrow. "I've decided something," she said, turning to Alex, her voice steady despite the tremor beneath it. "I'm going back to Stanford. I'm going to finish my studies."

Alex's nod was slow, his expression a blend of pride and quiet sadness, the lines of his face deepening in the fading light. "I think that's the right call," he said. "Clara would want you to keep going."

"I know," Maya replied, her fingers digging into the sand as if grounding herself. "But it's not just for her. It's for me, too. I need to keep going. I need to make sure her work—her legacy—doesn't die with her."

He reached for her hand, his grip firm despite the faint tremble in his fingers, a remnant of the injuries that still lingered. "You will, Maya," he said, his voice thick with conviction. "I know you will."

She squeezed his hand back, her chest tightening with a mingle of grief and determination. Returning to Stanford loomed like a mountain without Clara's voice on the other end of the phone—without her steady guidance, her quiet faith in Maya's potential—or the imagined laughter of little Elena to lighten the load. But it was also a reclamation, a refusal to let the Sons of Adam extinguish the light Clara and her unborn daughter had kindled. The world beyond was fracturing—research facilities burning, protests swelling into riots, fear threading through every headline—but here, where Clara and Elena's dreams had taken root, Maya felt a fire ignite within her. She'd finish what her aunt had started, not just to honor her, but to prove that hope could endure even in ashes.

The journey back to California was a hushed affair, Sydney's tension a faint hum beyond the plane's windows. Maya cradled a small vial of Clara's ashes—kept from the urn for a private scattering later, a ritual she wasn't ready to release—while another tiny vial beside it held a symbolic pinch for little Elena, a quiet promise to the child she'd never know. Alex's silence was a comforting presence, not an emptiness, as their shared purpose wove a thread through the darkness.

As the city's lights glimmered faintly beyond the curtains, Maya sat on the edge of her childhood bed, the room frozen in time—posters of DNA strands curling at the edges, a shelf of Clara's books gathering dust, a photo of her and her aunt pinned to the wall. She traced the vials with her thumb, her mind racing with the path ahead. Stanford beckoned—its labs a crucible, its libraries a vault for Clara's journals, the weight of two Elenas pressing her forward. The chaos outside loomed larger—another facility lost, another wave of unrest—but she pushed it aside, anchoring herself in the steady pulse of her own resolve. She'd return, transformed by loss into something fiercer, something unbreakable.

Alex appeared in the doorway, his silhouette softened by the hall's dim glow, his sling a stark outline against the light. "You okay?" he asked, his voice rough but warm, a lifeline from the man who'd stood by her through every fracture.

She nodded, her lips curving into a faint, resolute smile. "I will be. We will be."

He crossed to her, easing onto the bed beside her, their shoulders brushing in a quiet, unspoken pact. "She'd be proud of you," he said, his gaze drifting to the vials in her hands. "Both of them would—for not letting go."

Maya leaned into him, holding the pocketknife and the vials cool against her palm, her heart swelling with a love that pierced and a hope that refused to dim. The road ahead stretched vast and perilous—rife with danger, shadowed by loss, its horizon veiled in smoke—but she was ready to walk it. For Clara, who'd raised her from Elena's ashes; for little Elena, lost before her first breath; for Alex, who carried the same scars; and for a world still worth fighting for, one defiant, aching step at a time.

26

The Fire Within

A few weeks after the somber ceremony in Sydney, where Clara and little Elena's ashes were laid to rest beside Elena Hayes's grave, Maya stepped back onto Stanford's sprawling campus, her heart a heavy knot of grief yet pulsing with an unshaken resolve. The familiar pathways, once alive with the thrill of discovery and late-night debates, now stretched before her like a battlefield—each lecture hall and lab a front line in a war she hadn't chosen but couldn't abandon. The weight of her family's legacy bore down on her shoulders, a mantle forged from Clara's brilliance, Elena's sacrifice, and the fragile hope of a child lost before her first breath. Yet she carried it not as a burden but as a torch, its flame flickering with a fierce determination she could feel burning in her veins. In her dorm room, the unpacking was a quiet ritual—she set the whale-carved pocketknife Elena had given Clara on her desk, its worn handle gleaming faintly under the lamplight, a silent sentinel of the promise she'd inherited. Beside it, she arranged Clara's journals—some salvaged from the safe Alex had opened, others carefully transported from Sydney in a battered suitcase—their leather spines cracked but brimming with her aunt's meticulous notes, her dreams of a world made whole.

Her first act was to unlock Clara's cloud backups, a digital vault she'd only glimpsed in fragments before. Tucked among the journals, she'd found a scrap of paper in Clara's looping script—a password scrawled with a simple note: *"For Maya, the future."* The words stung, a lump rising in her throat as she typed them into the encrypted login, her fingers trembling over the keys. The screen flared to life, revealing rows of files that unfolded like a map to Clara's mind—research data meticulously cataloged, genetic sequences annotated with painstaking care, experimental logs spanning years, even personal musings she'd jotted in stolen moments. It was a treasure trove, a lifeline to the woman who'd raised her, and as Maya scrolled through it, her breath caught at a folder labeled *"Project Lazarus."* She clicked it open, her pulse quickening as pages of dense notes unfurled—Clara's secret ambition to reverse cellular aging and stabilize telomeres, the protective caps at the ends of chromosomes that frayed with each division. This wasn't just a side project; it was a parallel dream to her parthenogenesis work, a bid to heal the broader genetic wounds *Chromovirus-X* had carved into humanity's fabric. The scope of it hit Maya like a wave—Clara hadn't just been fighting for reproduction; she'd been fighting for survival itself, a future where decay didn't outpace renewal.

The days that followed were a grueling dance of ambition and exhaustion, a balancing act that stretched Maya to her limits. Her Stanford coursework—bioengineering seminars, advanced genetics labs—demanded precision and focus, but her own *CRISPR-XX* project consumed her nights, its audacious goal of stabilizing the X chromosome and halting the virus's mutations a relentless pull. She haunted the lab long after her classmates had gone, her eyes burning under the harsh fluorescent lights as she ran simulations late into the night, the hum of computers her only company. Clara's *Project Lazarus* files became a revelation, their insights sparking new pathways in her mind—telomere reinforcement could intersect with her X-chromosome work, weaving a dual shield against genetic collapse. Her laptop glowed with holographic DNA models, their spiraling strands twisting in endless permutations as she tested theories, her fingers rushing through the keys with a fervor that bordered on obsession.

Juniper, her steadfast anchor, was a constant presence through the haze, her Berkeley schedule a logistical puzzle she bent to fit Maya's needs. She arrived with steaming cups of coffee when the clock ticked past midnight, her hands steady as she proofread Maya's sprawling papers or debugged the AI algorithms crunching Clara's data. One night, as the lab's sterile air grew heavy with the scent of solder and burnt circuits, Juniper leaned against the bench, her voice cutting through the silence. "You're going to burn out if you keep this up," she said, her tone gentle but edged with worry, her arms crossed as she watched Maya tweak a stubbornly flickering simulation.

Maya didn't look up, her eyes fixed on the screen, her voice taut with exhaustion but unyielding. "I can't stop. Every second I waste, the Sons of Adam are out there, tearing down everything Clara built—everything she died for. I have to keep going."

Juniper sighed, her shoulders slumping, but she didn't push back. She knew Maya too well—knew the fire that drove her wasn't just ambition but a need to prove herself, to claw meaning from the ashes of her loss. Instead, she slid a granola bar across the bench, a silent truce, and settled into a chair beside her, her quiet presence a ballast against the storm raging within Maya.

The world beyond Stanford's ivy-clad walls was crumbling faster than she could track, its instability a constant drumbeat against her focus. News broke of a third attack by the Sons of Adam—this time in Shanghai, where a major genetic research hub went up in flames, its steel skeleton collapsing under a barrage of explosives. The government's response was swift, capturing most of the assailants and sparing lives, but the damage rippled outward, a shockwave that rattled the global scientific community. Research slowed to a crawl as nations slipped into emergency protocols, borders tightening and security strangling innovation. Whispers circulated through encrypted forums—rumors that the Sons were crafting a new virus vector, one aimed at the X chromosome itself. If true, it would be a dagger to the heart of parthenogenesis, a direct assault on the fragile future Clara had died to protect. The thought ignited a fury in Maya, a white-hot rage that seared through her grief. How could they be so blind, so reckless—gambling humanity's survival for a grudge against a world they refused to understand?

The news didn't break her—it forged her. She hurled herself into her work with a ferocity that startled even Juniper, her nights blurring into a relentless cycle of code, coffee, and Clara's journals. Those leather-bound pages became her lifeline, her late-night confessor, their words a beacon through the fog of her exhaustion. She traced Clara's handwriting with reverent fingers, piecing together the fragments of her aunt's sprawling vision—notes on telomere stabilization scrawled in hurried bursts, diagrams of CRISPR modifications sketched in margins, personal asides that revealed the woman behind the scientist. One evening, as the lab's lights buzzed overhead, Juniper slipped in with a tray of food—sandwiches, fruit, a thermos of soup—her quiet insistence breaking through Maya's haze. "You haven't eaten all day," she said, setting it beside the laptop, her tone firm but soft.

Maya glanced up, her eyes bloodshot but blazing, her voice trembling with a raw, electric excitement. "I've got something," she said, shoving a journal toward Juniper. "Clara's notes on *Project Lazarus*—she was modifying CRISPR to reinforce telomeres, to stop cellular aging at its root. If I can adapt that for *CRISPR-XX*, we could stabilize the whole genome, not just the X chromosome—block the mutations the virus keeps throwing at us."

Juniper's eyes widened, her breath catching as she scanned the page. "That's huge, Maya. But you can't do it alone. You need to sleep, eat, and take care of yourself. Clara wouldn't want you to destroy yourself trying to save the world."

Maya's jaw tightened, her fingers curling around the journal's edge, but Juniper's words pierced the haze. She exhaled, a shaky breath that carried the weight of her fatigue, and nodded. "You're right. But I can't stop now. Not when we're so close."

The world kept unraveling, its chaos a relentless tide against her efforts. Governments clamped down with draconian regulations, slashing funding for genetic research as fear of another attack took hold. Labs shuttered, projects stalled, and scientists retreated, their work choked by bureaucracy and paranoia. But Maya refused to bend. She turned to Clara's cloud backups, working in secret when the lab emptied out, her screen glowing in the stillness as she mined her aunt's files for answers. One night, buried deep in a log dated months before the bombing, she stumbled on a cryptic line in Clara's angular script: *"The key lies in the telomeres. Stabilize them, and we stabilize the future."* Her heart thudded as the implications crashed over her—if she could shield those fragile caps, halt the decay that left humanity vulnerable, she could rewrite the rules of survival. It was a thread, thin but unbreakable, tying Clara's dream to her own.

The hours stretched into dawn, the lab windows paling with the first light as Maya stood, the whale-carved pocketknife clutched in her hand. She crossed to the window, the darkened campus sprawling below, its quiet beauty a stark contrast to the fire roaring within her. The weight of the world pressed down—Clara's death, little Elena's loss, the Sons of Adam's relentless shadow—but it didn't crush her; it honed her, sharpening her into something fierce and unyielding. She pressed the knife to her chest, its cool metal a grounding pulse against her racing heart, and whispered into the stillness, "I won't let them win. For Mom and Dad. For Clara. For little Elena. For all of us."

The road ahead loomed vast and treacherous—littered with threats, shadowed by uncertainty, its end lost in the haze of a world on the brink. Governments faltered, labs burned, and whispers of a new virus grew louder, but Maya stood undaunted. She thought of Juniper's steady faith, Alex's quiet strength back in California, the journals cradling Clara's soul—and felt the fire flare brighter. It was fueled by grief, yes, but also by love, by the unshakable belief that hope—fragile, fierce, and defiant—was worth every fight. She was ready to walk that road, step by trembling step, to forge a future from the ashes of her past.

27

A Fragile Thread

The months after the Shanghai attack unraveled into a maelstrom of chaos and uncertainty, the world reeling as the Sons of Adam's campaign of terror escalated beyond isolated strikes. What had begun with the bombing of Clara's lab had morphed into a relentless barrage—smaller but no less devastating attacks peppering the globe like shrapnel. Research facilities crumbled under explosive payloads in Tokyo and São Paulo, government offices smoldered in Paris and Mumbai, even public squares—once sanctuaries of ordinary life—erupted in Madrid and Cape Town, leaving behind scorched earth and shattered lives. The world teetered on a razor's edge, its collective pulse quickening with every breaking headline, every wail of sirens cutting through the night. For the first time in decades, nations cast aside old rivalries, their leaders convening in shadowed rooms to forge a unified intelligence network—a desperate alliance pooling resources, sharing scraps of data, and tracking the elusive threads of a group that thrived in the margins. Bursting operations swept through hidden cells, netting a handful of the Sons of Adam in daring raids—gaunt men with hollow eyes hauled into custody in chains—but their decentralized structure slithered beyond reach, a hydra sprouting new heads with each severed limb.

The captured men posed a dilemma that gnawed at the marrow of a world already bled dry. With the male population hovering near extinction—a mere whisper hundreds of thousands scattered across a planet once teeming with billions—the question of their punishment ignited a firestorm of debate. Harsh measures loomed on the table—execution by lethal drones, life imprisonment in fortified bunkers, forced labor in remote outposts—and each sparked a visceral clash of ideals. Female-led governments, now the backbone of a reshaped society, wrestled with the scales of justice, their hands trembling as they balanced retribution against the fragile imperative to preserve humanity's dwindling genetic diversity. The streets erupted in a cacophony of protest—crowds swelling in city squares, their voices a discordant chorus. In Berlin, marchers hoisted signs demanding blood for blood, their chants a thunderous call for vengeance: "*Justice for Clara!*" "*No Mercy for Terror!*" In Nairobi, others gathered in somber vigils, their placards pleading for leniency: "*Save the Last Men!*" "*They Are Us!*"—their arguments rooted in the desperate hope that these men, however broken, were artifacts of a vanishing past, driven to extremism by a society that had turned its back.

In the gleaming halls of power—marble corridors now dimmed by flickering lights and the weight of decisions no one wanted to make—leaders grappled with an unanswerable question: What is the most humane punishment for those who threaten humanity's fragile thread? Proposals flew like sparks in a tinderbox—rehabilitation programs to rewire their rage into something salvageable, exile to barren colonies where they could neither harm nor be harmed, cryogenic stasis as a last-ditch bid to preserve their genes for a future that might never come. Voices clashed in late-night sessions, diplomats and scientists hurling statistics and ethics at one another, but no consensus emerged. The world watched, its breath held in a collective unease, as the fate of the captured men dangled in limbo—an emblem of a civilization fractured by its own survival.

Meanwhile, at Stanford, Maya teetered on the brink of collapse, her world a relentless churn of science and sorrow. The *CRISPR-XX* project—her audacious bid to stabilize the X chromosome and thwart the virus's mutations—consumed her every waking moment, its demands piling atop the ceaseless pressure to honor her mom and Clara's legacy and the raw grief for little Elena, the cousin she'd never hold. She haunted the lab like a specter, her frame thinning as she poured herself into her work, her eyes bloodshot from sleepless nights spent hunched over gene sequencers and glowing screens. Her hands trembled as she adjusted settings, calibrated simulations, her once-steady fingers now betraying the toll of her unbroken vigil. Juniper watched from the sidelines, her heart twisting with helplessness as Maya's vibrant spirit faded into a gaunt, hollow determination—a shadow of the girl who'd once laughed freely under California's sun.

One evening, as the lab's fluorescent lights buzzed overhead, casting stark shadows across the cluttered benches, Juniper stepped closer, her voice cutting through the hum of machinery like a lifeline. "Maya, you need to rest," she said, her hand settling on Maya's shoulder, firm yet tender. "You're going to collapse—you're already halfway there."

Maya shrugged her off, her movements sharp with a frustration that crackled in the air, her voice a brittle edge honed by exhaustion. "I don't have time to rest, Juniper. Every second I waste, the Sons of Adam are out there, trying to destroy everything Mom and aunt Clara worked for. I can't stop now." Her words trembled with a fury born of loss, her eyes glinting with unshed tears as she turned back to her screen, fingers flying over the keys with a desperation that bordered on mania.

Juniper's concern deepened, her brow furrowing as she studied the lines of strain etched into Maya's face. She knew this drive was more than ambition—it was love, grief, a need to claw justice from a world that kept taking. But she also knew no one could burn this brightly without breaking. With a resolve born of fear and care, she reached out beyond the lab's walls, dialing Alex's number in a quiet corner of the dorm, her voice low and urgent as she pleaded for his help.

Alex arrived a few days later, stepping onto Stanford's campus like a quiet storm breaking the horizon. His presence was a steady force, a tether to the life they'd shared before the bombing tore it apart. He found Maya in the lab, her silhouette framed by the glow of a microscope, her face pale and drawn, her dark hair falling in unkempt strands over her shoulders. The sight of her—so like Clara in her relentless pursuit, her jaw set with the same unyielding fire—pierced his chest, a pang of memory mingling with worry. He paused in the doorway, the hum of machinery filling the silence, then stepped forward, his voice soft but resonant. "Maya."

She jolted, her head snapping up, surprise flickering across her weary features. "Alex? What are you doing here?"

"Juniper called me," he said, closing the distance between them, his sling a stark reminder of the wounds he still carried. "She's worried about you. And so am I."

Maya's shoulders slumped, the weight of her exhaustion crashing through the walls she'd built, her resolve faltering under his steady gaze. "I'm fine," she said, though her voice cracked, betraying the lie. "I'm fine, Alex. I just... I have to keep going. For everyone."

Alex's hand found her shoulder, his touch gentle but unyielding, grounding her in the storm of her own making. "I know you do," he said, his tone thick with shared grief. "But you're not going to help anyone if you run yourself into the ground. Clara wouldn't want this for you. She'd want you to take care of yourself."

The dam broke then, tears spilling down Maya's cheeks as the weight of her loss—of Clara's warm laughter, little Elena's unrealized future, Elena's fading echo—crashed over her. "I don't know how to stop," she choked out, her voice raw and ragged. "Every time I close my eyes, I see them—Clara, the baby, Mom, Dad, all the faces we've lost. I can't let their deaths mean nothing."

Alex pulled her into his arms, his own grief surging as he held her close, their shared pain a bridge across the void. "You're not alone in this," he murmured, his voice steady despite the tremor beneath it. "We're in this together—me, Juniper, all of us who loved her. But you've got to let us help you. You have to let yourself breathe."

For a moment, she clung to him, her sobs muffled against his chest, the whale-carved pocketknife digging into her palm where she gripped it—a talisman of the family she'd lost and the fight she couldn't abandon. Alex's embrace was a lifeline, a reminder of the roots that still held her, even as the world spun out of control.

That night, he coaxed her from the lab's sterile confines, Juniper trailing beside them as they crossed the campus to a quiet café nestled near the quad. The warm glow of its lights spilled onto the street, a stark contrast to the lab's cold fluorescence, and the air carried the faint scent of roasted coffee and baked bread—a fleeting echo of normalcy. They settled into a corner booth, the clatter of dishes and murmur of sparse patrons a soft backdrop to their silence. For the first time in weeks, Maya let herself unclench, her shoulders easing as she picked at a plate of food Juniper insisted she eat, the warmth of the meal seeping into her bones.

As they sat, Alex shared fragments of news from Sydney—how the government wrestled with the captured Sons of Adam, their trials a tangle of ethics and survival. He spoke of the debates raging in council chambers—harsh punishment versus fragile mercy—and the protests splitting the city, voices clashing over justice and preservation. "They're talking exile now," he said, his voice low, his fingers tracing the rim of his cup. "Sending them to some island no one's touched in years. Others want them locked away forever—say it's the only way to keep us safe."

Maya listened, her mind churning as she sipped her tea, the steam curling upward like a ghost of thought. "It's not just about punishment," she said at last, her voice firm despite its quiet edge. "It's about why they're doing this. They feel erased, like the world moved on without them. If we don't figure that out—don't address the root—we're just kicking the fight down the road."

Alex's gaze softened, a flicker of pride breaking through his weariness. "You're right," he said, leaning back in his chair. "It's bigger than locking them up or letting them go. But change like that—it's a slow burn. It starts with people like you, Maya—people who won't stop fighting for something better."

The words settled over her, heavy but warm, a spark igniting in the ashes of her exhaustion. She thought of Clara's journals, their pages brimming with a vision that spanned beyond survival—of Elena's fierce hope, whispered in stories Maya clung to—of little Elena, a promise snuffed out too soon. The café's glow felt like a fragile shield against the chaos beyond, and for a moment, she let herself imagine a world where justice wasn't just vengeance, but understanding—a world worth building.

Later, as the campus slept under a blanket of stars, Maya stood on her dorm's balcony, the cool night air brushing her face like a whisper from the sea. The whale-carved pocketknife rested in her hand, its weight a familiar comfort, its grooves worn smooth by years of Clara's touch—a relic of the family she carried within her. Behind her, Juniper and Alex lingered in the room, their voices a soft hum as they spoke in low tones—Juniper's quiet worry, Alex's steady reassurance—a constellation of support holding her steady. She pressed the knife to her chest, its cool metal a heartbeat against her own, and whispered into the wind, "I won't let them win. For all of us."

The road ahead stretched vast and perilous—littered with the debris of a world unmoored, shadowed by the Sons of Adam's wrath, its horizon veiled in uncertainty. Nations faltered, their unity fraying under the strain of fear and division; labs stood empty, their work stalled by paranoia; and the whispers of a new threat—an X-targeting virus—grew louder in the dark. But Maya stood unbroken, her exhaustion tempered by a fire that refused to gutter. She thought of Juniper's unwavering care, Alex's unshakable faith, the journals cradling Clara's dreams—and felt that fire flare brighter. It was fueled by loss, yes, but also by love, by a belief that hope—fragile, fierce, and unyielding—was a flame worth tending, no matter the cost. She was ready to walk that road, step by trembling step, to forge justice from the chaos, a future from the ashes, for the family she'd lost and the world she still dared to save.

28

The Horizon of Hope

A few years had slipped by since Maya's return to Stanford, the passage of time etching subtle yet profound shifts into the fabric of the world she'd once known. The Sons of Adam's relentless assaults, once a jagged rhythm of destruction, had dulled to sporadic tremors, their frequency waning under the weight of a global counteroffensive spearheaded by Alex's ingenuity. His work in weaving artificial intelligence into the sinews of international intelligence networks had transformed the hunt for the terrorists—algorithms sifting through digital shadows, pinpointing patterns where human eyes faltered. Hundreds of operatives had been swept up in coordinated raids, their gaunt faces flashing across screens as governments trumpeted victories in a war that refused to end. Yet the group's leaders remained phantoms, their ideology seeping like a dark tide through the dwindling remnants of the male population—a whisper of rebellion that refused to be silenced. The world exhaled a cautious breath, safer but still perched on a precipice, the threat a smoldering ember that could flare anew at any moment.

Maya, now in her early twenties, had carved a path through Stanford with a ferocity that left her peers in awe, her life a relentless pursuit of the science that had claimed her family yet fueled her purpose. She'd fast-tracked her bachelor's degree in biotechnology, graduating with honors in a blur of sleepless nights and accolades, and now plunged into a PhD program that fused nanotechnology and genetic engineering into a daring frontier. Her research was nothing short of revolutionary—a tapestry woven from Clara's *Project Lazarus* and her own *CRISPR-XX*, its threads binding the past to a future she refused to let slip away. She'd unlocked a method to deploy nanoparticles and viral vectors as sentinels within the genome, stabilizing telomeres—the fragile caps at chromosome ends that frayed with age and stress—offering a shield against the genetic decay *Chromovirus-X* had unleashed. Her work hinted at slowing cellular aging, slashing the risk of genetic diseases that plagued a bottlenecked humanity, even teasing the edges of physical enhancement—stronger bones, sharper minds—though the ethical shadows of such power loomed large, a specter she wrestled with in the quiet hours.

Yet one barrier stood unyielding, a wall she battered against with every experiment: the Y chromosome's recovery. The virus had shredded it across generations, leaving a fragmented ruin no amount of ingenuity could fully mend. Her lab was a crucible of trial and error—rows of screens flickering with genetic sequences, petri dishes cradling fragile hope—but the results were stubbornly partial, a mosaic of half-formed successes that mocked her ambition. She'd sit late into the night, the lab's sterile glow casting her silhouette against the walls, staring at data that refused to yield, her fingers tracing the whale-carved pocketknife that had become her talisman. "We'll find a way," she'd mutter, her voice a quiet vow to the empty room, the knife's worn handle a tether to Clara's faith, Elena's fire, and little Elena's lost promise. "We have to."

Juniper had been her unwavering shadow through the crucible, a constant light in the storm of Maya's relentless drive. After earning her bachelor's in mechanical engineering at Berkeley, she'd eschewed further academia for a hands-on role, her skills a lifeline to Maya's sprawling vision. She'd crafted custom lab equipment with a precision that bordered on art—microinjectors humming with quiet efficiency, nanoparticle synthesizers whirring under her deft touch—and spent countless hours debugging the algorithms that parsed Clara's data, her mind a bridge between code and creation. Beyond the mechanics, she was Maya's emotional keel, her presence a steady hand pulling her back from the abyss when the weight of her work threatened to drown her. They'd sit together in the lab's dim hours, Juniper's quiet strength a counterpoint to Maya's frenetic energy, her voice a soft anchor in the chaos.

One evening, as the lab's fluorescent lights buzzed overhead, casting stark shadows across the cluttered benches, Juniper broke the stillness that had settled between them. They'd been poring over a holographic DNA model, its spiraling strands flickering as Maya adjusted parameters with a furrowed brow. "You've done more in a few years than most manage in a lifetime," Juniper said, her tone gentle but firm, her hand resting lightly on the bench beside Maya's. "You need to give yourself some credit."

Maya exhaled, a weary sound that carried the weight of her endless chase, her hand raking through her dark hair, now streaked with the faint gray of stress. "It's not enough," she said, her voice low and taut, her gaze fixed on the model as if it held the answer she couldn't grasp. "Not yet. The Y chromosome... it's like trying to rebuild a shattered mirror. Even if I can piece it together, the cracks will always be there."

Juniper's hand slid over hers, warm and steady, her fingers curling around Maya's with a quiet resolve. "Maybe those cracks are what make it beautiful," she said, her eyes meeting Maya's with a softness that cut through her defenses. "You're not just fixing what's broken—you're creating something new. And that's worth celebrating."

The words hung between them, a fragile bridge over the chasm of Maya's doubt, and for a moment, she let them settle, her shoulders easing under their weight. She squeezed Juniper's hand, a silent thank-you, her chest tightening with a gratitude she couldn't voice. Juniper's faith—unwavering, unspoken—mirrored the steady belief Clara had once held, a lifeline she clung to when her own faltered.

Alex, now brushing the edge of his late forties, bore the marks of a body outpaced by time, the virus's lingering echo etching premature age into his frame. His hair had surrendered to a near-total gray, a silver crown that caught the light in sharp contrast to the deepening lines carved into his face—testaments to decades of strain and the quiet toll of survival. His movements had slowed, a deliberate cadence replacing the easy stride of years past, and his hands—once steady as stone—trembled faintly as they danced across keyboards, a subtle betrayal he masked with a stubborn resolve. Yet his mind remained a blade, honed by necessity, and he'd thrown himself into his work with a fervor that defied his fading strength. His AI algorithms had become the backbone of global intelligence efforts, threading through networks to track the Sons of Adam with a precision that saved countless lives, earning him quiet accolades and a measure of peace amid the storm.

He'd confided in Maya once, late one night over a crackling video call, his voice a gravelly thread laced with pride and a shadow of regret. They'd been discussing a recent breakthrough in his tracking systems, the screen casting a pallor over his face that deepened the hollows beneath his eyes. "I'm not going to be around forever," he'd said, his gaze drifting somewhere beyond the camera, his words heavy with an acceptance she hated to hear. "But I want to make sure I leave this world a little better than I found it."

Maya had felt her throat close, tears stinging as she leaned closer to the screen, her voice breaking as she replied, "You already have, Alex. You've done so much—more than you'll ever know." She'd flown to him the next weekend, wrapping him in a hug that lingered, her arms tight around his thinning frame as if she could hold time at bay. His embrace was weaker than she remembered, but the warmth in it—the same steady love that had carried her through Clara's loss—remained unshaken.

One crisp autumn evening, the three of them—Maya, Juniper, and Alex—gathered for a quiet dinner at a small restaurant perched above

San Francisco Bay, its windows framing the city's lights as they danced across the water. The occasion was a solemn ritual, a remembrance of Clara and little Elena, whose absences carved a permanent hollow in their lives, yet bound them closer with every shared memory. The table was modest, laden with simple dishes—warm bread, a hearty stew, a plate of roasted vegetables—comfort woven into every bite. A single candle flickered at the center, its flame casting a soft, golden glow over their faces, a beacon in the dimness that mirrored the light they clung to.

They spoke of Clara as the meal unfolded, their voices weaving a tapestry of her life—her relentless determination that could bend steel, her sharp wit that cut through tension like a blade, her unwavering faith in a future worth fighting for. Maya's eyes glistened as she recounted a night from her childhood, her voice soft with nostalgia. "She stayed up with me once, all night, helping me finish a science project—even though she had a huge presentation the next day. She didn't even blink, just kept going, coffee in one hand, laughing at my terrible sketches." Alex's smile was faint but warm, his gaze distant as he added his own thread. "She always knew how to pull me out of the dark—some dumb joke or a look that said she'd never give up on me, no matter how bad it got." Juniper, who'd known Clara only briefly, leaned in, her eyes bright with secondhand reverence as she listened, soaking in the woman who'd shaped the people she loved.

"She'd be so proud of you, Maya," Alex said, his voice thickening as he set his fork down, his hand trembling slightly on the table. "Everything you've accomplished —the way you've taken her work and run with it—it's exactly what she fought for, what she dreamed of."

Maya's smile wavered, tears spilling as she brushed them away with her sleeve. "I just wish she could see it," she said, her voice cracking under the weight of longing. "And little Elena... I wish she could've been here, growing up with us, part of this."

Juniper reached across the table, her hand finding Maya's and squeezing it with a quiet strength, her voice steady despite the sheen in her own eyes. "They're here, Maya—in every step you take, every breakthrough you chase. In everything we're building together."

The words sank into Maya, a balm over the raw edges of her grief, and she nodded, her grip tightening on Juniper's hand. Alex's eyes shimmered, a rare crack in his stoic facade, and he raised his glass—a tumbler of water, his hands too unsteady for wine—his voice rough but resolute. "To Clara and Elena," he said, the names a quiet prayer. "And to us—for carrying on."

They clinked their glasses, the sound a fragile note in the stillness, a vow sealed in the candle's wavering light. The meal stretched on, their laughter mingling with tears, a shared remembrance that held the past close without letting it crush them.

As the evening waned, the restaurant emptying into the night, Maya drifted to the window, her breath fogging the glass as she gazed out at the bay. The city lights glittered like stars fallen to earth, their reflections rippling across the water—a mirror of the hope she clung to, fragile yet unyielding. The whale-carved pocketknife rested in her hand, its weight a familiar comfort, its grooves a map of the hands that had held it before her—Elena's, Clara's, now hers. Behind her, Juniper and Alex lingered at the table, their voices a low hum of camaraderie, their presence a steady anchor in the tempest of her thoughts.

"We're not done yet," she said softly, her voice a quiet vow carried on the night air, barely audible over the rustle of the wind beyond the glass. "There's still so much to do—to fix, to build. But we're closer than we've ever been."

Alex rose, his steps slow but purposeful as he joined her, his hand resting lightly on her shoulder, his voice warm with pride and resolve. "And we'll keep going—for Clara, for Elena, for everyone counting on us."

Juniper stepped beside them, her arm brushing Maya's, her presence a quiet promise. "Together," she said, her tone firm, unshakeable. "No matter what."

Maya's chest swelled, a tide of love and determination rising against the scars of loss. The road ahead stretched long and shadowed—littered with the wreckage of a world still healing, haunted by the Sons of Adam's lingering threat, its horizon veiled in questions she couldn't yet answer. The Y chromosome remained a fractured dream, the virus's echoes a persistent foe, and the ethical tightrope of her work loomed ever tighter. Yet in the cracks of that broken world, she saw glimmers of something new—a future forged not from perfection, but from resilience, from the stubborn hope that had carried her family through darkness. She pressed the pocketknife to her heart, its cool metal a pulse against her own, and felt ready—ready to walk that road, step by trembling step, with Juniper's strength, Alex's wisdom, and the ghosts of her loved ones whispering at her side. For Daniel, who'd sparked the fire; for Elena, who'd dreamed it first; for Clara, who'd made it real; for little Elena, who'd never had the chance; and for a world still worth saving.

29

The Shadow of Adam

The lab hummed with a quiet intensity, its sterile silence broken only by the soft drone of machinery and the intermittent beep of a monitor piercing the stillness. Maya sat hunched over her workstation, her silhouette a sharp contrast against the holographic display that hovered before her—a DNA strand spiraling in luminous threads, its intricate dance a puzzle she'd spent years unraveling. The whale-carved pocketknife rested on the desk beside her, its worn handle catching the dim light in faint glints, a steadfast companion through countless sleepless nights. Her fingers flew across the keyboard, adjusting variables with a precision born of desperation, her eyes—bloodshot and shadowed—scanning the simulation's flickering data. The nanoparticles she'd engineered were tantalizingly close to stabilizing the telomeres of the X chromosome, their microscopic lattice a fragile shield against the genetic chaos *Chromovirus-X* had wrought. But close wasn't enough—not now, not with the shadow of a new threat looming larger with every passing hour.

The door slid open with a whisper, and Juniper stepped into the lab, her presence a quiet disruption to Maya's focus. She carried a tray laden with food—a sandwich, a thermos of soup, a cluster of grapes—its simple offerings a stark counterpoint to the sterile complexity of their surroundings. She set it on the edge of the desk, her gaze narrowing as she took in Maya's slumped posture, the hollows beneath her eyes, the faint tremble in her hands as she typed. "You need to eat," she said, her voice a blend of firmness and tenderness, cutting through the lab's mechanical hum. "You've been at this for twelve hours straight."

Maya didn't lift her eyes from the screen, her voice taut with a resolve that bordered on obsession. "I can't stop now. Not when we're this close." Her fingers paused, hovering over the keys, then resumed their relentless dance, as if slowing would cede ground to the enemy she couldn't see.

Juniper exhaled a sigh that carried both exasperation and love, pulling a chair beside Maya with a scrape that echoed in the quiet. She settled in, her elbow propped on the bench, her eyes tracing the lines of strain etched into Maya's face. "You're not going to save the world by starving yourself," she said, her tone softening but unyielding. "Take a break, just a few minutes. You're running on fumes, and I'm not watching you collapse because you're too stubborn to listen."

Maya's gaze flicked to her, a flicker of irritation warring with exhaustion, but the fire in her eyes burned undimmed. "You don't get it, Juniper," she said, her voice rising with a raw edge. "They're close to finishing it. If they release the *Adamvirus*—" Her hands clenched into fists, the pocketknife's shadow trembling beneath her grip, a silent witness to her fear.

Juniper leaned closer, her hand hovering near Maya's shoulder before settling there, a steady anchor against the storm. "I do get it," she said, her voice softening into a lifeline. "I know what's at stake—I've seen the data, heard the briefings. But you're no good to anyone if you burn out before we even get a chance to fight. Eat something. Then we'll keep going—together."

The word together hung between them, a quiet vow that pierced Maya's armor. She hesitated, her resolve wavering under Juniper's unwavering gaze, then relented with a nod, reaching for the sandwich with a hand that shook more than she'd admit. As she took a reluctant bite, her mind churned—a relentless whirl of equations, variables, and the chilling specter of the *Adamvirus*. The name alone coiled ice around her spine—a derivative of *Chromovirus-X*, twisted by the Sons of Adam into a weapon aimed at the X chromosome, the fragile thread of humanity's future. If unleashed, it wouldn't just halt parthenogenesis; it would unravel the genetic code of women, sparking widespread infertility, cascading diseases, and a slow, inevitable slide into extinction. The Sons had distilled their rage into a final, apocalyptic creed: if they couldn't reclaim their world, they'd ensure no one else could either.

The first whispers of the *Adamvirus* had surfaced weeks earlier, a faint ripple in a sea of data that Alex's AI had snagged from the ether—an encrypted fragment referencing a "new strain" and "targeted degradation." At first, the intelligence community had waved it off as bluster, a scare tactic to bolster the Sons' fading morale. But the pieces had begun to align with a chilling clarity. A raid on a safehouse in Eastern Europe—crumbling concrete and rusted steel in a forgotten corner of the continent—had unearthed a trove of documents, their pages stained with coffee and desperation. Among them were schematics for a virus engineered to echo *Chromovirus-X* but with a lethal twist: it zeroed in on the X chromosome, a precision strike at the heart of female resilience. Dubbed the *Adamvirus* by its creators, it was still in its nascent stages, a beast not yet fully formed—but its potential was a nightmare made flesh. If perfected and released, it could doom humanity to a silent, sterile end.

The discovery had sent a seismic jolt through the global intelligence network, a wake-up call that reverberated from Sydney to Geneva. Governments that had once bristled at each other's borders now huddled in urgent conclaves, their rivalries buried under the shared weight of survival. The stakes towered higher than ever: the *Adamvirus* wasn't a threat to nations or ideologies—it was a guillotine poised over humankind itself. In labs and war rooms, the race was on—not just to stop the virus, but to outpace its creators before their endgame unfolded.

Across the globe, in a fortified facility in Geneva, Alex sat before a wall of screens, their glow casting stark shadows across his weathered face. His hair was a silver crown now, its gray a testament to years of strain and the virus's quiet toll, and the lines etched into his skin spoke of a body aging faster than time should allow. Yet his eyes burned with a clarity undimmed by fatigue, his fingers dancing over the keyboard with a precision that belied the faint tremor in them. His enhanced AI systems churned through terabytes of data in real time, a digital bloodhound sniffing out the Sons' encrypted trails. He'd poured years into refining these algorithms, weaving them into the backbone of the world's defense—a legacy born from Clara's faith and his own stubborn will.

"We've got something," he said, his voice crackling over the comms to Maya and Juniper, a gravelly thread cutting through static. "The AI intercepted a transmission from one of their cells—they're in the final stages of replicating the *Adamvirus*. We've pinpointed three labs: Siberia, the Amazon, and somewhere in the Middle East. If we move fast, we can hit them before they're ready."

Maya's heart thudded, a wild rhythm against her ribs as she leaned closer to the comms unit, her sandwich forgotten on the tray. "How much time do we have?" she asked, her voice tight with urgency, her mind racing to calculate the hours she'd need.

"Not enough," Alex replied, his tone grim, edged with a weariness he couldn't mask. "The virus is nearly complete. If they finish it and release it, even your *CRISPR-XX* might not be enough to stop it."

Her fists clenched, nails digging into her palms as she fought the panic clawing up her throat. "Then we need to move faster," she said, her voice rising with a desperate edge. "I'm close, Alex. So close. The nanoparticles are stabilizing the telomeres, but I need more time to lock it down."

"You'll have it," he said, his resolve a steel thread through the crackle of the line. "I'm coordinating with global intelligence now. We're launching simultaneous raids on all known locations. But Maya..." His voice faltered, a rare crack in his steady facade. "Even if we take these labs out, there's no guarantee we'll get them all. The *Adamvirus* is their endgame. They've scattered the replication process across the globe. If even one cell gets away—"

"I know," she cut in, her tone sharp with fear and defiance, her eyes flicking to the pocketknife as if it could anchor her. "Which is why I need to finish this. If I can stabilize the X chromosome, we might have a chance to counteract the virus before it spreads."

Alex's silence stretched a beat, then he nodded. "Then we'll buy you that time," he said, his voice firm again. "Just... be ready."

The news of the *Adamvirus* had jolted the world into an unprecedented unity, a fragile alliance forged in the crucible of existential dread. Governments that had once hoarded secrets now flung open their vaults, intelligence agencies pooling data in a frantic bid to outpace the threat. Military units drilled in lockstep across continents, their boots pounding a rhythm of urgency, while scientists from every corner of the globe funneled their expertise into a shared arsenal. The stakes were a clarion call: if the Sons succeeded, humanity's thread would snap, leaving nothing but silence in its wake.

In a high-security briefing room in Geneva, a constellation of leaders gathered—faces taut with strain, voices clipped with purpose—around a table dwarfed by the weight of their task. Alex stood at its head, his presence a quiet command amid the clamor, his screens a lifeline pulsing with real-time updates from his AI. "We've locked onto three primary labs," he said, his voice cutting through the room's tension like a blade, steady despite the tremor in his hands as he gestured to the map projected behind him. "Siberia, the Amazon, and a third in the Middle East—exact coordinates still fuzzy. We need simultaneous strikes—hit all three at once. Even one left standing could be the spark that ends us."

The room erupted into a flurry of voices—diplomats debating logistics, generals plotting routes—but the decision crystallized with a swiftness born of desperation. Within hours, multinational task forces coalesced, each a razor-sharp unit tasked with a single, unyielding mission. In Siberia, a joint force of Russian, American, and European operatives descended on a remote mountain facility, its entrance buried under ice and shadow. They breached it under a moonless sky, their boots crunching through snow as gunfire shattered the stillness, a brutal dance with the Sons' defenders that left the lab a smoldering husk. In the Amazon, another team hacked through dense jungle, their progress snarled by traps and ambushes, sweat streaking their faces as they closed in on a hidden bunker revealed only by Alex's satellite analysis—each step a testament to the knowledge that failure was unthinkable. The Middle East lab remained a ghost, its location a maddening riddle the AI could only narrow to a swath of desert; the team there relied on grit and interrogation, chasing leads through sand and silence as the clock ticked relentlessly downward.

Back at Stanford, Maya teetered on the edge of a breakthrough, her lab a crucible of hope and frustration. The nanoparticle system glowed with promise—telomeres strengthening under its lattice, the X chromosome holding firm—but it wasn't enough, not yet. She needed more than stability; she needed a counterstrike, a way to repair the damage the *Adamvirus* could inflict. Juniper hovered beside her, her hands deft as she adjusted equipment, her presence a quiet bulwark against Maya's spiraling intensity. ““What if we combine the nanoparticles with a modified version of the *CRISPR-XX*?” Maya muttered, her voice a low thread of thought as she stared at the screen, her mind racing through possibilities. “If we can target the telomeres and repair the damaged sequences simultaneously—dual-layer defense.”

Juniper leaned over her shoulder, her breath catching as she studied the data, her voice cautious but intrigued. “It's risky. But it might work.”

Maya's nod was sharp, her hands moving through the keyboard as she recalibrated the simulation, her pulse a wild drumbeat in her ears. "We don't have a choice," she said, her tone fierce with necessity. "It's the only way to stay ahead of them." The hours bled together, a relentless blur of code and coffee, but the solution danced just beyond her grasp, a maddening flicker that refused to resolve. Her frustration surged, a tide crashing against her resolve, and she gripped the pocketknife tighter, its grooves a lifeline to Clara's unyielding faith.

In Geneva, Alex tracked the raids from his command post, his heart pounding as updates crackled through the comms—Siberia down, the Amazon team breaching their target, the Middle East still a question mark. His screens glowed with a chaotic symphony of data, his trembling hands steadying only through sheer will as he relayed each success and setback to Maya. "We're buying you time," he said, his voice rough with exhaustion, a lifeline stretched taut across continents. "The Siberian lab's gone, Amazon's close—just hold on."

Maya's voice broke through the static, a thread of steel laced with desperation. "I'm close, Alex. So close. But I'm not there yet. I need more time."

"We'll buy you that time," he promised, his resolve a rock against the tide. "Just keep going, for all of us."

The world held its breath as the raids unfolded, a fragile hope trembling in the balance. Maya worked with a ferocity that burned through her exhaustion, the pocketknife a silent sentinel on her desk, its presence a whisper of the women who'd shaped her—Elena's fire, Clara's brilliance, little Elena's lost promise. Juniper's hands moved in tandem with hers, a quiet symphony of support, while Alex's voice anchored her from afar, a thread of faith across the chaos. The *Adamvirus* loomed like a shadow over them all, its threat a dark mirror to the hope they chased—a hope that flickered brighter with every telomere stabilized, every sequence repaired. The raids were a gamble, Maya's breakthrough a prayer, and humanity's fate hung in the scales, teetering between annihilation and a fragile dawn.

As the night deepened, the lab's hum became a heartbeat, the world beyond a distant echo of gunfire and resolve. Maya stood on the brink, her eyes locked on the screen, her hands steady despite the tremor in her core. The road ahead was a jagged expanse—littered with the Sons' wrath, shadowed by the virus's menace, its end veiled in uncertainty—but she faced it unbroken, her fire tempered by love and loss. She'd fight to the end, step by trembling step, until the shadow of Adam was no more.

30

The Last Lab

The world exhaled a tentative sigh as news of the successful raids rippled across its fractured surface, a rare victory snatched from the jaws of despair. Alex's AI systems, honed to a razor's edge over years of relentless refinement, had orchestrated a global symphony of precision—pinpointing and dismantling the Sons of Adam's labs in Siberia, the Amazon, and the Middle East with a swiftness that left the intelligence community reeling in awe. Satellite feeds had captured the aftermath: smoldering husks of steel and concrete swallowed by snow, jungle, and sand, their destruction a testament to a fragile unity forged in crisis. The captured leaders of the Sons—gaunt men with hollowed eyes and clenched fists—were whisked away to high-security prisons scattered across the globe, their fates a tangled knot of justice and necessity yet to be unraveled. Among them was Thomas, a name that flickered like a ghost from the past, etched into Elena's journals from the early days of *Chromovirus-X*. His presence stirred a restless curiosity in Maya, mingled with a conflicted ache she couldn't name, and after days of wrestling with the impulse, she resolved to face him—to seek answers, or perhaps something deeper, in the shadow of her family's legacy.

The prison was a fortress carved into the earth's bowels, a cold, sterile labyrinth buried beneath layers of rock and reinforced steel, its corridors patrolled by an army of drones that hummed with quiet menace. Maya walked its dimly lit expanse, her footsteps a staccato echo against the unyielding walls, her breath catching in the chill air that smelled faintly of metal and disinfectant. The whale-carved pocketknife rested heavy in her pocket, its familiar weight a talisman against the unease gnawing at her—Clara's touchstone, passed from Elena's hands, now hers, a thread binding her to the women who'd shaped her. She was led to an interrogation room, its stark confines a cube of gray steel, where Thomas sat chained to a table, his wrists bound by cuffs that glinted under the harsh light. He was older than she'd pictured, his face a weathered map of bitterness and loss—lines carved deep around his mouth, his once-sharp eyes dulled by years of grief and rage. Yet there was a flicker of something softer in his gaze as he looked up, a recognition that stilled the air between them.

"You look just like her," he said, his voice rough as gravel but laced with a quiet reverence that caught her off guard. "Elena. Your mother."

Maya eased into the chair across from him, her posture guarded, her hand lingering near the pocketknife as if it could shield her from the weight of his words. "You knew her?" she asked, her tone even but threaded with a curiosity she couldn't suppress.

"Not well," Thomas admitted, his eyes drifting to the table as if tracing a memory there. "And I also know Clara. They wanted to know why I was immune—thought there might be an answer in me, something to save them all. We never found it, but they..." He paused, a faint smile tugging at his lips, fleeting and bittersweet. "They never stopped looking." His gaze lifted, catching on the pocketknife as Maya drew it from her pocket and set it on the table, its whale carving a silent testament between them. "That was Elena's, wasn't it?"

She nodded, her fingers brushing its smooth handle, the wood warm against her skin from years of touch—Elena's, Clara's, now hers. "It's been passed down," she said, her voice steady despite the ache rising in her chest. "A reminder of what we're fighting for."

Thomas leaned back, the cuffs clinking softly as his hands settled on the table, his eyes searching hers with a mixture of exhaustion and defiance. "And what *are* you fighting for, Maya?" he asked, his tone sharpening. "A world without men? A future where we're nothing but a footnote in history?"

Her jaw tightened, a flare of frustration sparking beneath her calm, but she held his gaze, her voice unwavering. "I'm fighting for survival. For a future where humanity doesn't have to live in fear of extinction," she said, her words carrying the weight of every loss she'd borne. "The virus took so much—from you, from me, from everyone. We're not erasing anyone; we're trying to rebuild, to heal what's left."

A bitter laugh rasped from Thomas's throat, jagged and hollow, his head tipping back as if the ceiling held some answer she couldn't see. "Heal?" he echoed, the word dripping with scorn. "By erasing us? The moment parthenogenesis was announced, it was clear the world had moved on. Men were no longer necessary. We were relics, doomed to fade away. And you—you scientists—didn't even try to save us. You just... gave up."

The accusation stung, a barb that hooked into the guilt Maya carried despite herself, and her voice rose, sharp with the fire she'd inherited from Elena and Clara. "We didn't give up! We've been killing ourselves to stabilize the genome—to find a way to fix this. The Y chromosome—it's too broken, too shattered by the virus. We've tried everything, Thomas—everything—but it's like trying to hold water in your hands. We're doing all we can."

His eyes softened then, the anger draining from them like a tide receding, leaving behind a raw, unguarded sorrow that caught her off guard. He leaned forward, his voice dropping to a whisper that trembled with memory. "I lost my husband," he said, the words heavy with a grief that mirrored her own. "And our adopted sons—two boys we took in when the world started falling apart. The virus stole them all, one by one. I thought... if I fought hard enough, I could make someone see that we still mattered—that men weren't just ghosts to be forgotten. But it turned into this... this madness." His shoulders slumped, the weight of his choices pressing down, and he looked away, his gaze lost in the steel wall. "I never wanted to hurt Clara. She was different—she cared, even when I couldn't see it. But the others—the ones who took over after I stepped back—they didn't. They saw her as the enemy, the face of a future that didn't include us."

Maya's chest tightened, a pang of empathy piercing her anger—an unexpected bridge between them forged by shared loss. She thought of Clara's warmth, her relentless hope, snuffed out by the violence Thomas had helped unleash, and her voice softened, though it held an edge of steel. "I'm sorry for what you lost," she said, meaning it despite the fury simmering beneath. "But this—this violence—it's not the answer. You've taken so much from so many. Innocent people, Thomas. Clara... she died because of this. Little Elena, too—a baby who never got a chance."

Thomas flinched at their names, a crack splintering his stoic mask, his cuffed hands twitching against the table. "I didn't mean for it to go that far," he murmured, his voice fracturing. "I just wanted... I wanted them to listen. But it's too late for that now."

Maya leaned forward, her eyes locking onto his with a fierceness born of desperation and determination. "If you didn't mean it—if you really cared about Clara—then help me stop it," she said, her voice low and urgent. "Tell me what you know. Are there more labs? More plans?"

He hesitated, his gaze flickering back to the pocketknife, its whale carving a silent witness to their shared past. The room stretched taut with silence, his breath a ragged thread in the stillness, the weight of his guilt and regret a palpable force pressing against them both. Finally, he spoke, his voice a whisper that carried the gravity of confession. "There's one more lab," he said, his eyes meeting hers with a haunted resolve. "In Japan—hidden, off the grid. They've been working on the final strain of the *Adamvirus* there. If they release it..."

Her heart slammed against her ribs, a wild rhythm that drowned out the drones' hum beyond the walls. "Where in Japan?" she pressed, her voice rising with urgency, her hands gripping the table's edge. "Tell me everything, anything."

Thomas shook his head, a faint tremor in his shoulders as he looked away, his voice barely audible. "I don't know the exact spot—it's buried somewhere in the mountains, cloaked from sight. But it's real, Maya. And if you don't stop them, it'll be the end—not just for men, but for everyone."

The words crashed over her, a tidal wave of dread and purpose that left her reeling. She stood, her chair scraping against the floor, her mind a whirlwind of panic and resolve. "Thank you, Thomas," she said, her voice steady despite the chaos within, empathy warring with the fire driving her forward. "For telling me this."

He looked up, his eyes a storm of sorrow and resignation, a man adrift in the wreckage of his choices. "I didn't do it for you," he said, his tone raw with honesty. "I did it for them—for my husband, for my sons, for the future I wanted but won't see."

She nodded, understanding flickering through her anger—a shared thread of loss binding them, however tenuously—and turned to leave, her hand on the cold steel door. His voice stopped her, a final, fraying plea that echoed in the room's confines. "Maya... I'm sorry. For everything."

She paused, her back to him, her breath catching as the weight of his apology settled over her—a weight she wasn't sure she could carry or forgive. "I hope you find peace," she said quietly, her voice a whisper against the steel, then stepped out, the door sealing shut behind her with a clang that reverberated through her bones.

Back at Stanford, the lab thrummed with a frantic energy as Maya relayed Thomas's revelation to Alex and Juniper over a secure comms line, her words tumbling out in a rush as she paced the room, her sneakers scuffing the tiles. Alex, patched in from Geneva, redirected his AI systems with a speed that belied the tremor in his hands, his screens flaring with a cascade of data—satellite imagery sweeping Japan's rugged terrain, communication intercepts sifting through static, energy signatures traced across a frozen landscape. Juniper stood beside Maya, her hands deft as she adjusted equipment, her presence a quiet bulwark against the storm, her eyes flicking between the screens and Maya's taut frame. Hours stretched into a tense eternity, the silence punctuated only by the hum of machines and the occasional crackle of Alex's updates, the trio bound by a shared urgency that coiled tighter with every passing minute.

Finally, Alex's voice broke through the comms, taut with triumph and dread, his screen lighting up with a pinpoint on Hokkaido's jagged peaks. "Got it," he said, his tone grim, edged with exhaustion. "A facility buried in the mountains of Hokkaido—off-grid, no official footprint, but there's a heat signature and encrypted chatter spiking from the area. It's them."

Maya's fists clenched, her resolve hardening into steel as she met Juniper's gaze, the pocketknife a burning weight in her pocket. "We need to move—now," she said, her voice a blade slicing through the haze, her mind racing with the stakes—Thomas's warning, the *Adamvirus*'s shadow, the fragile hope she couldn't let slip away.

Juniper's hand found her arm, her touch steady but laced with caution, her eyes searching Maya's with a quiet intensity. "We've got a team ready—Alex is coordinating from Geneva, and I'll go with the strike force to help out with the comms," she said, her tone firm, unyielding. "You're needed here. You're the only one who can finish the *CRISPR-XX* modifications. If the *Adamvirus* is released, your work is our only hope. Let me handle this."

Maya's chest tightened, a surge of protest rising in her throat—every instinct screaming to join them, to face the threat head-on—but Juniper's resolve held her fast, and Alex's voice crackled through, a steady anchor from afar. "She's right," he said, his tone rough with fatigue but resolute. "You're the key, Maya—your work's what'll save us if we can't stop this in time. Stay put, finish it. We'll handle Hokkaido."

She exhaled sharply, her nod reluctant but firm, the weight of their trust pressing against her ribs. "Okay," she said, her voice steady despite the tremor beneath it. "But you both come back—promise me."

Juniper's smile was faint but fierce, her hand squeezing Maya's arm. "Promise," she said, then turned to gather her gear, her movements swift and sure.

The preparations unfolded in a whirlwind—Juniper assisting the strike team, Alex syncing his AI with global forces from Geneva—but Maya stole a moment amid the chaos, stepping into the lab's shadowed corner. Her fingers closed around the pocketknife, its weight a grounding pulse against the storm within, its whale carving a silent vow etched by the women who'd come before her—Elena's courage, Clara's brilliance, little Elena's lost light. "We're not done yet," she whispered, her voice steady against the hum, a promise to the air and the ghosts who lingered there. "Not while there's still hope."

As Juniper departed with the strike team, the plane slicing through the night toward Hokkaido's hidden fortress, Maya stayed rooted at Stanford, her lab a crucible of last-ditch hope. Alex's voice guided the mission from Geneva, his AI lighting their path, while Juniper's steady presence anchored the ground assault. The last lab loomed—a clandestine bastion cradling the *Adamvirus*'s final strain, the Sons of Adam's desperate endgame—and Maya faced it from afar, her fire forged from love and loss burning brighter than ever. The road ahead was a jagged expanse—littered with danger, shadowed by uncertainty, its end a question mark in the dark—but she stood undaunted, her hands steady on the keys as she pushed *CRISPR-XX* to its limit. For Clara, who'd died for this dream; for little Elena, lost before her breath; for Elena and Daniel, whose spirit pulsed in her veins; and for a world still worth saving—she'd fight to the end, step by trembling step, until the shadow of Adam was banished, and hope could rise from its ashes.

31

The Countdown

The operation to dismantle the final Sons of Adam lab in Hokkaido launched with a precision honed by desperation, a surgical strike cutting through the night's shroud with relentless urgency. Juniper, tethered to Alex's AI systems via a comms line that crackled with static, assist the infiltration under the cover of a moonless sky, the jagged peaks of the mountain range looming like silent sentinels against the stars. The lab was a fortress carved into the rock, its defenses a lattice of steel and shadow, but the Sons of Adam—caught off guard by the AI's pinpoint accuracy—faltered under the assault's swiftness. Juniper and her team moved like a blade through the chaos, their boots echoing on the cold stone floor as they neutralized operatives with a efficiency born of necessity—stun rounds cracking the air, bodies slumping in the dim corridors with minimal resistance. The air was thick with the tang of ozone and fear, but as they breached the inner sanctum, a chilling silence greeted them, broken only by the hum of machinery and a sight that drove ice into Juniper's veins: the vials of the *Adamvirus* were gone.

Her heart plummeted as she swept her gaze across the lab—a labyrinth of advanced equipment, gene sequencers whirring faintly, holographic screens flickering with data—but the sterile racks that should have cradled the deadly virus stood empty, their absence a void that screamed of foresight and betrayal. The Sons had anticipated the raid, spiriting their weapon away before the strike force could descend. Juniper's pulse thundered as she signaled her team, her voice taut over the comms, cutting through the static to reach Alex and Maya back at Stanford. "The vials are gone," she reported, her breath ragged with urgency, her flashlight slicing through the gloom. "They must have evacuated them before we arrived. But there's something else—a computer screen with a countdown. Ten minutes. And it's linked to a busy location in Hokkaido."

Alex's voice crackled back from Geneva, a gravelly thread laced with dread, his screens flaring with data as he processed her words. "A busy location?" he echoed, his tone grim, his mind racing through possibilities. "That could mean a public space—a train station, a market, somewhere packed with people..."

He didn't finish, the unspoken horror a weight they all felt—Juniper in the lab's shadowed heart, Alex in his command post, Maya listening from Stanford, her breath catching as the implications crystallized. The *Adamvirus*, even in its nascent form, could spread like wildfire through the air, its tendrils sinking into lungs and blood, seeding infertility and genetic ruin within hours. Juniper's jaw tightened, her voice rising with command as she turned to her team, their faces taut with the same realization. "We need to pinpoint that location—now," she spoke, her hands steady despite the tremor in her core, her flashlight sweeping the room for answers.

The countdown glowed on the screen, a relentless march of red digits slicing through the silence—nine minutes, eight—the tension coiling tighter with each tick, a noose around their hopes. The team sprang into action, their movements a frantic ballet of purpose—operatives tearing through files, hacking into terminals, their breaths sharp in the frigid air. Juniper's fingers flew over a console, her engineering instincts guiding her as she bypassed security protocols, her mind a whirl of code and fear. Finally, a shout broke the stillness, an operative's voice piercing the haze. "Got it!" he yelled, his screen flaring with coordinates. "Sapporo Station—it's one of the busiest hubs in Hokkaido. If they release it there..."

Juniper's blood turned to ice, the name a hammer against her ribs. Sapporo Station was a nexus of life—thousands streaming through its platforms every hour, a pulsing artery of humanity ripe for catastrophe. If the *Adamvirus* took root there, it would spread beyond containment, a plague racing across Japan and beyond. She relayed the intel to Alex, her voice a blade of urgency slicing through the comms. "Alex, it's Sapporo Station—they're targeting it. We need a full lockdown, now!"

Before Alex could respond, a deafening alarm shattered the lab's stillness, red lights flashing in a staccato pulse that bathed the room in blood-hued shadows. A robotic voice boomed through the corridors, cold and unyielding: "Self-destruct sequence initiated. Ten minutes to detonation." The words hung like a guillotine, freezing Juniper's team for a heartbeat before adrenaline surged them into motion. "We need to get out of here!" she shouted, her voice cutting through the panic, her hands snatching a drive with partial data as she waved them toward the exit. "Grab whatever intel you can and move!"

They scrambled through the labyrinth, boots pounding against steel as the countdown synced cruelly with the self-destruct timer, their breaths ragged in the tightening chokehold of time. Juniper's voice broke through the comms one last time, a desperate lifeline flung toward Alex and Maya. "The lab's rigged to blow—we're evacuating, but the virus is gone. Sapporo Station's the target—lock it down!" The line cut abruptly, static swallowing her words as the facility's systems winked out, the first tremors of collapse rumbling beneath their feet.

In Geneva, Alex's hands flew over his keyboard, his heart pounding as he relayed Juniper's warning to Japanese authorities, his voice a steady roar through the chaos. "Sapporo Station is the target. You need to lock it down immediately!" he screamed, his screens a frantic blur of alerts and maps, his gray hair damp with sweat as he patched into every channel he could reach. The Japanese government reacted with a speed born of terror—an emergency alert blaring across Hokkaido, forces surging toward the station in a tide of flashing lights and steel—but the response lagged, a fatal heartbeat too slow. Reports trickled in like poison—whispers of a strange mist curling through the station's platforms, followed by screams as passengers collapsed, coughing and clawing at their throats. The *Adamvirus* was free.

Alex's chest caved as he watched the live feeds from Geneva, grainy footage of panic unfolding in real time—bodies crumpling, crowds surging in blind terror, a gray haze spreading like a shroud. His hands trembled, the tremor he'd masked for years now stark against the keys, and he turned to the comms, his voice a ragged thread to Maya at Stanford. "It's out," he said, the words a gut punch, his face ashen as the feeds flickered. "Sapporo—they didn't lock it down in time."

At Stanford, Maya stood frozen beside her workstation, the whale-carved pocketknife clutched in her hand, its weight a lifeline as the world tilted beneath her. Her face drained of color, her breath shallow as Juniper's last words echoed in her skull—*the lab's blowing, the virus is gone*—and the silence that followed clawed at her heart. "Juniper..." she whispered, her voice fracturing, tears welling as she sank into a chair, her knees buckling under the weight of dread. "Is she...?"

Alex shook his head, his expression a mask of grief and uncertainty, his voice rough with strain. "Comms are down—we don't know if she got out. The explosion... it hit right after she signed off."

Maya's hands shook, the pocketknife digging into her palm as her mind reeled—Juniper lost in the blast, the virus loose, the world teetering on a precipice she couldn't pull it back from. The lab's hum faded to a distant drone, her vision blurring as grief and fear crashed over her, a tidal wave threatening to drown the fire she'd fought to keep alight. She thought of Juniper's steady hands tweaking her equipment, her quiet laughter cutting through late-night haze, her fierce promise to stand by her—and the void of her absence was a wound too raw to name. Yet beneath it, a spark flickered, a stubborn ember of resolve that refused to gutter, fueled by the women who'd shaped her—Elena's courage, Clara's brilliance, little Elena's lost light.

She turned to Alex's feed, his face a haggard mirror of her own on the screen, and her voice steadied, a thread of steel weaving through her anguish. "We need to accelerate *CRISPR-XX*—now," she said, her words a lifeline flung into the chaos. "If we can stabilize the X chromosome, counter the virus's mutations, we might still have a shot."

Alex nodded, his jaw tightening with a resolve that matched hers, his hands steadying against the console despite the tremor threatening to betray him. "We'll do everything we can," he said, his voice a quiet vow, thick with the weight of their shared losses. "For Juniper, for Clara—for everyone counting on us."

Maya rose, her legs trembling but her purpose unyielding, and returned to her workstation, the lab's glow a crucible where grief and hope collided. Her fingers flew over the keys, recalibrating the nanoparticle simulations she'd honed for years, her mind racing through the data—telomere stability, X-chromosome fortification, a desperate bid to outpace the virus's spread. She refused to believe Juniper was gone—somewhere, out there, her partner was fighting, clawing through rubble or racing against the same clock, her engineering mind a match to Maya's own. The thought fueled her, a flicker of defiance against the darkness, and she whispered it to herself like a mantra: *She's alive. She has to be.*

The news of the *Adamvirus*'s release tore through the world like a wildfire, igniting panic that spread faster than the mist itself. Governments scrambled, their voices a cacophony of orders—quarantines snapping into place, borders sealing shut, scientists racing to labs—but the virus slipped through their grasp, its tendrils curling beyond Sapporo into the night. Maya and Alex worked in tandem, their comms a lifeline across continents, his AI parsing outbreak patterns while her hands shaped a countermeasure from the ashes of despair. The world teetered, its pulse erratic as reports of collapsing lungs and faltering genomes flooded in, a grim tally of a future unraveling.

Yet amid the chaos, a single thread of hope glimmered—Maya's *CRISPR-XX*, a fragile beacon flickering in the lab's sterile glow. If she could perfect the modifications, weave the nanoparticles into a shield that stabilized the X chromosome and neutralized the virus's mutations, they might claw back a future from the brink. Time was a relentless foe, its seconds bleeding away as the outbreak spread, but she clung to the pocketknife, its whale carving a silent vow against her palm—Clara's faith, Elena's fire, little Elena's lost promise fueling her fight. "I won't let you down," she whispered, her voice a quiet thunder in the lab's hush, a promise to Clara's memory, to Juniper's unseen struggle, to the world trembling beyond her walls. "We'll find a way."

The night stretched endless, the lab a fortress of flickering hope as Maya and Alex pressed on, their hands steady despite the weight of grief and exhaustion. Juniper's fate hung in the silence, a question mark that gnawed at Maya's core, but she refused to let it break her. The *Adamvirus* loomed—a shadow born of rage and despair—but so did the possibility of dawn, a future forged from the embers of their fight. The road ahead was a jagged expanse, its end veiled in smoke and uncertainty, but Maya faced it with a fire that burned brighter than ever—forged by love, tempered by loss, unyielding in its defiance. She'd battle to the end, until the countdown stopped, and hope could rise anew.

32

A Glimmer in the Darkness

The lab lay cloaked in a heavy silence, broken only by the faint hum of machinery and the sporadic beep of a monitor piercing the stillness like a heartbeat on the edge of faltering. Maya sat hunched over her workstation at Stanford, her silhouette a stark outline against the holographic display that flickered before her—a DNA strand twisting in luminous threads, its promise taunting her with every failed simulation. Her eyes, bloodshot and shadowed from days without rest, burned as they traced the data, her fingers trembling over the keyboard as she adjusted variables in a relentless, futile dance. The *CRISPR-XX* modifications—her last bastion against the *Adamvirus*—had collapsed again, the latest in a string of failures that mocked her every attempt. The virus, unleashed in Sapporo Station, had spread with a ferocity no one had foreseen, its reach so far confined to Japan by a frantic quarantine, but within those borders, millions teetered on the brink—thousands already lost to its silent, suffocating grip. The weight of her failure pressed down like a physical force, choking the hope she'd clung to, her breath shallow as despair coiled tighter around her chest.

Across the room, Alex watched her from his own station, his graying hair catching the lab's sterile glow, his face etched with a deepening worry that mirrored the lines time had carved into his skin.

He'd patched in from Geneva days ago, returning to Stanford to stand by her side as the crisis spiraled, his AI feeds now a lifeline to the containment efforts half a world away. Maya hadn't slept in three days—maybe four—her determination teetering into an obsession that gnawed at her frame, thinning her cheeks and hollowing her eyes. He rose, his movements slow with the weariness of his own fading strength, and approached her, his hand settling on her shoulder with a gentleness that belied its firmness. "Maya," he said, his voice soft but steady, cutting through the lab's drone. "You need to rest. You're exhausted—you're pushing past what anyone could take."

She shook her head, the motion sharp and stubborn, her voice rasping from a throat raw with strain. "I can't, Alex—not yet," she said, her eyes never leaving the screen, her fingers resuming their frantic dance across the keys. "Not while the virus is out there, tearing through Japan. Millions are at stake—I can't stop."

Alex's grip tightened, his tone softening into a plea laced with resolve, his own fatigue threading through the words. "You're no good to anyone if you collapse," he said, his voice a quiet anchor in her storm. "Go home, Maya—get some sleep, even just a few hours. I'll keep the simulations running, tweak the parameters. You've got to trust me to hold this line for a bit."

Her hands stilled, hovering over the keyboard as her mind churned—a whirl of telomere stability curves, nanoparticle vectors, the relentless spread of the *Adamvirus* across Sapporo's quarantined sprawl. The exhaustion was a tidal wave she couldn't outrun, her vision blurring at the edges, and Alex's steady presence pierced her resolve. She relented with a reluctant nod, the motion heavy with surrender. "Okay," she murmured, her voice cracking as she pushed back from the desk, her legs unsteady beneath her. "Just... call me if anything changes."

He nodded, his hand lingering on her shoulder a moment longer, a silent promise in the gesture. "I will," he said, his voice firm despite the tremor in his own hands, a testament to the virus's lingering toll on his body. "Get some rest."

Maya stumbled from the lab into the cool night, the campus a quiet expanse under a starless sky, its stillness a jarring contrast to the chaos roiling within her. She drove home in a daze, the streets blurring past as her thoughts spiraled—Juniper's last transmission from Hokkaido, the explosion that had severed their comms, the virus's relentless march through Japan's millions. The house loomed dark and empty when she arrived, its silence a cavern that swallowed her footsteps as she wandered its halls, her mind too restless to settle. Her feet carried her upward, past framed photos of Clara and Alex on the stairs, to the attic—a dusty refuge of forgotten memories she hadn't breached in years. The air was thick with the scent of old paper and time, and her gaze landed on a cardboard box tucked in a corner, its label scrawled in faded marker: *ELENA—OLD STUFF*. She hadn't opened it in years, with a quiet compulsion she couldn't name, and she knelt before it, her hands trembling as she lifted the lid.

The box spilled forth a trove of her mother's life—leather-bound journals, yellowed photographs curling at the edges, keepsakes worn smooth by years of touch. A snapshot of Elena and Clara laughing in a sunlit lab slipped through her fingers, their smiles a mirror to her own lost lightness; a braided bracelet, its colors faded, whispered of a childhood she'd never known. Then, buried beneath it all, a sealed envelope caught her eye, her name—Maya—written in Elena's looping script across its face. Her breath hitched, her fingers shaking as she tore it open, revealing a letter penned in her mother's hand, its ink a bridge across twenty-three years of absence.

The words unfurled with a love that pierced her—a mother's final testament, written in the shadow of her own death, brimming with hope and unshakable faith.

"My dearest Maya,

If you're reading this, it means I'm no longer there to guide you. But know this: you are never alone. You carry within you the strength of our family, the legacy of those who came before you—your dad's bravery, your aunt Clara's fire, and my endless belief in you. Trust in yourself, my darling, and never give up. The world may seem dark, but even the smallest light can pierce the deepest shadows. I believe in you, always—more than you'll ever know."

Tears streamed down Maya's face, hot and relentless, as she clutched the letter to her chest, its paper crinkling against her shirt. For the first time in days, a flicker of warmth broke through her despair, a balm against the raw edges of her failure—Elena's voice, steady and fierce, whispering across the years.

She sank to the attic floor, her back against the box as she sifted through the relics of her mother's mind, her tears blurring the edges of photographs and notes. One journal caught her eye—its cover worn thin, its pages brittle—and she flipped through it, her fingers tracing Elena's hurried script. A sketch leapt from the margins—a DNA helix spiraling in rough ink, annotated with a scrawl that stopped her cold: "*Destroy the virus from within its own DNA. Use its structure against it.*" The idea was raw, embryonic, a spark from a mind that had burned bright before fading, but it seized Maya's attention like a lifeline. Her breath quickened as she devoured the notes—Elena's theory, unpolished but audacious: instead of shielding the genome from the virus externally, why not infiltrate its own structure, turn its weapon against itself? By anchoring nanoparticles to protect the telomeres, they could then deploy viral vectors to rupture the *Adamvirus*'s DNA from within, shattering its ability to replicate. It was a long shot, a gamble stitched from desperation, but with her current tech—*CRISPR-XX*'s precision, the nanoparticles' reach—it was feasible, a glimmer piercing the fog of her failures.

Exhaustion melted into a surge of adrenaline, her pulse racing as the idea took root, a wildfire sparking through her weariness. She grabbed her phone, her fingers fumbling as she dialed Alex, her voice trembling with a raw, electric excitement when he answered. "Alex, I think I've got it," she said, the words tumbling out in a rush. "My mom—she had an idea in her journals. We can destroy the virus from inside its own DNA—use its structure to tear it apart. We just need to tweak the parameters, refine the vectors."

Alex's breath caught on the other end, his voice steadying with a rekindled hope that mirrored her own. "That's brilliant, Maya" he said, his tone thick with pride and urgency. "But we've got to move fast. The virus is contained in Japan for now—millions still at risk—but if it breaks quarantine, we're out of time."

She nodded, her determination solidifying into steel, her grip tightening on the letter as if Elena's strength flowed through it. "I know," she said, her voice rising with resolve. "And we can't do it alone—we need help, Alex. Scientists, labs, every mind we can rally. If we pool everything, refine the simulations together, we might pull this off."

Alex's silence was a beat of agreement, then his voice crackled with purpose. "I'll get the word out—every channel, every contact. You write it up, Maya—make it clear, make it urgent."

She wasted no time, her attic refuge abandoned as she raced back to the lab, Elena's journal and letter clutched to her chest. The night air bit at her skin, but she barely felt it, her mind ablaze with the spark her mother had left her. At her workstation, she drafted a message—a clarion call distilled into stark, powerful words: "*The Adamvirus is contained in Japan, but millions hang in the balance. We've found a way to destroy it from within—nanoparticles and viral vectors to rupture its DNA—but we need your help. Share your data, run your simulations, join us. Together, we can save humanity.*" She sent it cascading across the globe—to scientists, research hubs, governments—a plea and a promise flung into the digital ether.

The response was a tidal wave, overwhelming and electric, a chorus of voices rising from the wreckage. Within hours, replies flooded in—researchers from Tokyo, London, São Paulo, Sydney, their screens lighting up with shared data, their labs humming with synchronized simulations. Geneticists in Osaka, reeling from the outbreak's proximity, patched in with real-time viral samples; engineers in Berlin offered nanoparticle tweaks; virologists in Cape Town ran parallel models, their findings streaming into Maya's console in a flood of collaboration. It was a unity forged in crisis, a testament to humanity's stubborn will, and Maya's chest swelled with a fragile, fierce hope as the pieces converged.

The lab became a crucible of relentless effort, Maya and Alex working in tandem as the world's minds bent to their cause. Her fingers danced over the keys, integrating datasets with a precision born of desperation—telomere stability curves sharpening, nanoparticle lattices tightening, viral vectors calibrated to pierce the *Adamvirus*'s core. Alex's AI parsed the influx, his screens a symphony of flickering hope, his voice steady over the comms as he coordinated with global teams, his graying frame a rock against the tide. Hours bled into days, the simulations evolving with each refinement—Elena's primordial sketch blossoming into a tangible weapon, a counterstrike clawing back from the brink.

But time was a relentless foe, its shadow lengthening as the virus held Japan in its grip—millions quarantined, thousands lost, the death toll a grim drumbeat in Maya's ears. Containment held, a fragile dam against the outbreak's spread, but reports of breaches loomed—whispers of infected air slipping through cities, a specter threatening to unravel their efforts. She turned to Alex, her voice steady despite the exhaustion carving hollows beneath her eyes, her hands clenched around the pocketknife as resolve burned through her fatigue. "We're close. So close," she said, her words a quiet thunder. "But we need to test it. If this works..."

Alex's nod was resolute, his hand resting on her shoulder, his own eyes glistening with a mix of pride and fear. "It'll change everything," he said, his voice rough but unwavering. "Let's do it—everything we've got."

The final test was a breathless plunge, their hands trembling as they launched the simulation—the lab's screens flaring with data, the world's eyes watching through shared feeds. Nanoparticles wove a shield around the telomeres, viral vectors slipping into the *Adamvirus*'s structure like silent assassins, rupturing its DNA with a precision that stole Maya's breath. The results crystallized in a heartbeat—the virus's replication stalled, its lethal spiral collapsing into silence. "It worked," Maya whispered, sinking into her chair, tears streaming down her face as relief crashed over her. "It actually worked."

Alex's hand tightened on her shoulder, his voice breaking with awe and exhaustion. "You did it, Maya—your mom, Clara, they'd be so proud."

The lab erupted into a quiet frenzy—coordinates relayed, production protocols dispatched—as Maya and Alex coordinated with governments and medical teams to deploy the treatment across Japan's quarantined cities. The virus remained contained for now, millions still at risk within its borders, but the solution was a lifeline, a glimmer piercing the darkness that had threatened to swallow them whole. The road ahead stretched long and treacherous—years of recovery looming, the scars of the outbreak a wound that would linger—but for the first time in weeks, hope flickered, fragile yet fierce, a flame rekindled from ashes.

Maya drifted to the lab's window, the dawn breaking over Stanford's quiet campus, its golden light spilling across the glass. The whale-carved pocketknife rested in her hand, its weight a steady pulse against her palm—Elena's courage, Clara's brilliance, little Elena's lost promise woven into its grooves. She thought of Juniper, her fate a gaping void since the Hokkaido blast, her steady hands and fierce heart an absence that gnawed at Maya's core. Refusing to surrender to despair, she whispered a vow into the stillness—She's out there, fighting, just like me—and beyond that, to Clara, to Elena, to the partner she wouldn't let go: "We're not done yet. Not while there's still hope."

The lab hummed behind her, Alex's voice a steady thread as he guided the global effort, their hands joined by countless others across the world—scientists, survivors, strangers united in defiance. The *Adamvirus* loomed, contained but clawing at Japan's millions, its shadow a reminder of how close they'd come to silence. Yet in that glimmer—Maya's spark, Elena's dream, humanity's will—a future flickered, fragile and fierce, a dawn worth fighting for, one trembling step at a time.

33

Reunion and Renewal

A few days had slipped by since Maya's breakthrough with *CRISPR-XX*, and the world exhaled a cautious breath, its pulse steadying as the shadow of the *Adamvirus*—still confined to Japan but gripping millions—began to recede. Production of her solution had surged into a global crescendo, laboratories from Seoul to São Paulo humming with a relentless rhythm as they churned out vials of the nanoparticle-laden countermeasure. Governments, their voices a unified chorus for the first time in decades, funneled resources to the hardest-hit regions, Japan's quarantined cities a priority etched in urgency—hospitals overflowing with the afflicted, streets silent under lockdown, a nation clinging to the fragile lifeline Maya had forged. The virus had clawed its way through millions, its toll a grim tally of lives teetering on the edge, but her innovation glimmered through the darkness—a beacon of hope stitched from the threads of Elena's vision, Clara's sacrifice, and her own unyielding fire. Yet amid the progress, a hollow ache gnawed at her core, a silence that drowned out the lab's hum and the world's tentative cheers: Juniper.

Since the Hokkaido lab erupted in a blaze of steel and ash, no word had pierced the void where Juniper's voice should have been. Maya had buried herself in her work, her hands steady over keyboards and vials as she pushed *CRISPR-XX* to its limits, but the absence was a relentless echo—a deafening quiet that stretched each hour into an eternity. She'd sit in the lab's sterile glow, her phone a constant companion on the desk, its screen dark and unyielding as she willed it to flare with news—any sign that Juniper had clawed her way out of the rubble. Alex had been her anchor through the vigil, his steady presence a bulwark against the storm in her mind, his reassurances a quiet refrain: *"She's tough, Maya—she'll make it."* But even his calm couldn't unravel the knot of dread twisting in her chest, a fear that grew sharper with every unanswered call, every report of the explosion's aftermath—a facility reduced to a smoldering crater, its secrets buried beneath tons of debris.

The lab had become her refuge and her prison, its walls a fortress where she could drown the silence in data and simulations, her fingers tracing the whale-carved pocketknife—a relic of Elena's, passed to Clara, now hers—as if it could summon Juniper back. Late in the evening, as the sky beyond the lab's windows deepened to an inky bruise, her phone buzzed—a sharp jolt that nearly sent it clattering to the floor. She fumbled to answer, her heart slamming against her ribs as the caller ID flashed: *Japanese Government Authorities*. Her voice trembled, a fragile thread as she pressed the device to her ear. "Hello?"

The voice on the other end was measured, professional, a calm that belied the storm within her. "Dr. Maya Hayes?" it began, the accent clipped and precise. "This is Officer Tanaka from the Japanese Ministry of Health. We have news regarding Juniper Nakamura."

Maya's breath snagged, her free hand gripping the pocketknife as if it could steady the world tilting beneath her. "Is she..." she choked out, the words a jagged plea. "Is she alive?"

"Yes," Officer Tanaka replied, his tone softening, a crack of warmth breaking through his formality. "Juniper and several members of her team were rescued from the lab explosion. They were injured but are now in stable condition, receiving care at a secure government facility. Juniper sustained some injuries—concussion, a fractured arm, minor burns—but nothing fatal or severe. She's recovering well."

Relief crashed over Maya like a tidal wave, her legs buckling as she sank into her chair, tears spilling hot and unbidden down her cheeks. Her breath shuddered, a sob breaking free as the knot in her chest unraveled, the weight of dread lifting to reveal a fragile, radiant joy. "Thank you," she whispered, her voice fracturing with gratitude. "Thank you so much. Can I… can I speak to her?"

Officer Tanaka's pause was gentle, regret threading through his response. "Unfortunately, the quarantine remains in effect," he explained. "We're taking every precaution to ensure the *Adamvirus* doesn't breach containment—Japan's holding it, but it's a delicate line. Juniper will need to stay in isolation until she's cleared, likely a few more weeks. But we can arrange a video call for you—would that suffice?"

Maya nodded, the motion instinctive though he couldn't see it, her voice steadying as relief anchored her. "Yes," she said, a faint smile breaking through her tears. "Please—I need to see her."

The call came within the hour, a lifeline stitched through the chaos as Maya settled before her laptop in the lab, her hands clasped tight to still their trembling. Alex lingered nearby, his presence a quiet pillar as he watched from the shadows, his own relief etched into the lines of his face. The screen flickered, then flared to life, and Juniper's face filled the frame—a sight that sent a wave of emotion crashing over Maya, a tidal surge of love and gratitude that stole her breath. Juniper looked weary, her forehead wrapped in a stark white bandage, her left arm cradled in a cast, her skin mottled with faint bruises—but her eyes sparkled with the fierce light Maya had always known, and her smile, though tired, was a sunrise breaking through the dark.

"Hey, you," Juniper said, her voice warm but hoarse, a thread of her usual mischief weaving through the fatigue.

Maya choked back a sob, her hands pressing against her chest as tears welled anew, her voice fracturing with relief. "Juniper… I thought I lost you."

Juniper's smile softened, her eyes glistening as she leaned closer to the camera, her casted arm resting awkwardly on the table. "You can't get rid of me that easily," she said, her tone a gentle tease that belied the weight behind it. "I'm tougher than I look—takes more than a lab blowing up to keep me down."

A laugh broke through Maya's tears, a shaky sound that mingled with her relief, her hands wiping at her face as she steadied herself. "You have no idea how worried I was," she said, her voice trembling with the memory. "When I heard about the explosion—when the comms went dead—I didn't know if..."

"I know," Juniper cut in, her voice softening, a balm against the raw edge of Maya's fear. "It was too close. The blast hit right as we got out, threw us into the snow. I thought... I thought I wouldn't make it back to you. But I'm okay, Maya. A few bumps, a broken arm, some burns, but I'll be on my feet soon." Her gaze sharpened, a flicker of curiosity threading through her exhaustion. "How about you? How're you holding up?"

Maya's breath hitched, her smile faltering as she brushed away the last of her tears, her voice steadying with the anchor of Juniper's presence. "I've been better," she admitted, her fingers tracing the pocketknife's grooves—a habit born of nerves and memory. "But we're making progress. The solution's in production—Japan's getting it first, as fast as we can ship it. Trials are showing viral loads dropping, and vaccinated people are immune. It's not perfect—there's resistance in some strains—but it's a start, Juniper. A real one."

Juniper's eyes lit up, a spark of pride breaking through her weariness, her smile widening despite the strain. "I knew you'd do it," she said, her voice thick with admiration. "You're beyond incredible, Maya. You've pulled us back from the edge."

Maya shook her head, her throat tightening as she met Juniper's gaze through the screen, the distance between them a palpable ache. "We did it together," she said, her words a quiet vow. "I couldn't have gotten here without you—your gear, your brain, your... you. This is ours."

The days that followed wove a fragile rhythm of renewal, the world inching back from the brink as *CRISPR-XX* took root. Juniper's recovery unfolded in stolen video calls, her injuries mending under the care of Japan's medical teams—her concussion fading, her arm healing beneath its cast, her burns softening into faint scars. She remained in quarantine, a precaution against the *Adamvirus*'s lingering threat, but her spirits lifted with each conversation, her laughter a lifeline threading through the screen to Maya's weary heart. Maya, at last, surrendered to rest, the weight of Juniper's survival lifting the fog that had clouded her mind. She slept in fits and starts—hours snatched on the couch, the lab's hum a distant lullaby—her body and soul grateful for the reprieve, her dreams of Clara's smile, Elena's voice, and Juniper's steady gaze.

The solution's production surged, a global symphony of effort as facilities churned out vials around the clock—Tokyo's labs glowing with urgency, Osaka's factories a relentless pulse, even distant hubs in Berlin and Buenos Aires joining the chorus. Japan bore the brunt, its millions under siege, but the countermeasure flowed like a tide—administered to the infected in sealed wards, injections as a preventative method in crowded quarantine zones. Reports trickled back like faint stars piercing a storm—viral loads plummeting, new infections slowing, the *Adamvirus*'s grip loosening inch by inch. Containment held, a fragile dam against a flood that threatened millions, and for the first time since Sapporo's fall, a tentative hope bloomed, its roots fragile but reaching deep.

The breakthrough deepened as weeks unfurled, *CRISPR-XX* proving a blade sharper than Maya had dared dream. The *Adamvirus* faltered, its instability a flaw her solution exploited—its DNA rupturing under the assault of her vectors, its adaptability crumbling against her ingenuity. Japan's government steadied, its cities exhaling as the death toll plateaued, and other nations watched, their own reserves bolstered by the vaccine's promise. Maya didn't rest on the victory—her mind raced beyond containment, the technology a key to broader vistas: stabilizing the human genome against a litany of genetic scars, a shield for future generations of parthenogenesis. It was a leap forward, a ripple that could reshape humanity's horizon, born from Elena's scribbled spark and carried by a world that refused to break.

The call came after weeks of quarantine, a quiet dawn when the world felt less brittle—Juniper cleared to return, her isolation ending as tests confirmed the virus's retreat from her blood. Maya waited at San Francisco's airport, her heart a wild drumbeat as she paced the terminal, her fingers tracing the pocketknife in her pocket—a ritual of nerves and memory. The crowd parted, and there she was—Juniper stepping through the gate, her arm in a sling, her face etched with faint scars, but her smile a sunrise that lit the gray morning. Maya ran to her, heedless of the stares, and pulled her into a fierce embrace, her breath shuddering as she pressed her face into Juniper's shoulder, the scent of antiseptic and warmth a lifeline she'd feared lost.

"I missed you so much," Maya whispered, her voice trembling with a relief that spilled over, her arms tightening as if to hold Juniper against the world's chaos.

Juniper held her close, her good arm wrapping around Maya's back, her own eyes glistening as she buried her face in Maya's hair. "I missed you too," she murmured, her voice thick with emotion, a quiet laugh breaking through. "Thought I'd never get out of that hospital bed."

Maya pulled back, her hands framing Juniper's face, her gaze tracing every line, every scar—a map of survival she'd feared she'd never see again. "You're here," she said, her laugh shaky with joy. "You're really here."

Juniper's smile softened, her hand finding Maya's, their fingers lacing together with a quiet certainty. "Always," she said, her tone a vow. "But we've got work to do—can't slack off now, can we?"

Maya laughed, a sound bright and unburdened, the weight of weeks lifting as she shook her head. "Always the pragmatist," she teased, her voice warm. "But first... let's have a break for a little while. We've earned it."

Juniper's nod was gentle, her eyes shining with a shared understanding, a promise stitched into the silence between them. "Deal," she said, her voice a quiet anchor.

They left the airport hand in hand, stepping into a sunset that spilled gold across the bay, its light a mirror to the hope flickering within them. The road ahead stretched vast and shadowed—Japan's millions still healing, the virus's scars a lingering echo, new challenges rising on the horizon—but for the first time in years, Maya felt a peace settle over her, a stillness born of reunion and resilience. The *Adamvirus* had struck a brutal blow, its containment a fragile victory over millions, but it had summoned humanity's finest—its ingenuity, its unity, its refusal to yield. She thought of Clara, her fierce spirit guiding every breakthrough; of Elena, her quiet courage etched into the journals; of little Elena, a lost light that fueled her fight; and of Juniper, her partner in every sense, alive and unbroken beside her.

The whale-carved pocketknife rested warm in her pocket, a symbol of a legacy forged through loss and love, a tether to the women who'd shaped her and the future they'd dared to dream. The world was still broken, its cracks deep and raw, but it was mending—thread by thread, breath by breath—and Maya knew she'd face what came next with Juniper at her side, their hands clasped against the dusk in hues of renewal, a promise they'd shape together.

34

A New Dawn

Several years had unfurled like a quiet tide since the shadow of the *Adamvirus* receded, leaving a world transformed in ways Maya could scarcely have dreamed in the darkest days of its reign. The virus, once a specter poised to unravel humanity, had been tamed—its threat extinguished by the relentless spread of *CRISPR-XX*, a solution born from her hands and refined by a global chorus of minds. Laboratories across continents had honed it into a shield, its applications stretching far beyond the initial crisis that had gripped Japan's millions. Parthenogenesis, once a fragile lifeline teetering on the edge of failure, now boasted a success rate nearing ninety-five percent, a triumph etched into the X chromosome's stability—a legacy of Maya's tireless work, a thread pulled from Elena's earliest sparks and Clara's unyielding faith. The world was no longer a patchwork of despair; it was rebuilding, brick by painstaking brick, and hope had shed its distant shimmer to become a tangible pulse, a rhythm beating through cities once silenced by fear.

Maya stood on the stage at Stanford University, her heart swelling with a pride that trembled beneath her calm exterior as she accepted her PhD—an achievement forged in sleepless nights, tear-streaked breakthroughs, and the echoes of those she'd lost. The auditorium thundered with applause, a roar that rippled beyond its walls to screens worldwide, a testament to a journey that had reshaped humanity's horizon. Yet her gaze sought only one face in the sea of clapping hands—Juniper's, radiant in the front row, her smile a beacon that anchored Maya amidst the storm of sound. This moment was theirs, a victory carved from shared scars and unwavering resolve, a testament to the partnership that had carried them through the abyss. Juniper's eyes, bright with pride and love, mirrored the light Maya felt within—a light that had flickered but never faded, even when the world seemed poised to crumble.

In Sydney, the Advanced Genomics Institute had raised a new edifice to honor the Hayes family—a towering structure of glass and steel christened the Hayes Building, its silhouette a quiet monument to the women who'd shaped its legacy. Statues of Clara and Elena flanked its entrance, their bronze faces cast in serene determination—Clara's hands poised as if mid-experiment, Elena's gaze lifted to a horizon she'd never see. Maya visited often, her steps echoing through its polished halls, her heart a tangle of pride and sorrow as she traced the names etched into plaques and walls. Clara's fierce spirit lingered in the labs bustling with young scientists, Elena's quiet courage in the archives preserving her journals, and little Elena's lost promise in the silence that draped their memory. Their absence was a wound that never fully healed, a hollow ache that pulsed with every triumph, but their legacy thrived—not just in stone and steel, but in the work Maya poured herself into, a living testament to the hope they'd died to protect.

The Sons of Adam had faded into a shadow of their former threat, their ranks shattered by years of relentless pursuit. The remaining immune men—Thomas among them—had been swept up in the global dragnet or vanished into hiding, their ideology a fading ember in a world that had moved beyond their rage. World leaders, after years of fractious debate, had forged a fragile consensus on their fate—a punishment that balanced justice with the vestiges of compassion. They were confined to high-security facilities, not dank cells but places of quiet dignity—spacious quarters with access to books, screens, and medical care, a gilded cage where freedom was a memory but survival was assured. It was a decision that sparked murmurs of dissent—some cried for harsher reckoning, others for mercy's full embrace—but it stood as a testament to a humanity striving to heal rather than rend. Thomas, his once-sharp eyes dulled by regret, had accepted his confinement in silence, a man adrift in the ruins of his fight, his final act of aid to Maya a faint redemption he'd never fully claim.

The male population had dwindled to a whisper—hundreds of thousands scattered across a globe once teeming with billions—accelerated aging from *Chromovirus-X* claiming them faster than time should allow. Alex had been among them, his gray hair a silver crown by his early fifties, his body bowing under the virus's quiet toll. A year ago, he'd slipped away—his death a gentle fade in a hospital bed, his hand clasped in Maya's as he refused the *CRISPR-XX* treatment that could have slowed his decline. "I've lived a good life," he'd told her, his voice a rasp of peace as he smiled faintly, the lines of his face softening in the dim light. "I want to rest now—beside Clara and little Elena, where I belong." His words had cracked her open, a grief as raw as the day she'd lost Clara, but she'd honored his choice, her tears falling silently as he drifted into the quiet—her rock, her father in all but name, gone to join the family she'd mourned too long. Losing him carved a hollow in her chest, a piece of herself buried with him beneath Sydney's windswept earth, but his legacy lingered in the AI networks still guarding the world—an echo of his quiet strength she'd carry always.

The lab at Stanford had quieted in the years since, its frenetic pace giving way to a steady hum as *CRISPR-XX* wove itself into humanity's fabric—Japan's cities healing, their scars softening under the balm of recovery, the global genome fortified against the shadows of its past. Maya's work had ripened into something vast, a foundation for a future she'd once only dreamed—a shield against genetic ruin, a promise of resilience for generations yet to come. Yet her life had blossomed beyond the sterile confines of science, its roots sinking deep into the soil of renewal. She and Juniper had built a home together—a modest house overlooking San Francisco Bay, its walls lined with Juniper's blueprints and Maya's journals, its rooms alive with laughter and the quiet moments that stitched their days together. Their partnership, forged in the crucible of crisis, had deepened into a love that anchored them both—a bond unspoken in its certainty, a lifeline that held firm against the world's storms.

On a crisp afternoon, Maya and Juniper stood on a rocky outcrop above the Sydney ocean, the waves crashing below in a restless hymn that mingled with the wind weaving through the cliffs. The mission—the long, brutal fight against the *Adamvirus*—had been fulfilled, its shadow banished by the light they'd kindled together. In Maya's hands rested two small vials, their contents a whisper of ash: one for Clara, one for little Elena, kept from the urns buried years ago for this moment of closure. She'd carried them through the chaos, a promise to scatter them when the world was safe, when their sacrifices bore fruit. Juniper stood beside her, her presence a steady warmth against the sea's chill, her hand resting lightly on Maya's arm as they faced the horizon.

Maya uncapped the first vial—Clara's—her fingers trembling as she tilted it toward the waves, the ash catching the wind in a silver swirl that danced briefly before sinking into the ocean's embrace. "For you, Aunt Clara," she whispered, her voice steady despite the tears welling in her eyes, "for every fight you won, every hope you held. Rest now—the world's healing because of you." She turned to the second vial—little Elena's—its weight a quiet ache in her palm, and let its ash spill free, a finer dust that shimmered in the sunlight before vanishing into the sea. "And for you, little Elena—my cousin, my star. You never got your chance, but you're part of this dawn. I feel you with us."

The wind carried her words, a soft echo against the cliffs, and Maya felt a presence beyond the tangible—a whisper of Daniel, her father, his bravery a shadow in the air beside Elena's courage, Clara's fire, and little Elena's lost light. "Dad," she murmured, her voice breaking as she pressed the pocketknife to her chest, its whale carving warm against her skin, "you're here too, aren't you? Watching over us, proud of what we've done." The ocean sighed below, its rhythm a cradle for their spirits, and for a moment, she swore she felt them all—Daniel's quiet strength, Elena's fierce love, Clara's unyielding resolve, Alex's steady anchor, little Elena's gentle promise—woven into the breeze, a family reunited in the stillness.

Juniper's arm slipped around her waist, pulling her close, her voice a low, grounding thread against the wind. "They're with us," she said, her tone soft but certain, her gaze tracing the waves where the ashes had vanished. "Every step, every fight—they've been here. And now they can rest, Maya. We've made it."

Maya leaned into her, her tears falling freely now, a release of grief and gratitude as the ocean swallowed their remnants—a final farewell to the ashes she'd held, a closure that felt like wings unfurling in her chest. "We have," she said, her voice trembling with peace, "and there's still so much to do—to build, to heal. For them, for Kalina, for everyone."

They turned from the cliff, hand in hand, the vials empty in Maya's grasp, their contents surrendered to the sea—a ritual of renewal that bound the past to the future. Before them stood the graves in Sydney's cliffside cemetery, a solemn row beneath the eucalyptus trees: Elena Hayes, her name weathered but resolute; Clara Hayes, her statue's echo in bronze above; little Elena Hayes, a smaller stone cradled between them; and now Alex, his resting place fresh, the earth still soft beneath a simple plaque. Maya's hand rested on her stomach, a gentle swell beneath her jacket where a new life stirred—a baby girl they'd named Kalina, a melding of Clara and Elena's names, a promise born from the ashes of loss. The child was theirs, conceived through parthenogenesis refined by Maya's hands, a testament to the future they'd fought to secure.

"We've come so far," Maya said, her voice soft but steady, a quiet thread against the wind as she traced the curve of her belly, her gaze drifting across the graves. "So much pain, so much fight—but we're here. And there's still so much to do—to build, to heal. I promise you—all of you—I'll make the future better. For Kalina, for everyone who's left."

Juniper's hand found hers, their fingers lacing together with a warmth that steadied her, her grip gentle but firm as she squeezed—a silent vow in the touch. "We'll do it together," she said, her voice a low, resolute melody, her eyes shining with a love that mirrored Maya's own. "Just like we always have."

Maya's smile broke through the ache, a bloom of peace unfurling in her chest as she leaned into Juniper's side, the wind tugging at their hair in a shared dance. The graves stood as sentinels to a past carved by sacrifice, but they were more than markers of loss; they were roots, grounding her in a legacy that pulsed with hope. The world beyond the cliff was healing—its cities rising from the *Adamvirus*'s scars, Japan's millions reclaiming breath and laughter, humanity knitting itself anew with threads of resilience and kindness. It wasn't perfect, its cracks still raw, but it was stronger, a tapestry rewoven with the lessons of its breaking.

They lingered there as the sun dipped low, its gold spilling across the ocean in a shimmering path that stretched to the horizon—a mirror to the road ahead, vast and shadowed but radiant with possibility. Maya's hand tightened around the pocketknife, its whale carving a silent vow pressed against her palm—a relic of Elena's courage, Clara's faith, now hers to carry forward with Daniel's spirit whispering alongside. She thought of Alex's quiet farewell, his smile as he slipped away; of Clara's fierce pride in every breakthrough; of little Elena, a whisper of what could have been; of Elena and Daniel, their love a lantern through the dark. And she felt Juniper beside her—her partner, her anchor, her home—a presence that made the weight bearable, the future tangible.

The wind sighed through the trees, a gentle hymn to renewal, and as they turned from the graves, hand in hand, Maya's steps felt lighter, her heart fuller than it had been in years. The world had been broken, its seams torn by virus and rage, but it was mending—thread by thread, breath by breath, a dawn born from the longest night. Kalina stirred within her, a flutter of life that mirrored the hope pulsing in her veins, and she knew she'd face whatever came next with Juniper at her side—their hands clasped, their spirits unbroken, ready to shape a future worthy of the past. The nightfall brushed the sky in tones of promise, a canvas they'd fill together, and as they walked into its glow, Maya whispered a vow to the fading light: "*We're not done yet—not while there's hope.*"

www.ingramcontent.com/pod-product-compliance
Lightning Source LLC
Chambersburg PA
CBHW060803310726
48980CB00002B/221

* 9 7 9 8 9 9 2 8 4 4 7 2 6 *